THE SUPERSTAR
PATRICIA LOGAN

AUTHORPATRICIALOGAN.COM

WARNING:

The unauthorized reproduction or distribution of this copyrighted work is illegal. Criminal copyright infringement, including infringement without monetary gain, is investigated by the FBI and one of their finest agents, Cody Redsun, who will hunt you down, and is punishable by up to 5 years in federal prison and a fine of $250,000!

REMEMBER:

This book is a work of fiction. All characters, places and events are from the author's imagination and should not be confused with fact. Any resemblance to persons, living or dead, events or places, is purely coincidental.

PLEASE BE ADVISED:

This book contains material that is only suitable for mature readers. It contains scenes of a sexual nature between two or more consenting men.

ropes and other convenient methods of restraint. ~ *Petronella Ford*

"Patricia Logan is a walking contradiction that may be baking cookies with her grandchild one moment and writing an e-stim sounding scene the next. Known famous as being a cat lady, she picks up more and more strays as she goes along through life. I am just happy to be one of them. ~*JP Adkins*

"Even since stumbling across Patricia Logan through Silver Ties, in an ever widening search to find my kink in reading, I have been held captive - yes, tied up, ball gagged and whipped into submission. Patricia has an understanding of the Dominant/submissive relationship (formalised or not) and can take you from a gentle simple starter level to some hardcore BDSM scene's with humour, pathos, attention to detail and awareness of her responsibilities to her readers and the characters who inhabit her worlds. (*whispers* - Mistress Logan... Can I come now?)~Mary Phillips Wallace

"Patricia Logan has hair as red as the red hot passion that dominates all of her books. Ready for a wiener roast? ~*Patricia Nelson*

ACKNOWLEDGEMENT

I would like to thank GA Hauser for directing Storm Ellison in his first major motion picture "Silver Bullets" based on the book by Patricia Logan. He tells me she was an incredible director, magnificent producer, a good sport, and an all around force of nature. He had a lot of fun with her. I'd also like to thank her for allowing me to mention her full length major motion pictures, "Capital Games" and "Naked Dragon" Check her work out at AuthorGAHauser.com.

PROLOGUE

Balthazar Grant blew out a huge breath as he pounded down the hill toward his small Hollywood apartment. At least the last two hundred yards of his daily five mile run were downhill and for that he was grateful. Even though it was September in Los Angeles and the rest of the country was preparing for a brisk fall, Taz had become accustomed to the sweltering heat of the southland in the two years since he'd relocated from his home in the Bay Area. He still cringed when he thought of the last time he'd seen his former boyfriend Gregor board a plane and fly out of San Francisco International Airport and his life forever. Taz had become attached to the man in the two years they'd dated, though neither would call it love. Taz had never really been in love, but having Gregor around a few nights a week had become comfortable. *Comfortable? You're getting old.*

At twenty-nine, Taz was happy with his new life in Los Angeles. After serving four years in the Marine Corps in Afghanistan, he'd come home ready for just about anything. In the Corps, his job had been working as a liaison for one dignitary after another, coordinating security, so it hadn't been a giant leap to go into the private security business once he was Stateside. It had only taken a few calls to firms recommended by veteran buddies, and he'd soon been employed. The freelance work included everything from working security for parties of the rich and famous to acting as a bouncer at several of the more popular nightspots in Hollywood. The glittery exuberant celebrities of southern California loved to party and they all seemed to have the money to do it. Taz was happy to wear a fancy suit, stand at attention, and watch the crowd for trouble from behind black sunglasses. Of course he was always armed to the teeth. His .45 caliber Glock G41 was one of his best friends.

When he reached the locked lobby door of his modern apartment building, he stopped as a neighbor exited the building. The lanky blonde with large boobs was dressed in tight running shorts, and her hair was pulled up into a tight ponytail. When she smiled sexily at him, Taz smiled back and he caught the door, holding it open as she passed by to begin her morning run. One of the things Taz loved about Los Angeles was the vibrant beauty of the place. Though girls were not his thing at all, you certainly couldn't tell by looking at him. There was not a stereotypical gay thing about Balthazar Grant. He stood almost six foot six and was built like the side of a building and just as hard. He knew he was a good-looking man. Hell, he'd been told what a stud he was by both men and women. Everyone seemed to love his silver eyes. He knew they were a stark contrast to his milk chocolate-brown skin and complemented him well.

He pushed the elevator button in the lobby and took it up the four flights to his small clean studio where he stepped inside to cool air-conditioning. As he headed toward the bathroom, Taz heard his cell ring. He walked to his kitchen counter and picked up the smartphone, swiping the screen and smiling when he saw a name he recognized.

"Rome? How you doin' man?" Rome Wilkins was a good friend whom Taz had met working a private security gig in Beverly Hills.

"I'm good, man, good. How's it hangin'?"

Rome lived in Westburg, Texas just outside of Austin. After retiring from the military several years before, he'd gone into the private security business. The last time Taz had talked to him he'd just taken on a full time job working at a new BDSM club in Austin. Rumor had it the club catered to all kinds of kink, both gay and straight. Though the thought of using his handcuffs on a lover got Taz off, he wasn't really a kinky dude beyond that. "I'm good man. You know, takin' things one day at a time. What's up? How's the new job?"

"I really like it, Taz," his friend replied.

"Yeah, you kinky fuck." Taz chuckled.

"Well, you know, it's a living." Rome laughed. "Hey, but listen, I called you for a reason. You know Herman Morrow? Well, he just dropped me a line on a really sweet full-time private bodyguard job out in LA and of course you're the first person I thought of."

Herman Morrow had hired Taz and Rome to work security for visiting royalty a couple of years before. They'd become fast friends and had kept in touch even after Rome had returned to Texas.

"You know I like freelance," Taz said.

Rome chuckled. "I know but this deal was so nice I thought I'd pass it on before Morrow had a chance to job it out to someone else."

"I appreciate that, Rome. What's so great about it?"

"You ready for this? You'd be Storm Ellison's private bodyguard," Rome replied.

"Storm Ellison? The seriously overrated gay teen superstar, Storm Ellison? Famous for that reality show, 'Trapped on an Island' Storm Ellison?"

"One and the same and he's hardly a teen. He's almost as elderly as you."

"What… twenty?" Taz laughed.

"According to his bio, he's twenty-five and not as overrated as you think. I bet you've never even watched his show. Pepper is addicted to it," Rome said, sounding serious.

Taz knew Rome had recently married an FBI forensic specialist named Pepper Rawlings, but it was rumored there was another man in their lives. Taz respected Rome and considered him one of his best friends. Whatever made Rome happy made him happy, but it still gave him pause to think that Rome was in a three-way relationship with anyone, much less a girl and a guy. Of course, the lure of big money and luxury accommodations had him interested. But from what he'd heard about the superstar, he was destined to be a one-shot wonder, washed-up by the time he was thirty. Well, Taz had worked a lot of less glamorous jobs in the past.

"Okay, okay, I suppose it's worth a phone call to Herman, Rome. I'm tellin' you now, if this guy turns out to be a pain in the ass, I will haunt you." Taz sighed.

Rome laughed. "They're always a pain in the ass, Taz, but as long as you're careful on the job, you won't have to haunt anyone and I promise you'll have fun at it. If I were free, I'd love it. All you have to do is hold off the crowds, stand there and look pretty, and be on the lookout for overzealous fans."

"And put up with a spoiled child who's constantly chasing the latest fashion trends while doing lines of coke, right?" Taz asked.

"If anyone's up to the challenge, it's you, buddy. And who knows, you might even learn to like the guy," Rome added.

"Thanks for thinking of me, Rome. I really do appreciate it."

"Any day, Taz. Stay safe out there."

"You too."

CHAPTER ONE

Taz waited while the applause died down as Storm exited the stage. Another year of the Emmy Awards was a wrap, and Storm had done a nice job of emceeing the show. He'd also picked up his own Emmy for best actor in a drama for his portrayal of Trevor Manix in "Trapped on an Island"; the hot gay twenty-something actor and the popular show were the talk of the town. Storm looked up and spotted Taz nodding at him as he passed by, grabbing a bottle of water from his agent, Alan Steinberg, and twisting the top. Taz took up the rear behind the two men, settling his bulk between the stage and Storm while the men walked rapidly toward Storm's dressing room. If anyone was planning on getting close to Storm it would be only because Taz allowed them to.

When they got ten yards from the room, Taz looked over Storm's shorter form at the crowd of people that had gathered just beyond the dressing room, behind the red velvet rope blocking them from getting any closer. One of Taz and Rome's friends and another former Marine, Ranger Corrigan, stood in front of the velvet rope, guarding Storm's dressing room door to make sure no one could slip in unnoticed. Taz nodded at the handsome tatted hunk, decked out in black leather from head to toe, and felt a wash of gratitude that he'd hired him on as additional security for the night. It was good working with people he trusted and Ranger was definitely that. Ranger had also worked for Herman Morrow and he and Taz had met on the job. Taz knew the Emmys would be a madhouse, what with Storm's popularity, and since he'd only had a few weeks to prepare for ensuring his client's security after accepting the job with the celebrity, it certainly felt good to have someone he really counted on to guard his back.

As soon as Storm was recognized, a roar went up from the teeming crowd behind the velvet rope and Ranger stuck out a thickly muscled bicep, blocking a couple of enthusiastic fans who decided to try to jump the rope and get close to their idol.

"Step back behind the rope, douche," Taz clearly heard as Ranger growled at a twinkish man with hair the combination of neon pink and black, as he tried to vault over it with a pad of paper and a pen in his hand. It was all Taz could do to keep from bursting out in laughter at his friend's apt description of the small man. The guy looked up at Ranger's sinister dark features with wide eyes and took three steps back while gulping so loud it was nearly audible above the cries of the crowd.

"Storm! You're my hero!" one fan cried out while waving a pad of paper. The mostly older teen to twenty-something crowd was dressed wildly, some with multicolored hair, most with autograph books and eight by ten glossy photos for the star to sign. As Storm and his agent walked up to them, Storm turned and threw a look over his shoulder, making eye contact with Taz. Taz felt a wave of satisfaction run through him when he realized the star was aware of his presence at his back. Taz nodded at him again and Storm smiled a bright smile before turning toward the throng of his fans given backstage passes to meet the celebrity. If it were up to Taz, he wouldn't allow his client anywhere near his fans but he also understood that Storm would be nothing if it weren't for those who adored him. The whole thing creeped him out just a bit. Taz couldn't imagine having so much adulation showered down on him every time he turned around, and frankly he couldn't quite understand why anyone would want it. Celebrities like Storm Ellison and others seemed to have the paparazzi swarming around them everywhere they went. He wondered how they could ever find any peace at all but Storm seemed to thrive on his fans and as he stepped up and began signing autographs while Ranger held them back, Taz noticed how the fans responded to him.

"Oh, Storm, I just love you!" one man said, dreamily. "If you want, I'll go down on you right here."

"Back the fuck off, Sunshine, or you're *gonna* be going down and not in the fun way," Ranger growled, balling his fist and showing it to the man.

The guy looked over at Taz's friend, gave him the up and down look and then did a finger snap in his face. "You're too rough for me, Brutus," he lisped.

Taz grinned when Ranger reached out and swallowed the fan's much smaller fingers in his gigantic paw, squeezing. The guy yelped before Ranger let go but to his friend's credit, the guy stepped back.

Storm chatted with his animated fans as his manager stood beside him, talking in his ear the whole time. Taz had to hand it to the star; he was polite to his admirers and tried to sign all the autographs and photos he possibly could in the five minutes Taz had allowed him to spend with them. When the time came,

Taz leaned in and spoke to Alan Steinberg who looked over at him and nodded.

"So sorry, Storm has to get ready for the after-parties, guys. Thanks for being here!" Alan yelled over the crowd.

They groaned as a unit and some threw small pieces of paper at Storm when he stepped back. Taz knew most contained phone numbers and room numbers from surrounding hotels. When Storm stopped to talk to a pretty blond boy, the celebrity looked back over his shoulder at Taz and made eye contact. Taz was pretty certain what Storm was telegraphing but as the celeb brushed past him, he quietly said, "You can let him back in half an hour."

WTF? I'm supposed be your pimp now? Taz was slightly surprised but he knew discretion was part of the job description and he realized helping Storm get laid was part of that too. He wondered for the hundredth time if taking the bodyguard position had been a mistake but Rome had been right, the money was killer and the accommodations were posh. Because he only had to go out when Storm went out was a bonus, though the guy liked visiting the gay bars at night and that was no problem when the eye candy was just so damned pretty to watch. So far nothing bad had happened and though Taz checked through large bags of Storm's fan mail to make sure he didn't miss anything suspicious, everything had been quiet on the security front so far.

When he'd first sat down with Alan Steinberg and Storm's business manager, Anthony Kincaid, at the initial job interview and toured Storm's Malibu home, he'd offered up some suggestions that would not only ensure the superstar had better privacy, but also keep him safer. Alan agreed to Taz's suggestions readily and he'd installed extra security cameras for the perimeter of the property set on the cliffs overlooking the picturesque Pacific Ocean. Taz thanked his lucky stars Storm hadn't bought a beachfront place that would be extremely difficult, if not impossible, to keep secure. Taz had updated Storm's existing security cameras, added a state of the art video surveillance system to replace his outdated one, and set up a protocol for accepting deliveries at the gated entrance to the property. The delivery men were to ring through directly to Taz's cell with a special code, and Taz would respond in person.

Taz followed Storm and Alan into the dressing room and shut the door, closing out the noise from the corridor beyond. The room was filled with flowers from well-wishers, the largest arrangement from Storm's producers on "Trapped on an Island". Storm had been informed that the show had been picked up for a fourth season, and Taz knew that as his client's popularity grew, so would the security concerns around the star. He stayed with his back to the door and watched as Storm sat in front of the large lighted vanity mirror and began removing his stage makeup while Alan took up a chair beside him. The middle-aged agent was holding a script and waving it at his meal ticket as he spoke animatedly beside him.

"I am telling you, Storm, this is the biggest thing yet!" he gushed. "A starring role in what promises to be the most romantic gay film since 'Brokeback Mountain'. No one is making these types of movies, Storm."

Taz watched as Storm eyeballed his manager skeptically.

"What do you mean gay movies? There's lots of them, Alan."

"Not like this. This one is pure romance and a lot of intrigue. There's action, love, and best of all, hot man on man sex with a happy ending. Gay movies rarely have happy endings, you know that. It's right up your alley, baby; you're gonna be famous!"

Storm's eyebrow lifted as he pinned his manager with a surprised look. "It's porn? Alan, you told me to not even contemplate porn."

"Porn? Hell no, Storm. This is all about love. Your character, Michael Francis, is a supermodel who falls for a hot cowboy cop. The story takes place in Los Angeles and Texas and it's produced and directed by GA Hauser," Steinberg said. The manager was practically bouncing in the chair and Taz had to firm his lips to keep from smiling at the spectacle.

"But you said man on man love," Storm replied, watching his manager while wiping away makeup with a towelette.

"Yes, but there's no frontal nudity and only implied sex, though I must say, the way the screenwriter, Patricia Logan, wrote it, makes it look steamy." Alan thrust the screenplay at his client. "Please, Storm, don't say no until you read it. This could be your big break."

"Hello? Earth to Alan. I just won an Emmy for best actor in a drama. What do you call that?" Storm said haughtily, taking the script from his manager.

"I'm talking the big screen, baby! This is your big break. Look what it did for Heath Ledger or Jake

Gyllenhaal. No one knew who the hell they were before that film. Storm, you have to trust me; have I steered you wrong so far?"

The star looked over at his manager and became serious, finally throwing down the tissue he held and taking Alan's shoulder as he looked into his face. "Okay, Alan, I'll give it a read through tomorrow." He let go of Alan's shoulder and looked back at the makeup mirror for a second, brushing a manicured finger under one eye before sighing heavily. "I'm tired, Alan."

The manager stood up and put both hands on Storm's shoulders, meeting his gaze in the mirror as he looked over the star's head. "Thank you. You won't regret it, Storm." Steinberg swiveled and walked a few steps toward Taz before turning back to his star. "Finish what you need to do, Storm, and have a Red Bull… or do you need something stronger? We've got four after-parties to hit before we quit tonight."

"I don't do drugs, Alan. You know that!" The star pinned his manager with an exasperated look and Alan nodded.

"Fine, fine, just be ready in fifteen minutes."

Taz glanced at Storm over the manager's shoulder and watched him slump in his chair as Alan walked back toward him. When Steinberg stopped in front of him, Taz moved to the side to open the door. He didn't expect the manager to lean in and speak to him.

"Don't let him dally too long with the twink outside. Sure the kid needs to get laid, but his public waits," he said under his breath.

"I'll do what I can," Taz growled, unhappy to be thrust into the role of keeper and disgusted by the agent's offering of drugs to his client. The last thing he needed was to have to peel Storm off the pavement after overdosing and as far as the sex thing? Like hell was he going to cock block the star but timing him was a whole other issue. *Am I supposed to tell him, "Okay, Storm, you have three minutes to get off. Your public waits."?* The thought was comical at best. Taz opened the door and let the manager out, sticking his head into the corridor where he spied the blond Storm had spoken with earlier. The boy's eyes looked glassy and Taz wondered what the kid was on, hoping he didn't want to share it with Storm. Though he hadn't seen Storm so much as smoke a joint, he'd accepted the job ready to face the fact he did drugs... they all did.

"He's ready for you," Taz grunted to the kid. He looked up at Ranger who still held the crowd back with the velvet rope and rolled his eyes. Ranger smirked knowingly and raised the rope, letting the slight form of the kid slip underneath. Taz moved between the kid and the door, glaring down at him, stopping him in his tracks.

"Raise your arms."

The kid stared at him for a moment before raising his arms over his head.

Taz reached out and patted him down, satisfying himself that the kid wasn't carrying a weapon before stepping back. "Lemme see your ID."

The twink's mouth dropped open in surprise for a second before reaching into a fanny pack he carried, producing a California driver's license. Taz checked it, noting the kid was nineteen, older than he thought. He handed it back.

"You got ten minutes; leave your fanny pack with me, Colby Duncan," he growled.

The kid complied, handing him the fanny pack and Taz opened the door, letting the kid into the room, before following him inside. The boy waved enthusiastically at Storm who stood looking unbelievably sexy in a silk robe beside a couch in the room. A rolling screen was nearby and would provide all the privacy they were going to get; Taz had no intention of leaving a total stranger alone with his client. The star's short blond hair stood off his head in spikes and he'd applied a fresh coat of guyliner in the short time Taz had been outside the door. His lips were plump and blushing pink and when he smiled a dazzling white smile at the boy, Taz's stomach did a flip-flop. Storm Ellison was probably the sexiest man he'd ever seen and he had to make a conscious effort not to let himself get hard when he thought of what the star and the twink were about to do.

****

God, his bodyguard was good-looking. Storm had been walking around with a hard-on since he'd first laid eyes on his new bodyguard nearly a month before. The fact he was standing beside the door looking sexy as hell as he let the twink into the dressing room for their encounter had Storm all worked up and ready to shoot his wad. In fact, the moment he'd seen Balthazar Grant, better known as Taz, he'd wanted to drop to his knees and service the huge hunk of manhood. He glanced up and down Taz's body, looking right past the twink who was

14

trying his best to look sexy. He paled in comparison to the dark bronze God who towered over him. Storm estimated Taz to be nearly six and a half feet tall and even though he wore a suit and tie, Storm guessed they had to be specially tailored just to conceal the hard muscle beneath. The fact he'd never even gotten a glimpse of Taz behind the dark mirrored glasses he wore drove Storm crazy. How could he tell if the man was interested if he couldn't look in his eyes?

"Hello, Storm," the twink said.

Storm dragged his gaze away from his beautiful bodyguard and focused on the blond who'd stepped up to him. When he smiled down at the guy, he tentatively lifted one hand and began rubbing it up and down Storm's chest while gazing at him with a combination of lust and adoration.

"I can't believe I'm touching you," he sighed dreamily. *It's always the same. They love the actor; they don't give a damn about me.*

"Oh, you're touching me, sugar, just in the wrong places," Storm said, taking the guy's hand in his and moving it lower to cover his growing erection. He looked back over the boy's head and noted Taz's unmoving form. For all he knew, the bodyguard was sleeping but he doubted it. From what he'd seen, the guy was the consummate professional.

"Oh, Storm, you're so big," the twink said.

"Let me give us a little more privacy… what's your name?" Storm asked, reaching for the privacy screen.

"Oh, it's Colby but you can call me Coke," the boy said.

Storm rolled the screen, cutting off the bodyguard from his view. The moment Taz's face was obscured, Storm was almost certain he heard a chuckle coming from the other side of the curtain. He looked over at the twink who gazed at him adoringly. The boy's hand was now inside the folds of his robe and wrapped around his cock and Storm found himself annoyed by the fact he had to concentrate on getting hard because he was so distracted by his gorgeous bodyguard. He reached out and took Coke's jaw with his ring covered hand. His skin was smooth as a girl's and just as pretty as heck. He would love to fuck this kid but time didn't allow for that.

"Kiss me, Coke," he said.

The boy moaned as Storm touched his lips with his own. They kissed for only a second before Storm felt the guy's tongue. He immediately broke the contact between them. Storm rarely ever kissed his tricks but the kid had a pretty face and he lost himself for a moment. The minute he felt Coke's attempt to deepen the kiss, he ended it.

"Don't you wanna kiss me, Storm?" the kid whimpered, looking at him with glazed eyes.

Shit. The kid's on something. The urge to end the encounter right there was almost overwhelming and if Taz hadn't been listening to the whole thing from the other side of the screen, Storm would have. Hell, he had a reputation to protect, even in front of his bodyguard. He looked into the kid's eyes again and made a decision. Reaching out, he put both hands on Coke's shoulders and began pushing. "Suck me off," he said, ignoring the guy's question.

The kid nodded vigorously. "Oh, man. I'm gonna suck Storm Ellison's dick!" he cried enthusiastically, dropping to his knees without any effort and baring Storm's cock from between the folds of his robe.

Storm watched as his dick, long and hard, stood out from his shaved groin. Coke expertly grabbed the base with one hand and his ball sac with the other. It was only a second later before he leaned in and took the head of Storm's cock into his mouth. Storm closed his eyes and pictured Taz on his knees in front of him. His dark sunglasses were gone and he was naked, his dark brown skin glistening as he leaned in and began sucking Storm. His thick soft lips slid over the shaft of Storm's cock and the contrast between dark and light skin was so beautiful. Storm felt a tug on his balls and listened to the slurping sounds coming from beneath him. *Yeah, that's right; suck me, Taz.*

Storm floated away on fantasy for the next minute as his balls were rolled and his cock sucked. The urge to come rose fast in him as the image of Taz sucking his dick played out behind his closed eyes. Storm reached down to touch Taz's bald head. When two handfuls of hair ended up in his fists, Storm's eyes flew open and he looked down. Coke's hand was still on his balls, his mouth sucking hard on Storm's dick with hollowed cheeks, and with his other hand, he was jacking himself off. Storm tried hard to ignore the small dick Coke held in his hand and closed his eyes tightly, wanting to sink back into his own fantasy as he came.

"Give me your load, Storm." Storm could almost hear the deep cadence of Taz's voice as his orgasm erupted from his balls. His eyes flew open as he shot

only to look down and see Coke eagerly swallowing his come, his large Adam's apple bobbing as he groaned and emptied a puddle of his own come at his feet. The fantasy dissolved instantly and he was left with the vision of Coke's vacant eyes as he looked up and connected his gaze with Storm. *Get the fuck away from me!* Storm let go of Coke's head and stepped back, instantly breaking the kid's connection with his cock as it slid out of his mouth. Fortunately, the kid let go of Storm's balls at the same time.

"That was hot," the kid said.

"Thanks, but I need to get going," Storm said, adjusting the tie on the silk robe as he covered himself. He watched as the kid tucked his own cock back inside his jeans and stood up. The boy was grinning from ear to ear.

"Hey, Storm, I'd like to do that again. Will ya call me?" the boy asked, closing the gap between them until he was nearly touching Storm with his body.

Storm shivered, suddenly very uncomfortable. He couldn't wait for the kid to leave. "Look, you're a nice guy and all but I'm really busy, Coke. Thanks though. It was hot." Storm forced himself to lean in and peck the guy on the lips, quickly pulling away.

The kid finally stepped back and then reached into his back pocket, yanking out an autograph book. He thrust it at Storm. "Please sign it, Storm. I never want to forget this night," he said dreamily.

Storm took the autograph book and scribbled in it before giving it back to Coke. He turned away before the kid could say thank you and rolled the screen aside. His eyes went straight to the tall beautiful bodyguard who stood staring straight forward with his arms folded across his massive chest. Storm noted the way the coat of his suit bulged where his biceps stretched the fabric and a wave of lust shot through his veins. *Bet you heard that whole thing. Serves you right, you smug bastard.* Storm watched briefly as the bodyguard relaxed his stance, turned, and pulled open the door before he dragged his gaze away and walked to a rack of clothes his wardrobe girl had set aside for him. When he turned back to see if Taz was watching, he was surprised to see the guy following Coke out into the hall and shutting the door. *Well fuck you too!*

****

Taz was so fucking hard his suit pants were bulging at the groin. He shut the door as soon as the twink was outside in the hallway and took up a stance in front of it, making sure his crotch was covered by the coat of his suit. Ranger had cleared the hallway of Storm's fans and was nowhere in sight. Taz was happy he'd called in his friend to help. Ranger was nothing if not efficient. He felt sweat bead on the top of his shaved head and tickle his back as it rolled down between his shoulder blades. He was hotter than hell buttoned up with a dress shirt and tie, and his gun hung heavy at his armpit. Uncomfortable wasn't even the way he'd describe himself at the moment. He wanted to get the hell out of there but he knew Alan Steinberg had several parties where he expected Storm to make an appearance. Taz would be accompanying them to every last one so it promised to be dawn before Taz would be able to quit for the night. Hell, it was a lot of work, but he'd signed up for it.

Watching his strikingly beautiful client getting sexed up and ready for his encounter with the twink hadn't been a fun experience. As a matter of fact, it was extremely uncomfortable. When Taz accepted the job, he knew he'd be in close proximity to the gorgeous superstar and he realized at the time that he'd be expected to watch over Storm at all times, even those when he had booty calls. What Taz hadn't counted on was the attraction he felt toward the star. Storm was beyond beautiful. He was stunning. About six feet tall, lean but beautifully muscled, his body and face had an undeniable aura about them. It was more than charisma. There was some sort of an inner glow Storm possessed that made wanting to be in his circle of light necessary beyond measure. The only thing Taz could think to compare it to would be how he'd felt about being in the presence of something larger than himself. One time in his career, he'd accompanied a client to London. When the client was invited to a state dinner at Windsor Castle, he'd felt something approaching awe, being in the Queen's palace. Though he wasn't allowed in the same room as the monarch, it had still been amazing for Taz to stand in a castle which was over twelve hundred years old. He knew if he ever had the opportunity to meet the US President, he'd feel much the same.

He hadn't been certain if Storm was going to order him out of the room when the twink entered but judging by the talk they'd had the day he'd been introduced to Storm, the star realized he did need protection and insulation from his more overtly adoring fans. Taz had been clear about his commitment to the young star—he would do everything in his power to keep Storm safe—and the star had to accept his expertise and listen to his directions when it came to questions about security when they were out in public. So far, the relationship had progressed without incident but Taz knew it was only a matter of time before his client defied him at some point... they always did.

With Storm, his first openly gay client, being in the room with him and his trick while they had sex hadn't been an easy thing to take. It hadn't been the first time he'd acted as unwilling voyeur, but it had been the most uncomfortable, primarily because he was attracted to the handsome star himself. It was difficult not to be. The fact that Taz could get laid anytime and anywhere he wanted to made no difference. He certainly wasn't short on offers but was particular in his tastes and hadn't been in any sort of meaningful relationship since Gregor and before that, high school. Even then, he'd been a young kid who seemed to have a crush on every guy in school. His first boyfriend at sixteen had broken his heart and Taz had stayed single since then, not considering Gregor to actually be a boyfriend but more like a regular booty call. Taz simply existed, carefully avoiding relationships that would drag his focus away from his goals in life.

Taz was disturbed from his musings when he saw Storm's agent coming back down the mostly empty hallway toward the dressing room. Alan Steinberg had been the first person in Storm Ellison's entourage he'd spoken to when Rome had first referred him the position and he seemed like a decent guy, though Taz was the kind of person who didn't let first impressions be his compass. The short, balding older man had hired him as soon as he'd seen him, anxious to fill the position, explaining how Storm was destined for the big screen and would need a personal bodyguard more than ever.

"Is he ready?" Alan asked, walking up and pointing to the door.

"Getting there," Taz answered.

Alan eyeballed him a moment before nodding and rapping on the door. "Storm, you decent?" Alan asked.

The door opened, revealing Storm in all his beautiful glory. The star had donned a skintight pair of olive green pants and a camouflage T-shirt that hugged his defined pectorals beautifully. Over that, he wore a smooth tan leather jacket and matching leather boots. He'd gelled his hair so it spiked up from the top of his head and he wore the sexy guyliner and silver rings on nearly every finger and thumb, a silver neck chain that resembled a dog collar, and had changed out a stud in his nose for a ring and had added a silver eyebrow bar above the left eye. He was stunningly handsome and it was all Taz could do not to drool.

"Ready, Alan," Storm said, throwing only a cursory glance toward Taz as he walked out of the room, closing the door behind himself.

Taz turned his back on them as they followed him down the hallway toward the exit in front of them. Steinberg's cell rang as they exited the stage entrance on the side of the building. Taz noted Storm's stretch limousine waiting for them just outside the large Nokia Theatre and he held out an arm halting the pair, looking side to side to make certain that no fans had crossed over the barriers LAPD had set up to hold back the throng of admirers who sent up a cheer the second they spotted their favorite star. He motioned for Storm and his manager to move quickly toward the limousine and watched Storm's expression transform with a beauteous smile as he waved toward the crowd before ducking into the car followed by his manager. Once they were inside, Taz shut the door and the driver, David, greeted him as he climbed into the front beside him. As soon as the doors were locked, David started the car and headed off to the first after-party venue at the Beverly Hills Hotel on Sunset Blvd, not far from the theater. Taz happened to glance in the rearview mirror and caught the mischievous eye of Storm who watched him closely while the manager jabbered away on the phone. The moment he caught Taz watching, the star winked and flashed him his famous million dollar smile. Taz couldn't help but smile back at him in the mirror.

"You won't believe who just died!" Alan said, excitedly, swiping his phone to end his call.

Storm's expression turned serious as he looked at his manager. "Who?"

"Jill Gibbons!"

"The comedienne?" Storm asked, his expression awash with surprise. "Oh, I loved her," he pouted.

"Me too, but now we have a problem!" Steinberg said, biting his lip.

"What problem?" Storm asked.

"Seriously? Did you forget the slurs she made against transvestites two months ago, calling them trannies? This puts you in a very precarious position, Storm!"

"How so?" the star asked his manager.

"How so? Storm, according to her daughter, Monica, her mother's final request was that all of Hollywood be invited to her funeral so she can go out with a bang."

Taz watched the star's face for some sort of reaction.

"Okay, and so, what does that have to do with me?"

"Storm! You are the high profile public face of the gay community and if you haven't realized after tonight, you are an A-list celebrity! Everyone will be watching to see if you show up and give your support to her."

Taz watched Storm's expression in the dark car. "Jill was a friend of mine. She was one of the first people to interview me on her late night television show. Of course I'm going, Alan! You got me that gig on her show. Oh, how sad she died; she was a really nice lady."

"Storm, you will face ridicule and may even be blackballed from gay Hollywood if you show up in support of her!" The agent seemed mortified but Taz watched a look of determination cross the star's features.

"Seriously, Alan, I'm going. I liked her very much. She raised millions for homeless causes, hunger causes, and AIDS causes in the past. She rode in Pride parades across America. She loved gay men and was very public about it. She was a comedienne, Alan, and she was joking when she made the tranny comment. I know it was offensive but she was in her eighties for Heaven's sake, and she probably didn't mean it the way she said it; they honestly need to give her a pass. I loved her like a grandmother. If gay Hollywood doesn't like the fact that I go to her funeral, then fuck gay Hollywood! Besides, I doubt that would happen."

Taz watched as the agent twisted his hands in his lap, obviously unhappy that his star had a set of balls and couldn't be as easily manipulated as some.

"Oh, hell, fine then. I'll put out a press release with a statement from you, explaining your decision," Steinberg finally said.

"Good, but you let me read it first, Alan. I don't want anything disparaging said about that woman. I genuinely liked her."

The agent seemed to look very frustrated but he finally capitulated to his client's wishes. "Okay, Storm. I'm only looking out for you."

You're looking out for your meal ticket.

"Thanks, Alan," Storm replied.

Taz watched the star turn away and look out at the bright lights that lit Sunset Blvd as they whizzed through the streets of Los Angeles. Traffic had finally cleared and when they pulled up to the valet at the Beverly Hills Hotel, Taz was the first person out of the car. He walked to the back and opened the door for Storm while David did the same for his manager. The moment Storm stepped out onto the red carpet, flashbulbs went off and a roar went up from the fans, once again held back by a velvet rope. Storm glanced at Taz and leaned in as he soon as he stood up.

"What do you think, Taz? I should go to Jill's funeral, shouldn't I?" His face was open and honest as he asked.

"It's not my place to do your thinking for you, sir," Taz answered.

Storm's features instantly transformed as hurt washed across them a moment before a blank mask slid into place wiping it away as though the expression had never been there. Taz could have kicked himself the moment he saw it and he instantly regretted it.

"Of course it's not. Don't forget that," the superstar shot back through gritted teeth.

Taz instantly felt as though he'd been punched in the stomach and as he watched Storm turn away with glistening eyes, he suddenly wished Storm had done just that.

CHAPTER TWO

Storm pulled on his yoga pants and stood checking himself out in the full-length mirror in his large opulent bedroom the next morning. He'd watched his intake of alcohol the night before and even though they'd made the rounds of all four after-parties and had gotten home just before dawn, he was filled with energy and ready for what the day would bring him. Rebecca, his maid, had sent up a plate of melon and multigrain toast along with his favorite ruby red grapefruit juice, and Storm was feeling quite rested after only a few good hours of sleep. Of course, the glass of water and the vitamin packet of Emergen-C he shook into it, had prepared him for his workout with Guru Shamsa whom he was expecting any time. He worked out with the guru a few days a week and had been following a rigid diet along with his yoga and a regime of weekly colonics for the last six months. The guru assured him that his internal cleansing was as important as his physical workout and diet and Storm had taken the advice seriously, following the routine to a tee.

Storm smoothed the yoga pants over his muscled thighs and made a turn, checking out his ass in the mirror, assessing the tight muscles that were impossible to hide in the skintight spandex. As he did, he caught sight of the white lines appearing on the inside of his left forearm. The scars had faded but Storm meticulously covered them with his long-sleeved clothing, ashamed to let anyone learn of his cutting ritual of the past. It had been months since Storm had cut, but something in the way his new bodyguard had distanced himself from Storm the night before had cut him even deeper than the razor blade he used to draw across his skin. The urge to cut again had been strong and as he looked into the mirror, seeing them as fresh as if they were still new on his body, all of the old insecurities Storm had felt came rushing back. In reality, Storm had lived with fame for so short a time it was easy to forget he was one of the most famous and beloved stars in the country at the moment; it was much easier for him to fall back into the old way of thinking which told him he was worthless and untalented, wanted only for his body and face and he had no redeeming qualities other than the physical. He turned, walked to the large ensuite bathroom, and reached into the medicine cabinet to pull out the box of large bandages. He yanked one out and put it on to cover the old scars just a second before there was a knock at the bedroom door.

"I'm coming," he called out, leaving the bathroom and crossing the bedroom to pull open the door.

Taz stood in the hallway outside wearing a freshly ironed dress shirt and black suit. Storm noted his own pale blue eyes, circled with fresh guyliner, reflected in the bodyguard's black mirrored sunglasses. *Doesn't he ever take the fucking things off?* "Oh, it's you," he remarked, still stung by Taz's remark the night before. He stepped into the hallway and shut the bedroom door.

"Your guru is in the foyer, sir," the bodyguard said formally.

Storm stared at him, almost certain a smile hinted around the gorgeous lips of his smug bodyguard. He ignored him and walked past, feeling the bodyguard's stare on his ass. For the millionth time he speculated at Taz's sexuality and fantasized about fucking the big man, or better still, being fucked by the man. *He's gotta be six foot five if he's an inch. I bet he's got a huge cock. I wonder if he's cut or uncut.* Storm felt his yoga pants begin to stretch as the blood rushed to his dick. He reached down to adjust his package as he walked and was relieved to see Butch come charging down the hall at him. He stopped in his tracks, grinning widely as he bent to scoop up the small black French Bulldog. Butch reacted to Storm by excitedly licking his face.

"Butchy boy," Storm said, nuzzling the dog's neck as he wiggled excitedly in his arms. Barely more than three, Storm had received the dog as a gift from Alan when he'd won the part on "Trapped on an Island". Ironically, the role's shooting schedule meant he had little time to spend with his four-legged friend so when he was able to play with Butch, he made the most of it. He kissed the dog, letting him lick all over his face, wondering if he were to take the part to the new movie that Alan proposed he'd be spending even more time away from Butch. His insane schedule didn't leave Storm a lot of time for his dog or a boyfriend for that matter. He'd never had anyone serious in his life, nor wanted anyone, if he were to be entirely honest with himself.

"Atta boy, Butch. Who's my lover? Who's my lover?" He kissed the dog and put him down. Butch jumped up on his back legs and did a circle as Storm laughed. He glanced over at Taz who walked beside him down the hall, catching him grinning. The relaxed expression lit up the man's whole face bringing out a dimple in each cheek. He was stunning. *So, you do have a heart, you cold bastard.*

Storm allowed himself to smile as he walked down the length of the hallway with Butch and the bodyguard and took the stairs down to the first floor where his guru waited for him in the marble floored foyer of his palatial mansion. The second Butch saw the man waiting for him, he began barking like crazy, running up to him. Guru Shamsa had been his yogi for the last three months and he enjoyed his company. They got along well and Storm appreciated the reserved nature of the man. He seemed to exude a quiet positive energy even though he kept his thoughts to himself. Storm couldn't really call him a friend… they hadn't opened up to each other that way, and that was fine with Storm. He wasn't looking for a friend in the guru, only a companion and someone who could guide him through the taxing yoga exercises they both liked. The guru looked down at the dog as he ran up and Storm was instantly embarrassed when Butch tried to nip at the guru's feet. The man stepped back as Storm ran up and scooped the dog into his arms.

"Butch, what the hell is wrong with you?" he chided. "That's no way to treat a guest," Storm said. "Let me put him outside," he said shamefully, and he turned, walking to the patio door, opening it, and putting Butch on the ground outside. "Stay here, bad boy," Storm said. He closed the screen as Butch started barking again and turned, walking back to where the guru and Taz stood.

"Namaste, Guru," Storm greeted, walking up, pressing both flat palms together in front of him as he bowed slightly at the waist. Guru Shamsa was as Caucasian as Storm but he had a dark tan as though he spent hours in the sun, coloring his skin golden brown. His light blue eyes were a contrast against his tanned skin and though not classically handsome, Guru Shamsa had an appealing look to his hawk-like features.

"Namaste, Storm," the guru replied, bowing back. "Are you ready for a workout?"

"I am so ready," Storm said, turning toward a hallway as he began walking with the tall, thin bald man beside him. He sensed Taz following the two of them but put the thought to the back of his mind as he geared up for the punishing exercise session ahead of him. They got to the workout room where meditation music was already playing softly and Storm stopped, turning back to Taz.

"Why don't you take your lunch? We'll be fine from here," he said to the bodyguard.

Taz seemed to bristle a little at being told what to do but to his credit he nodded, walked out of the exercise room, and shut the double doors behind them, leaving Storm and his guru alone. It was a full hour and a half before they were finished and Storm was absolutely certain that every single cell in his body was screaming in pain. The yoga exhausted him but was invigorating at the same time. His doorbell rang as he and Guru Shamsa were walking out of his home gym. Rebecca answered the door. The second she pulled the huge oak door open and he heard the high-pitched voice of his best friend Juliana Ortiz, he found himself grinning.

"Storm! Storm Ellison. Where's that gay ass of yours?" she called out before spotting him and his guru standing twenty feet away. "Oh, Oops!" she burst into giggles. "Sorry, I didn't know you had company," the little spitfire said. Juliana Ortiz was his soul mate… if a female in Storm's circles could be called a soul mate.

"Jules!" Storm said, walking up to her. He threw his arms around her petite form and squeezed. She was nearly a foot shorter than him with a glorious mane of brown curls that skimmed the top of her shapely butt. He accepted her hug back and then let her go, stepping back to admire her outfit. She wore a bikini top stretched across her generous breasts and the bellybutton ring she sported with its sparkling diamond accent highlighted the Hawaiian inspired sarong swirling around her ankles. Sandals and an expertly done pedicure finished off her bohemian look. Juliana's father was a highly placed official in the Puerto Rican government and her mother a perfectly coiffed society princess. Though they tried reining in their only daughter, Jules was a free spirit and Storm realized because they loved her so much, she was allowed a lot of slack except when it was required she attend the occasional political function at their insistence.

"How are you?" she asked. "God were you ever beautiful last night! All my friends were jealous of me. They kept asking who you're dating and I had no idea what to tell them," she chattered excitedly. "Oh, hello, Guru," she said, making the proper bow as she turned toward Guru Shamsa.

Storm smiled at his friend as the guru bowed back. "Namaste."

"Meester. Storm, ju lunch, she ees ready. Ju like to eat outside on the pool deck?" Rebecca asked with her thick Cuban accent.

Storm turned toward her, smiling at Rebecca who'd been with him for two years as a housekeeper, maid, and cook, since he'd first become famous in his short run on a popular daytime soap opera. When he'd moved into his current residence after landing his TV series, she'd come with him and had taken up residence during his waking hours. She didn't live in the mansion and he knew she had a husband whom she complained about all the time with no real malice. He suspected she loved him very much.

"I think we'll take our lunch by the pool, Rebecca," Storm said. He turned toward his guru. "You are welcome to join us, Guru."

The darkly tanned man looked past him to the yard where Butch barked at the screen and then turned back and bowed to him again. "No, thank you, Storm. I have a client to meet down at the temple. Namaste." The expression on his face was unhappy and Storm could only think he was put out by the way Butch was behaving.

"Namaste." Storm bowed and moved to stand beside Jules, watching as the guru let himself out.

"Fuckin' creepy," Jules said the moment the door was closed.

Storm turned toward her, his mouth dropping open. "Jules!"

She grinned at him, showing off her perfect straight white teeth. "Well, there's something weird about him, Storm. Even Butch agrees."

He burst into laughter and then was distracted as Taz walked into the entryway, looking scrumptious in his buttoned-up suit. It occurred to him that Jules had yet to meet the bodyguard, though she was practically a fixture around his house. "Jules, this is Balthazar, my new bodyguard," he said, making introductions as the beautiful black man walked up.

"Balthazar? Well, you're a big one," she said, grinning madly, sticking out a petite hand. Taz took it and her palm was instantly swallowed in his gigantic mitt.

"Please, call me Taz," he said, the bodyguard's low voice rumbling as he smiled at Jules. "It's nice to meet you."

"Taz! Oh!" Jules said, exaggeratedly, looking over at Storm and nodding like a bobblehead as she widened her eyes, sending a silent signal to him. He could read the lust in her eyes instantly and Storm didn't even try to hide his smile. She cracked him up. "Join us for lunch, Taz," Jules said flirtatiously, taking the bodyguard's arm as she completely ignored Storm and walked away toward the sliding glass doors leading to the back yard. Storm grinned and shook his head, following his bodyguard and his best friend.

"I just ate, ma'am," Taz said.

Storm watched as Jules slapped his arm. "Please, my mother is ma'am. Call me Jules, big boy."

Taz chuckled.

Well, it didn't take much for her to give him her stamp of approval! The fact was, Jules was a good barometer for Storm. Her judgment of a person's character mattered very much to him. He'd met Jules when they were taking acting classes at Pierce Community College in the San Fernando Valley before Storm became famous and she'd been his best friend, encouraging him in his endeavors every step of the way since that time. He knew her heart inside and out and with Storm, trust was a major issue. It was so easy for him to be fooled by false friends because truthfully, no one in Hollywood was who they claimed to be. Jules, on the other hand, was a genuine friend, one who'd known Storm before he'd hit the big time, and he valued her friendship above all others. If she liked Taz, that was good for huge bonus points in Storm's mind, though he did think her opinion of his guru was flawed.

"So, you think you can keep my boy safe?" Storm heard Jules ask.

"Taz, please keep my Jules entertained while I shower. I'll be two minutes," Storm told Taz. He pointed at Jules. "You… behave!"

Jules giggled. "Not on your life, Storm. Run along and freshen up," she said, grinning. "Taz and I will talk about you behind your back while you're gone. Come on, sugar," she said.

Storm smiled at her and watched as his best friend and his handsome bodyguard walked outside. The look on Taz's face was perfect. The big man didn't know what to make of Jules but that was a common occurrence when it came to the hot little Puerto Rican.

****

Taz and Juliana stepped out onto the patio. Butch had relaxed and Taz reached down to pet him.

Jules petted him too as the dog's little stump of a tail wagged furiously and Taz turned away, looking out at the one hundred and eighty degree view of the gorgeous Pacific Ocean which could be seen from Storm's yard. His infinity pool seemed to drop off the face of the cliff at the edge of his property and the crystal clear water was stunning in the bright California sunlight. Rebecca had laid out a luncheon for two on the teak wood table under Storm's patio cover and Taz noted the assortment of fresh fruit including Storm's favorites, juicy red watermelon and cantaloupe. A platter of brie and other cheeses had been set out, two glasses of sparkling white wine had already been poured, and Jules began humming when she caught sight of the spicy mango chicken wings that were one of Rebecca's specialties.

The maid had preceded them out to the patio and was dishing up Greek salads with a light vinaigrette dressing, cucumbers, and kalamata olives which Storm was crazy about. Taz noted the absence of a third plate and he wondered how Rebecca had guessed correctly that Guru Shamsa would decline the invitation to join them. The guru was an interesting guy but as Taz stood behind Juliana's chair to pull it out for her, he put all thoughts of the guru aside and focused on Storm's friend. He'd learned to observe his clients' friends and acquaintances, knowing he could learn a lot about a client's personality from the people they spent the most time with.

Juliana took the chair Taz offered and continued humming, making yum-yum sounds as she inspected the afternoon's fare. When she looked up at Taz and smiled, her face was stunningly gorgeous. If

Taz were into women, she'd be precisely the kind of woman he went for. He loved personality and she had it in spades.

"Sit down and join me, Taz," she said, holding out a hand to Storm's empty chair.

"Ju want to eat, Meester Taz?" Rebecca asked Taz.

"No, thank you very much. I ate," Taz answered, knowing very well that Rebecca had seen him in the kitchen. He liked the older woman. She had a motherly persona and Taz appreciated that very much. He was very close to his own large family and he saw them often whenever he had days off.

"Well, at least have some juice," Juliana said, lifting the pitcher and pouring him a glass of the fresh squeezed orange juice Storm loved.

"Thank you," Taz said, taking the glass from her and pulling out a chair to sit beside her, leaving Storm's chair across from her untouched. He watched as she picked up a bottle of Tabasco sauce and dribbled some into her glass of tomato juice. After squeezing a lemon wedge into the tumbler, she picked up a small spoon and stirred the concoction together before lifting the glass and downing it in one gulp. Taz shivered. Sure he liked his Louisiana hot links as much as the next guy, but he wasn't a huge fan of hot sauce on or in everything.

"Storm's lucky to have found such a great bodyguard," Juliana said. "He says you came highly recommended."

Taz blushed a little, feeling grateful that Herman and Rome had given him such a good recommendation.

"So how many people have you shot?" she asked, batting her long eyelashes in his direction.

Taz coughed and almost spit his juice clear across the table. Storm took that moment to reemerge from the house. Taz looked up only to see his employer looking handsome as heck, dressed in tan and brown camo shorts and a beige wifebeater T-shirt. He also wore sweatbands on his wrists which looked out of place, but Taz ignored them as he got a closer look at Storm's body. His chest muscles were defined through the shirt and Taz could make out two nipple rings underneath the thin fabric. He swallowed hard and dragged his gaze away from Storm's body to focus on his eyes. The damn gorgeous guyliner was back along with the nose ring and eyebrow bar and the star was looking as scrumptious as he possibly could.

"Are you terrorizing my new bodyguard, woman?" Storm asked, picking up Butch and kissing him as Taz got to his feet, setting down the juice glass. Storm pulled out a chair and sat at the table, setting the dog down as he looked at the offered fare.

Juliana blinked innocently as she grinned. "I just asked him how many people he's shot, Storm, a perfectly innocent question."

Taz watched as Storm's mouth dropped open before he began to laugh. Storm looked up at him, a slight curiosity in his features.

"I am a former Marine, ma'am," Taz answered without committing to a number as he looked away from Storm's gaze and forced himself to smile at Jules. He knew he probably couldn't count anyway.

"He's a former Marine, Jules," Storm repeated, admiring the delicious looking salad on the plate in front of him. It sounded very non-committal coming from the superstar, though Taz could detect a hint of interest in the way Storm said it.

"Oh, how lovely, a military hero," Jules said, humming again before taking a delicate bite of her salad. Taz retreated several feet and positioned himself with his back to a column, tuning out the conversation the two friends carried on. The sound of the ocean was soothing as he listened to Jules giggle at something Storm said.

"You have got to be kidding, babe, a colonic? The guru says that you need a colonic? Don't you take care of the internal cleansing as part of some routine anyway?"

Taz's ears perked up as he watched Storm turn his head and shoot him a sideways glance before answering. He knew Storm couldn't see his eyes behind the dark aviator sunglasses he wore but it was fun watching him react.

"I swear sometimes you need a muzzle, Jules," Storm answered his friend, frowning slightly. Taz could see he struggled with the expression he threw his friend, noting the smile that played around his mouth. "And, just for your information, yes… I have the cleanest colon in town but that's not the point. The guru says that regular colonics will clean all the internal toxins from deep within. Do you realize how many parasites live inside our bodies?"

Taz watched as Juliana dropped the fork she was holding over her salad and pushed the plate of wings away. "Well, that takes care of lunch," she said, sounding disgusted.

Taz held back a smile.

Storm reached over to her plate and pointed at her wings with his fork while he chewed. A perfectly shaped olive was speared on the end. "Eat up, babe," he said around the bite of food in his mouth. "We have a big night ahead of us and a busy day of shopping before that," he told his friend.

She stared at Storm for a few seconds before reaching out and pulling the plate of wings back toward her and smiled before picking one up, taking a dainty bite. "Oh, where are we shopping?"

Storm took another bite of his salad and gestured with his fork. "I thought we'd start off at Jimmy Choo's and then there's this amazing leather coat I saw at Gucci. Enrique told me he'd have it in my size by today," Storm said.

Taz listened to the two of them banter as he wondered at the money so easily thrown around by the rich and famous. It seemed like a waste to him. Though he'd grown up in a poor area of town, his mother, father, two brothers, two sisters, a brother-in-law, and a niece had all lived in the large hundred year old house his great-grandfather had built. Money was always tight but they'd all contributed and it had been a happy life, even with the financial struggles.

"Oh, that sounds like fun," Juliana said. She looked over at Taz. "Will you be coming with us, Taz?"

"Yes, ma'am," Taz answered.

"He insists on going everywhere I go," Storm said, looking over at him and winking. Taz stared at him stoically.

"Do you ever smile, big boy?" Juliana asked, a smile playing around her pretty full lips.

"No, ma'am," Taz answered.

"Ignore him, Jules. He's way too serious," Storm added.

"What's on the agenda for tonight?" Juliana asked.

"I thought we'd start at The Abbey and then maybe make it over to The Red Room," Storm suggested, stuffing a forkful of salad into his mouth before chewing.

"Oh, that drag club. I love that place," Juliana said.

"I do too, though I miss Ricky LaGrange. He was the best."

"Oh, I agree," Storm's friend added. "He was so beautiful, you couldn't tell he was a guy."

"Rumor has it he married a genuine cowboy and moved to Texas," Storm said.

"Wow… a cowboy. I had me a cowboy once," Jules said, her eyes sparkling.

Storm chuckled as he bit into a bite of salad, dripping in dressing. "I think you've had more than one, Jules. Tell the truth," he said.

"Well, a girl has to be social, doesn't she?" Jules asked, grinning from ear to ear. She continued as Storm nodded. "So, who will it be for you tonight, Storm? Twink or bear? What's my boy in the mood for?"

Storm seemed to ponder the question and then glanced over at Taz, letting his gaze rake the length of him from head to toe. Taz warmed under Storm's appraisal and suddenly felt the afternoon heat through his suit. "I think I'll see who strikes my fancy, Jules… though I do love the bears," Storm drawled.

Jules reached out a manicured hand and slapped Storm on the bicep. "Ain't that the truth. You aren't any too picky but somehow all your dates make mine pale in comparison," she said, lightheartedly.

Storm grinned. He was stunning even when he wasn't trying. Taz thought he was probably one of the best looking men he'd ever seen and Taz had seen some absolutely gorgeous men.

"I do have good taste, Jules but trust me; your dates are no ogres." He took another bite of salad and chewed. "So, are you bringing anyone?"

"No, Tony had the bad taste to break up with me last night," she said with a smile.

"You don't seem too upset about it, Jules," Storm remarked.

"I can't remember when I was broken up about a breakup," she giggled, "though I had high hopes for Tony."

Storm chuckled. "Yeah, right! You'd been dating Tony what two weeks?"

"Ten days, but that's practically a record for me," she said, tossing her beautiful curly hair as she grinned.

"I'll say," Storm said. "I bet your mom was devastated."

"My mom wants me settled down giving her grandchildren yesterday, Storm. That doesn't mean it's happening anytime soon. Do you know she had the nerve to tell my father that she was going to find me a suitable husband if I didn't find one on my own?" she said, throwing Storm a look of feigned shock.

"Sweetie, she just wants grandchildren, the same as any red-blooded mother," Storm said, tongue in cheek.

"For Pete's sake. The next time she comments on my dating status, I'm going to tell her I'm a lesbian. Let's see how well that goes over," she remarked, sounding serious.

"You?" Storm asked before bursting out laughing. "You couldn't live with taco if your life depended on it." The remark earned the star a slug to the bicep.

"Shut up. I could do girls if I wanted to," she said, trying to sound outraged.

Storm continued laughing. "God help the woman who bedded you. You'd eat her alive," he said.

"Lesbians love that, Storm," Juliana said, rolling her eyes as she bit into another wing and chewed.

It was Storm's turn to tap Juliana's arm with his fist. The touch was gentle and Taz watched her eyes light with mirth. "Oh, and you're such an expert on lesbians."

Juliana leaned forward, speaking quietly. "Do you really think I've never been in bed with a woman, babe?"

"Not unless you were sharing a guy," Storm said with a giant grin on his face.

"Who told you?" she gasped. "Ernesto? Did Ernesto tell you? Rat! I never could trust him," she protested loudly.

"You dated him for a week," Storm added, a smile playing around his lips. He pushed his empty plate away and refilled his juice glass before relaxing back in his chair.

"It was a long weekend, actually." She grinned and waggled her eyebrows. "A hell of a long weekend."

"And you call me a player," Storm smirked.

"And you love me for it," she said, putting down her chicken bone and picking up a napkin. "Let's get going," she said, looking over at Taz. "Are you ready to go shopping, tall-dark-and-lovely?"

"I vibrate with anticipation, ma'am," Taz said.

She laughed before looking back at Storm who was once again checking him out. "Oh, Storm, you need to keep Taz around. Not only is he drop-dead gorgeous, he's got jokes," she said.

Storm laughed and it was everything Taz could do not to join them.

CHAPTER THREE

A thumping beat pounded out of the large speakers on either side of the DJ booth in the dark club. The Red Room featured a large dance floor which doubled as a stage when the drag performers entertained the wall-to-wall audience. Tonight, Storm was out to have fun. With Jules along as a companion it was hard not to have fun, even when there was the chance their night would be cut short by paparazzi and overzealous fans. Though Storm loved the fame and the fortune that came along with it, he sometimes longed for the anonymity he'd enjoyed before becoming famous for his role on "Trapped on an Island". The popular television show was a reality/fiction hybrid, combining real life personalities and a scripted storyline. The concept was new in that the target audience knew it was scripted though it was pretty well known that the producers of most "reality" shows scripted their participants' situations… who ended up with the rose on any given night or who ended up in whose bed and the like. They had to keep it interesting so they made sure the drama their fans craved was always present.

As Storm and Jules wound their way through the crowded club, the superstar was happy he hadn't been recognized yet. He knew it would happen eventually, probably sooner rather than later; he was confident that his tall, gorgeous bodyguard would provide a barrier between them and the fans for a little while at least. The first drag show had concluded and the club goers had crowded onto the dance floor, moving in time to Beyoncé. Fortunately the club was dark and Taz had paid the host to secure Storm and Jules a booth against a far wall close to the club's back room where they could watch what was going on in relative privacy. The club was located in the center of the rainbow district of West Hollywood on Santa Monica Blvd and was a popular hangout for all types of gay men, young and old. Tonight, Storm noted the bar seemed to be populated with his personal favorite, bears. Though Storm wasn't particularly picky and wasn't into the leather or daddy scene, he liked men who were larger than he was... men like Taz. *Dammit.* He didn't even know if Taz liked guys.

Storm knew he'd been gay from a very young age. He'd started out in foster care and had been one of the lucky kids; he'd found a good family to adopt him after his mother had abandoned him when he was just a toddler. His parents had adopted through a placement agency called The Children's Home Society after his drug-addled mother had signed away her parental rights. Storm had never known his biological father. His adoptive family, the Ellisons, had named him Stephen and even though Storm had never been told his birth name, he hadn't missed it; the Ellisons had been devoted to him. When his father had passed away from a heart attack just after Storm graduated middle school, he'd been devastated but when his mother had been killed in a car accident while Storm was in acting school, he'd gone into a deep depression. It was during this time that Storm had landed his role on a daytime soap opera and not being able to share his fame with his mom had hurt deeply. He'd formed an even tighter bond with his friend Jules who was like a sister to him. The bonus of having Jules as a friend was that she shared his love of beautiful men. He looked over at her and listened as she leaned in, animatedly describing a hottie she'd seen on the way to their booth.

"There! There he is, Storm. Isn't he perfect?" She pointed to a tall, handsome bear who turned Storm's way, openly appraising him as they passed by him and his two companions. Storm managed to smile at the bear before arriving at their booth where Taz waited. He glanced at the bodyguard and then slid into the booth followed by Jules before Taz sat down, boxing in Storm's pretty friend between them. A waitress walked up, took their orders, and had just walked away when the tall bear sauntered up to the booth. Storm looked up at him, noted his good looks, and smiled as the man stuck out a hand.

"Hello, gorgeous," he said with a European intonation. Storm guessed the man was French or Belgian judging by his accent.

"Hi," Storm said, taking the offered hand and shaking it. The man was very handsome with a dark goatee, closely cropped hair, and expensive looking clothes.

"Would you dance with me, cher?" the man drawled, holding out an arm in a sweep of the dance floor.

Storm smiled and then glanced over at Taz to see what his reaction would be… not that he needed the bodyguard's permission to dance, but he was almost hopeful the big man would shake his head no and then stand and pull Storm into his own arms and out onto the dance floor. Taz sent him a blank look and Storm felt instantaneous disappointment. *What the hell are you thinking, wanting this guy?* The thought took Storm off guard and angry with himself, he sneered at his bodyguard before turning back to the bear and holding out a hand.

"I'd love to." He slid out of the booth when the man grinned widely and Storm stood up, gripping the man's hand, refusing to look back at Taz and Jules in the booth. He felt the weight of his bodyguard's eyes on his back as he walked away but stubbornly ignored the urge to let go of the bear and rush back to his table. They let the crowd swallow them up and as soon as they found a place where he knew Taz couldn't see them, and he turned, letting the bear surround him in his long arms. The man wore a denim jacket and he smelled good and Storm loved feeling the heat from the man's body as he pulled him close. They'd moved together for about a minute when the man whispered in his ear.

"My name is Henri and I know you are Storm Ellison," he said.

For just a moment Storm was surprised; he'd really hoped the man hadn't recognized him but he realized how foolish that was. Storm knew he was probably famous all over the world after his appearance on the Emmys; Alan had told him the fan mail was pouring in along with offers of movie deals, television parts, and personal appearances. He leaned back in the man's arms and smiled at him, looking up the two inches difference in their heights. Up close the man was good-looking but not fabulous like he'd originally thought. He was also slightly older than Storm had first guessed, approaching forty and his attraction waned a little.

The man smiled back and looked down at Storm's lips. "I want to kiss you, Storm. May I?" Henri asked.

Storm's first inclination was to say no but as he glanced past the man's shoulder only to find Taz watching him through the crowd with a very unhappy expression on his face, he gave in, turning his attention back to Henri's face.

"Please," he breathed.

A second later, Henri was kissing him and grinding a hard dick against his groin as he did so. Storm let himself fall into the fantasy of having sex with Henri, the tall, handsome European and he began to become aroused himself. *How do you like watching me now, Taz?* Storm suddenly ended the kiss as the unbidden thoughts snuck into his mind, taking over all sexy thoughts of Henri, and he found himself pissed as hell that he couldn't help but look in the bodyguard's direction. When he remembered that he'd purposely put the crowd between him and Taz, he got irritated. Angry with himself, Storm had let Henri's kiss go on a little longer than he'd wanted to and when he finally pulled away from the Frenchman, the guy was smiling widely.

"Ah, cher, you are so beautiful. Please let me take you home with me," he said sexily.

Storm noted the look of lust on his face which matched the hard cock persistently rubbing against Storm's groin. When Storm pictured the two of them in bed together, his thoughts of a night of fun suddenly evaporated. *This man is not who I want. I want Taz.* Storm sobered instantly and stepped back so fast Henri was thrown off balance as he was forced to let go. His frown was instantaneous and the sneer that accompanied it was as unexpected as could be. A bolt of fear shot through Storm as the bear cursed under his breath in French. Storm was stunned when Henri's arm shot out landing a gigantic hand on his shoulder.

"Where do you go, you rich tease?" he growled. "No one rejects Henri!"

Storm felt a sharp pain as the guy's grip on his shoulder became punishingly painful. He yelped. Only a second passed before Storm was nearly lifted off the dance floor as a strong arm came around his middle, pulling him back where he slammed against a hard body. It happened so fast, Storm was barely able to register the look of shock on the bear's face when Taz's fist connected with Henri's jaw, propelling the guy backward only for him to land on his ass. As if in slow motion, Storm felt himself being gathered into the safe cocoon of Taz's embrace as he heard Jules's raised voice from beside Taz.

"Let's get out of here, boys," she practically yelled over the crowd.

Before Storm could even reply he and Jules were being steered out of the club as the stunned crowd of gaping onlookers parted like the Red Sea in front of them. When a bold fan tried to block their path, Taz's thick elbow came up and connected with the man's nose. Though the motion appeared accidental, Storm had a sneaking suspicion it was not. A second later, he heard a crunching sound, cringing as he heard it break. Thankfully, Taz's jacket blocked his face from further view of what was in front of him as the man's arm surrounded him while they moved out of the club.

Once they were outside, Taz dropped his arm and Storm took a deep breath, getting his bearings as the cool fresh air hit him in the face. The heat of Taz's huge body instantly disappeared as the man let Storm's waist go and when he finally located Jules a few steps behind them, she was laughing like crazy. Storm heard Taz whistle loudly and then spotted his limo when the driver pulled up, screeching to a halt. He reached out for Jules as Taz yanked open the door, shoving her inside onto the seat before piling on in after her. He'd barely gotten inside when his door was unceremoniously slammed shut and Storm watched as Taz climbed into the front before the limo peeled off through the parking lot. Storm was flattened against the back of the seat by the car's momentum as it lurched forward, stopping at the entrance to Santa Monica Blvd, and then pulling out onto the busy street, making a sharp, quick turn. He looked over at Jules who continued to roar with laughter and forced a frown around the smile he couldn't hold back.

"Stop laughing, you ass," he said which only made her crack up even harder.

"That was awesome," she gasped. A second later, she jumped off the seat and crawled to the front of the limo. She reached up and slid back the privacy screen, sticking her head into the driver's compartment where Taz and David sat. "You are magnificent, Taz," she said breathlessly as Storm watched his best friend. He heard the bodyguard chuckle.

"Thank you, ma'am."

Jules looked back at Storm and winked, a gigantic smile on her face as she made her way back down the length of the limo and flopped on the seat beside him, letting her head rest against the cushion as she stared at him. "Let's go dancing every night," she said, giggling again.

Storm couldn't help but laugh at her. "You ass," he said, "I was this close to getting laid." He held up his index finger and thumb with the spread of an inch between them.

"Funny, it looked like you were that close to getting manhandled and not in a good way, lover," she chuckled.

Storm smiled broadly and laid his head back against the seat again, turning to stare out the window as the lights whizzed by them.

"Where to, sir?" the driver asked.

He glanced over at Jules who simply smiled and shrugged. "Home, David," he replied, looking forward.

"Yes, sir," David answered.

A second later, Storm caught Taz's gaze in the mirrored visor in front of him. Though he had every right to gloat, the bodyguard's expression was only filled with concern. *Dammit. Does nothing faze you?* Of course it didn't. Taz was a former fucking Marine and the consummate professional. Storm relaxed again, closing his eyes as he let the smooth movements of the limo lull him into a meditative rest. It was quiet for the remaining half hour of the drive home and it gave Storm a lot of time to think. The fact was, he probably wouldn't have gone home with the French bear even though he'd been attracted to him. He'd had no real interest in him anyway and it was becoming clear to Storm that his recent interest gelled in one area only… a handsome bodyguard.

****

Storm took a deep breath and ducked his head in the water of his swimming pool as he approached the side. He touched the smooth tile wall and flipped, making the turn in the water with ease as he pushed off, looking straight ahead underwater. The clear blue of the rippling cool water was refreshing and he stroked hard and kicked, increasing his speed as he approached the middle of his pool. Coming up for air, he glanced at the sliding glass door where Jules was emerging from the house before looking forward as he plunged his face back in the water and took three more long strokes. He surfaced for air again just as he approached the far side of the long expanse of cool water and came to a stop, sucking in a huge gulp of air as he tried to slow his breathing down while hanging on to the side. His long legs bobbed in the water and he enjoyed the buoyant feeling for a full minute with his back to his best friend as he looked out over the gorgeous Pacific Ocean, appreciating the oranges and yellows as the southland was bathed in the beauteous rays of light.

"Good morning, fishy!" Jules finally yelled from the patio table where she sat drinking her favorite tomato juice which Rebecca had just set out for her. She'd obviously gotten tired of being ignored.

Storm grinned, wiping the water out of his face as he turned and waved at her. "Hello, bitch!"

"Hey," Jules protested with a laugh. "You're still mad that you didn't get French ass last night, aren't you?"

"Ha! Hardly," Storm protested, hoisting himself out of the pool and rising to a standing position as he reached for a towel Rebecca had laid out for him on a teak chaise lounge. He began rubbing it over his chest as the water sluiced off his body while he walked toward the house. He looked over Jules's shoulder noting Taz's presence for the first time that morning as he got closer and nodded to him before turning his attention back to his friend. She was gazing at him with an evil twinkle in her pretty brown eyes and he instantly knew she was up to something. He grinned at her as he reached for his orange juice. "What are you up to? I recognize those rusty gears turning again."

"Nothing, nothing," she said and then she set down her juice, leaning in closer. "Taz is looking quite stunning, Storm," she said.

He noted she was almost purring and it suddenly struck him that his best friend was nearly as enamored with the bodyguard as he was. His mouth dropped open as he leaned in, pinning her with a gaze. "You like him, don't you?"

Her smile faded instantly.

"Well, he's cute but you know me… I don't do gay guys… it's always when they're on the rebound from a bad boyfriend breakup and honestly… I don't like anyone's sloppy seconds… besides they can't hardly ever get it up and keep it up for me unless we're doing doggy because then they can imagine it's a guy and…"

"God, do you ever listen to yourself?" Storm asked, chuckling. "What vitamin are you taking anyway? You know that Red Bull shit will rot your brain, Jules."

She tossed a piece of a croissant at him across the table before continuing with a grin on her face. "You're a fine one to talk, superstar boy. You like him too. Don't lie to me… you're a terrible liar, Storm."

He leaned in again, shushing her with the frown he sent her direction. "Yes, I like him and if you repeat it to him, I'll kill you. I know how nosy you can be and I don't want him knowing it."

She simply grinned.

"Nod if you understand and promise me, Jules."

She simply grinned.

"Oh, you're so frustrating," he grumbled, stabbing a cantaloupe wedge with his fork.

"And you are fucking transparent, Storm," she mumbled around the mouthful of croissant she was chewing. "God, these are good," she said.

Storm chuckled and then looked up as he heard a loud voice coming from the bowels of the house. Taz turned his head and stared inside and then Storm recognized Alan's voice just before his agent whizzed by the bodyguard and stepped out onto the patio. He was holding his smartphone to his ear and talking loudly into it.

"I told you, Marty. I will get an answer from him… yes… yes… Jerry's Deli? Good. Good. Noon. I will see you at noon… right… ciao!" Alan swiped the phone and looked up, smiling at Storm as he got to the table. "Do you know who that was?" Alan asked, excitedly.

"Good morning to you too, Alan," Storm said, dryly.

"Good morning. Good morning," Alan said, flopping into a chair as he reached for a croissant and a butter knife. Storm watched his agent butter up his breakfast and shovel it inside his mouth. He wondered if Alan ever ate anything healthy at all. He had a gigantic gut on him and Storm knew he was only in his early fifties. It was truly a miracle he hadn't dropped dead yet. Storm glanced over at Taz. There was nothing flabby about the bodyguard and once again he found his thoughts turning decidedly sexual as he pictured the muscles under the black suit and white shirt Taz wore. *I'd love to unwrap you one piece of clothing at a time. I bet I couldn't get you entirely naked before I start licking.* It was an effort, but Storm shook himself out of his fantasies and looked back at Alan who was buttering up a second croissant and slathering it with whipped cream cheese.

"Did you have a chance to look over the screenplay?" Alan asked, coming right to the point of his visit. The man had a one-track mind but that was what Storm paid him for after all.

"Yes, actually, I did," Storm answered, stabbing a square of watermelon. "I like what I've read so far."

Alan dropped his croissant. "Oh thank God! I knew you would. You'll do it then?"

"I'm considering it, if it works into the shooting schedule of 'Trapped on an Island'," Storm replied. The attraction of making a major motion picture appealed to Storm but he'd never thought of gay films. In fact, most gay films had sad endings and were very dark. The idea of making one with a happy ending that may actually appeal to a wide audience and not simply a gay audience, intrigued him. "Do you really think it will become a crossover film from the gay community to the straight audience?"

"Think it? I know it!" Alan replied, excitedly. "Silver Bullets has everything one might like, a murder mystery, a love story, and hot hot sex; what more could you possibly want?"

"Well, it's really what the audience wants, now isn't it, Alan?" Storm asked.

"I think it sounds amazing. I love watching gay guys in love," Jules remarked, picking up her glass of juice to take a dainty sip.

"Oh, it will be amazing and more," Alan said around the bite of croissant in his mouth. "So, if I can get the TV producers to agree to work around your shooting schedule, you'll do it, right?"

"If they agree and we're not stepping on their toes, that's fine, Alan. You know I don't want to put out any of the other actors on the show," Storm said. He was very close to the cast on "Trapped on an Island" and the last thing he wanted to do was put them out. He'd hated it when one of the co-stars on the daytime soap he'd been on had done the same thing and thrown all of his co-stars under the bus. The actor had lost a lot of friends because he'd been selfish. Storm understood anyone wanting to put their career first, but he'd always hated the fact some did it without thought to the other actors in a production, whether television or film. There was enough selfishness in Hollywood to go around and Storm believed in Karma. He wasn't about to piss off that bitch if he could help it.

Alan's face lit up. "Excellent," he said, brushing off his hands and standing up. "Can I use your computer? I need to Skype the producer right now."

"Of course. You can use the one in the library, Alan. You know where it is," Storm replied.

"Perfect."

Alan turned and rushed into the house, passing by Taz who stepped off to the side to let him go. Storm let his eyes linger on the handsome bodyguard for a minute before turning back to Jules. She threw him a shit eating grin.

"I knew it! You like him!"

"Alan?" Storm asked.

"Taz!" she said, slapping him on the bicep. "You can barely take your eyes off of him."

"Shh," Storm said, hushing her. "He's going to hear you." The truth was, Storm did like his bodyguard but he wasn't about to let his attraction get the better of him. The jury was still out when it came to trusting the man completely. Just because he'd gotten him out of a precarious situation the night before didn't mean Storm was about to throw all his self-control to the wind and take up with a man who worked for him. Besides, he realized he might just be incorrectly reading the subtle signals he'd picked up from his bodyguard. Perhaps Taz wasn't really interested in him the way he hoped he'd be. It was nearly impossible to guess what the man was thinking with his eyes behind his dark sunglasses. *Why don't you ever take them off, Taz? What are you hiding?*

"So, what are we doing tonight?" Jules asked, cutting into his musing and changing the subject.

"I don't know. What do you want to do?" Storm asked, focusing on his friend.

"I know, let's go dancing! I hear the French soccer team is in town," she giggled.

It was Storm's turn to smile. "Bitch."

"You wouldn't have it any other way, Storm."

****

Taz watched the two friends at the breakfast table. He really liked what he saw of Jules. Not only was she pretty and funny, she was devoted to Storm and though he really didn't know why that pleased him, it did. Somehow, seeing the two banter back and forth was not only amusing, it reminded him very much of the get-togethers with his own large family. Growing up in a household with four generations including his grandparents when they were alive, siblings, his sister's husband, and their daughter, made him aware of other families and the dynamics between them. It was easy to spot a loving family and Taz knew Jules was good for his client. He got the idea that Jules liked him too and not in the Biblical sense. Though Taz wasn't in the closet at work, he kept his sexuality private just like his love life. The last thing he needed was to be distracted by the gorgeous superstar he'd sworn to protect.

Taz looked to the side and across a courtyard. The house was laid out in a U pattern with a bubbling fountain in the center of a courtyard which was open to the pool area. On the one side were double French doors leading onto the patio where he stood, to the left of this was the fountain in the courtyard, and beyond that was Storm's study/library where he could see Storm's agent sitting at a large, ornately carved desk in the room. When Taz had taken the initial tour of Storm's large mansion, he'd been surprised at much more than the size of the rooms and the antiques Storm had collected. He'd been very surprised to find Storm's library with its twelve foot ceilings and bookcases that covered three of the four walls. They were stocked with books of every genre, romance and gay romance sitting right alongside classics and contemporary literature. It seemed his young client was very well read indeed.

Beside the library was a media room with a fully equipped home theater which sat twenty people in luxurious reclining leather theater seats. There was also a candy counter, soda fountain, Thermador sub zero refrigerator, and popcorn maker. When Storm had first seen the room, images of Michael Jackson's famous home theater with much the same accoutrements as those at his Neverland Ranch came to mind. When Taz had seen the setup, he'd been absolutely certain he was coming to work for a vapid, spoiled Hollywood child but somehow, Storm Ellison was turning out to be much more. Frankly, that surprised Taz. He really didn't expect the superstar to have a brain to speak of and he certainly didn't think the man would be thinking with anything above the waist.

Storm's reputation as a hard-partying gay playboy was common knowledge, but his quiet routine of morning swims, yoga, and solitary meals with his best friend had thrown Taz for a loop. Of course Storm and Jules did hit the club scene almost every night, but any evidence of Storm using drugs or even excessive use of alcohol hadn't appeared on Taz's radar so far. Storm hadn't had any overnight guests since Taz had been there and for that matter, he hadn't been asked to escort the star to any rendezvous so far. Though there had been the one encounter after the Emmys, as far as

Taz knew, Storm wasn't prone to taking advantage of his fans or groupies, which was unusual among the clientele Taz had before. Though he'd never had a client as famous as Storm Ellison, he had acted as bodyguard and security for more than one high profile company executive and politician. As a rule, most had affairs on the side of their relationships, whether they were married or committed, and cheating was rampant with the expectation that Taz would provide security for his client's trysts. Though he hadn't had any female clients to this point, Taz could only guess they'd be much like the men he'd worked for.

"I'm telling you, Dante! This one is going to happen! Just spot me on this bet and you won't be sorry." Alan Steinberg's raised voice carried out through the open triple-paned windows of Storm's library all the way to Taz, who stood a good thirty feet off. He seemed to be having a heated conversation with someone, probably his bookie, trying to get his point across. Taz could see the sweat beading on the older man's head all the way across the courtyard where he was standing. He glanced back at Storm and Jules. The two had risen from the table and walked over to the pool where they were rubbing tanning oil on each other's chests while laughing. When Storm's fingers dipped into Jules' cleavage, she screamed, slapped his hand away, and giggled, diving into the pool with a huge splash.

"You're not getting away that easily," Storm yelled, diving in right after her.

"Please, Dante, just one more time. Check with Quinn. Tell him it's just this once. I promise this horse is going to take it all. I have a tip from his jockey."

So, someone likes the ponies, huh? Sounds like this isn't the first time Alan's made promises he couldn't keep. Taz had never understood some men's obsession with gambling, though he didn't consider it the worst vice in the world. Taz wasn't addicted to anything though he was much more familiar with the destructive nature of alcohol and drugs. He'd had clients who abused both and had witnessed the poor choices they'd made while under the influence.

"Thank you, Dante," Alan said, sounding relieved. "If he says it's all right, put me down for ten grand on Mirabelle to win in the fifth… yes, thank you." Taz watched the agent swipe his smartphone and then turn his attention to the computer monitor. When he began to tap on the keyboard, Taz looked back at the pool. Storm and Jules were racing down the length of the blue expanse, trying to best each other to the end and it seemed his client was beating his best friend by almost a length.

"Meester Taz, I breeng ju lemonade," Rebecca said, walking up with a frosty glass in her hand. He smiled at the smaller older woman and reached out to take the cold glass from her hand.

"Thank you, Rebecca," he said, then took a sip. The woman seemed nice enough and in the waning hours of the morning, the day promised to be hot again. California was mild most of the year but the late summer and fall months were most definitely the hottest.

"Mees Jules, she's a nice girl, no?" Rebecca asked, looking up the almost twelve inches between them.

Taz took another sip of the cold drink and smiled down at her. "Ah, I guess. I hadn't really thought about it much," he answered.

"Meester Storm, he no like the girls," Rebecca said with a smile.

Pretending not to know what she was talking about, Taz only nodded. "Oh?" he asked.

"No, Meester Storm, he ees a gay."

Taz nearly choked on the lemonade. *A gay?*
"Yes, I've heard the rumors," he said, noncommittally.

"Well, he has no… how ju say? A boyfriend."

Taz wondered why it was any of the maid's business anyway. She kept her client fed and his house clean. When he'd first been hired, Taz had gone through all of the personnel files Herman Morrow had given him and he'd learned that Rebecca had been working for Storm for two years, since before the star had purchased the mansion. He'd checked out her other references and they'd turned out to be legitimate which was important to Taz. Storm's previous bodyguard had retired, and hadn't kept great records. Herman Morrow had been retained by Alan Steinberg for Storm's security needs and though Herman had made recommendations for the upgrades in security; nothing had been done until Taz had been hired; when he insisted they be implemented, Storm's business manager had seen to it Taz had all the funds required to do the job.

It was clear to Taz that Storm trusted Anthony with his checkbook and Alan with his career opportunities and he had no idea how close the men were. Taz nevertheless made note of the agent's gambling obsession. If Storm asked his advice in the future, Taz might be inclined to let him know. He didn't have a dog in the hunt at present, so he was unwilling to insert himself into Storm's business affairs. As long as his paycheck cleared the bank, Taz was okay with whatever the star decided to do.

"Well, Storm's personal life is not my business, Rebecca," Taz sighed. "My business is to keep him safe, that's all."

The cook eyeballed Taz with a raised eyebrow before finally nodding. "Si, ee's no mine either, Meester Taz, but ju should know."

"That he's gay? I don't see how that should matter. I'll keep him safe regardless of his sexual orientation," he said, growing irritated at the subject.

"Si," the cook said, shaking her head as she turned to walk away. "But Meester Storm, he ees so nice man… good man."

Taz opened his mouth to say something to her and then closed it, realizing everyone would have their opinions about Storm whether they were wrong or not. Jules's squeal drew Taz's attention back to the pool. Storm had her around the waist and was laughing as he attempted to dunk her head under the water. When she came up sputtering, they were both laughing. Taz couldn't help but smile. Regardless of what the housekeeper thought of Storm, Taz was really beginning to like the superstar, in spite of his reservations.

CHAPTER FOUR

Taz sat in the front seat of the limousine taking Storm and Jules to Carnal Knowledge, the club they'd chosen for the evening. During the ride in the limousine, Taz listened closely to the pair in the back. Storm was excited about his meeting with the producer of "Silver Bullets", the movie Alan wanted him starring in. It was scheduled for later in the week.

"Looks like the boss is going to be even more famous than he is," the chauffer remarked. Taz looked over to the handsome younger man from where he sat in the front passenger seat. David was a nice enough guy. Taz had learned through personnel records that David was another struggling actor, hoping to land his big break. They'd conversed about the many auditions David had tried out for. Currently, he was up for an orange juice commercial that promised to run nationwide. Taz knew if David were lucky enough to land it, he could make more money than some working actors. Each time the commercial ran, he'd earn royalties. He had been called back for more than one commercial, missing out by a hair each time and Taz really hoped David would land this one. It might mean he'd have to vet another man for the job of chauffer since the job entailed coming into close personal contact with Storm, and therefore was a security concern to the star, but he honestly wished David good luck.

"Well, from what I gather, his manager is happy about it," Taz replied. It really wasn't his place to speculate on his client's fame or his career.

"Yeah, I like working for him. I'll miss it if I get famous some day," David said, hopefully.

"Well, maybe I'll be working for you some day," Taz said.

David looked over at him with a serious expression on his face. "Man, Taz, you should go into acting or at the very least, modeling. Hell, the photographers would go insane over you. How many muscles do you have anyway? You must work out like crazy!"

Taz chuckled. "You have the same muscles I have, David. Mine are just bigger."

"How'd that happen? It must take years to build that bulk," the chauffer asked.

"Yeah, humphed it across a thousand miles of desert in the Marines. That was a start. The maintenance came easy after that. Trust me, there's nothing like carrying a hundred pound pack for twenty miles to tone and build muscle. We did that sometimes every day for weeks."

"Holy shit, Taz. I can't even imagine that. You must have some stamina."

Taz watched as David turned his head and let his gaze slide over his seated form from top to bottom, pretty much confirming his suspicion the chauffer was gay. When he turned his gaze to the road and grinned to himself, Taz was convinced of it.

"So... you dating anyone right now?"

Taz smiled. "Nope. No one."

David nodded. "Yeah, didn't think so. You gay?"

Taz looked over at him when David turned his head to glance in his direction. "Yep," he said.

David grinned widely. "Wanna be dating anyone?" He waggled his eyebrows.

"Nope." Taz chuckled.

"Ah, a man of few words. I like that," David said. "I hope you know I don't give up easily."

"Thanks, David," Taz said. He was flattered. If he didn't work with David, he might have taken the handsome man up on the offer. As it was, he really wasn't looking for romantic entanglements and in his experience from watching others, office romances rarely worked well. "I'll let you know when I'm on the open market," he chuckled.

"Good."

"Yay! There it is!" Jules cried from the backseat. Taz looked over at the neon lights spelling out the name of the club in bright pink letters. The long line out the door of Carnal Knowledge wrapped clear around the building and as David eased the long limousine into the line of cars pulling up to the club entrance, paparazzi ran up to the car, flashbulbs going off. Taz knew their limo, with its darkly tinted windows, didn't allow them to see who was inside, but the photographers anxiously waited for the door to open and reveal the prize. As David pulled up to the curb, Taz glanced in the rearview mirror.

"Ready? You have a crowd already waiting," Taz said.

"Yep, let's go," Storm answered, glancing at his reflection in a makeup mirror Jules held up for him.

"You look beautiful, babe," Jules said, as Taz opened his door and stepped out.

David did the same, walking to the back of the limo. Taz and David glanced at each other over the roof of the car and bent to open the doors at the same time. Jules stepped out first and then came running around the side of the curb where Storm was emerging from the limo. Flashbulbs went off, instantly blinding Taz as he reached down and took Storm's hand, pulling him out of the car as Jules came to stand beside him. She and Storm had dressed in matching outfits, her in leopard striped leggings and a fuzzy shirt of some sort, and Storm in leopard skinny jeans and a tan suede jacket with fringe.

"Storm!" a woman screamed, and Taz turned to see the fan waving frantically. Taz instantly inserted himself to protect Jules and Storm as the fans rushed forward.

"Back up," he said, loudly, holding out an arm as two burly security staff from the club rushed forward to assist the star's walk into the popular venue. Between Taz and the two men, Storm and his companion made the short few steps into the club with minimal trouble while the catcalls and whistles continued until they'd ducked inside. Once in the darkened space, Taz and the security staff cleared a path to the roped off VIP space where their reserved table waited. Once they were seated, the security staff nodded at Taz, leaving him alone with the pair.

"Whew, I never tire of that," Storm said with a sparkling grin. His short hair was gelled into a fauxhawk tonight and Taz thought he looked good enough to eat with the sexy guyliner he loved to wear.

A starry-eyed waitress walked up and fawned over the patrons as Storm and Jules ordered well drinks. Taz asked for a Coke and caught Storm watching him as the waitress walked away.

"You can have alcohol, Taz," the star remarked.

"I'm good," Taz said, declining the offer, "none too keen on alcohol and I am working, sir."

"Please… sir?" Jules asked, with a grin. "Storm's no gentleman. I have it on good authority," she joked.

Storm threw his friend a grin. "I can be a complete gentleman when I want to be," Storm laughed.

The three sat there listening to the DJ, watching the bright lights and the gyrations on the dance floor until the waitress returned with their drinks. After she'd walked off, Storm picked up his glass and lifted it high. "To Taz for getting us from place to place in one piece," he said.

Taz smiled and picked up his Coke, bending his head and taking a sip through the bright red skinny straw. "Just doing my job, Mr. Ellison."

"Now see, that's gotta stop," Jules said.

"I agree; please call me Storm," the star said, taking a sip of his watermelon sakitini. "Damn this is good," he added, holding it out to look at the pink liquid in the frosted glass.

"I really prefer it if you let me call you sir," Taz said, looking over at his charge. If he let his guard down with Storm the way the man wanted, he'd regret it.

Storm opened his mouth to protest but stopped when a handsome bear walked up to their table. The man was flanked by two tall men who seemed to be blocking the gawking onlookers from what was going on at the table. Taz immediately bristled, sizing up the two huge men and silently calculating the shortest path to the front door. Taz was absolutely certain the two men were packing heat and the thought didn't sit well with Taz one bit. The bear honed in on Storm instantly and Storm looked up from his drink and smiled.

"Hello there," the bearded man said with a low voice, "I would be honored if you would dance with me, Mr. Ellison." He offered his hand which Storm reached out and took, scooting to the edge of the booth's seat.

"That would be lovely. Are they joining us?" Storm asked, lightly. Taz didn't like the interest in Storm's voice and he was instantly angry with himself for feeling possessive of his boss.

The handsome bear's low chuckle filled the space as his wide fingers curled around Storm's. "They are just here to make sure I get in an out with no trouble."

"Oh, you must be famous," Storm said. "What's your name?" he asked, standing up. Taz focused all his attention on the man as he answered.

"Petros… and no, not famous, only wealthy," he said.

Taz took an instant dislike to the man as he surrounded Storm's back with a huge arm and began leading him away toward the dance floor. Taz noted the man leaning down and saying something in Storm's ear to which the star threw back his head and laughed just a second before turning and glancing over his shoulder at Taz. When Storm turned back and said something back to the tall bear, aggravation filled Taz something fierce. He didn't like the way the pair had so intimately connected right off the bat and he certainly didn't like being talked about. It was everything Taz could do to keep himself planted in his seat.

"Calm down, big guy," Jules said, drawing his attention away from Storm and the bear who'd begun to dance. He looked down at where Storm's pretty friend had her hand on his sleeve and then up at the concern etched in her features.

"You know what they say?" she asked. "If you love something you have to let it go. If it comes back to you, it loves you too." She smiled.

Taz opened and then closed his mouth and then did it again, a little unnerved by what she was suggesting. "I don't love your friend, Jules," he finally said.

"No one's sayin' you do… yet," she replied, staring at him and then turning to look back onto the dance floor. "Besides, if you did, Storm would be in trouble."

"Why do you say that?" Taz asked, irritated beyond measure watching the two men locked in an intimate embrace as the bear whispered in Storm's ear and fondled his ass with a massive paw. Storm didn't seem bothered by the manhandling in the least and that only served to annoy Taz even more.

"I say that because Storm doesn't know what he wants. He thinks it's that big bear out there. What Storm really wants is a man to take care of him… a man who has the capacity to love him. He needs a hero. I have a feeling if Storm got to know the man who is the real Balthazar Grant, he'd fall in love with you," she said, pinning him with a knowing look.

Ludicrous. "No offense, but you don't know me, ma'am."

71

"No? I know all about you, Taz. Storm told me you were a Marine. He told me you served your country honorably. He told me you've saved fellow Marines' lives and he told me you're fearless."

How the hell? Had Storm read his employment folder? Herman Morrow had insisted Taz list his military service and commendations in the folder including the purple heart he'd earned pulling a comrade out of a burning Humvee after they'd run over an IED. He'd suffered a gunshot wound to the thigh when they'd come under fire which ultimately resulted in him being sent home early. One thing he did know was that nowhere in the folder was there any mention of him being fearless. He examined Jules's expression. He didn't note a bit of humor. She was serious when she said Taz would be good for Storm. She honestly believed it. Once again, he wondered how transparent he must be if she was aware he was gay. He dragged his gaze away from the pretty woman as a cute lesbian walked up and asked her to dance and looked back out at Storm and the man. One of the man's hands was skimming Storm's ass while the other was wrapped around the back of Storm's head. He held his face close and was kissing Storm for all he was worth.

Fuck this job! For the first time in his career, Taz hated his job. He realized how attracted he was to Storm as he saw the big handsome bear groping him and he didn't like it at all. Swallowing hard, he turned back to the table, watching Jules smile at the girl, shaking her head. The girl walked away seeming disappointed and then Taz's attention was drawn back to Storm just as he broke his kiss with the bear. He watched the bear lean down and say something in Storm's ear and then saw Storm blush as he nodded, gazing into the man's eyes. A second later, the man grinned, straightened, and caught sight of his two companions. He snapped his fingers to get their attention, speaking something to them as Storm broke away from him and walked up to the table. Taz scooted out of the booth and stood up before he got there and Storm looked right at him.

"Change of plans," he said to Taz. "You can let David take you and Jules home."

Anger coursed through Taz. "I don't think so, sir," he growled, staring down at the superstar as he balled his fists at his side.

"Excuse me?" Storm asked with his mouth dropping open.

The bear walked up behind Storm, flanked by the two guards. He bent and leaned down, kissing Storm's neck as Storm canted his head, giving him room. He never took his eyes off Taz.

"May I speak to you alone, sir?" Taz said, through gritted teeth. The truth was, the star had every right to go home with whomever he wanted but he most certainly wasn't going without Taz accompanying him.

Storm glared at Taz for a second and then wiggled out of the wealthy Petros's arms. He sent the handsome man one of his gorgeous smiles. "Please give me a moment, lover. My bodyguard wants to talk to me."

The bear looked down at Storm and then straightened, throwing a dangerous sneer at Taz. Taz bristled. He was beginning to seriously dislike the obnoxious man. The man stepped back ten feet and began speaking to his men as Storm turned his attention to Taz.

"Okay, what is it, Taz?"

"You can send Jules home with David but you will not be going anywhere without me, sir."

"I don't need you, Taz," Storm said. "Petros's men will make sure we are safe from the paparazzi and fans."

"It's not the paparazzi and fans I am worried about, Mr. Ellison," Taz said, stoically.

Storm's mouth fell open as he stood there for a few seconds. "Fine. Maybe you'd like to join us in bed too, Taz," the star said, testily.

"No, sir," Taz answered. It took every bit of restraint he had not to say what he was really thinking about the big bear and his aggressive ways. He really didn't like the way the guy looked down his nose at Taz but he wasn't going to let it bother him. At the same time, there was no way on earth, Taz was letting Storm walk off with a total stranger and two rough looking armed companions. For all Taz knew, Storm would be gang raped and murdered. There was no way Taz was going to let that happen.

"Fine!" Storm said, nastily, quite out of character from the way the star had been only a half hour before when he'd been teasing and fun with his friend, Jules. "But, you're not allowed to say anything or get in the way," Storm said.

"Very well, sir," Taz replied coldly, feeling hollow in his victory. He watched Storm roll his eyes and as Jules hugged him, whispering in his ear, Storm nodded at her, leaning down to kiss her cheek. She turned to Taz, reached up, and pulled his collar until he leaned down.

"Take care of him. The guy seems kinda huge, Taz," she said, worrying her lower lip.

"I will, ma'am," he replied. He watched as the bear threw his arm around Storm's middle and walked behind his two big guards who cleared a path out of the club the way the club's security guys had cleared a path for Storm and Jules. Taz placed his hand on Jules's back, leading her behind the entourage until they were out on the street.

"I'll be one moment," Taz said to Storm.

Storm nodded as Taz escorted Jules to Storm's waiting limo where David held open the door at the curb. She blew Taz a kiss before getting into the car and David closed the door, turning to Taz where he waved, before walking around and getting inside the car, pulling into traffic. Taz turned and walked back. One of Petros's men stood waiting by the side of the front seat as Petros and Storm climbed into the back.

Taz climbed in the front seat followed by the huge guard while the second man opened the driver's door and climbed in behind the wheel. Taz scooted to the middle of the front seat flanked by Petros's men and looked up into the rearview mirror. The bear had Storm beneath him on the long seat where he was laid out and he was grinding his groin against the star's. Storm was moaning and seemed to be liking it very much. Taz's heart did a little twist in his chest as he realized they'd most likely be naked before ever reaching their destination. Watching Storm get fucked by another man was the last thing Taz thought he could stand and it was at that moment he realized just how desperately he wanted his young client.

****

Petros kissed Storm for all he was worth and he couldn't remember being this turned on in a long time. He tasted so good and the bear's erection grinding into his groin was driving him just a little bit crazy. It had been months since Storm had agreed to go home with someone and his body was craving release. His last sexual encounter in his dressing room at the Emmy awards was nothing compared to the way he wanted the big hairy bear who was groping him in the back of his long black limo. The fact he knew nothing about the man other than the way his large body felt against his didn't bother him at all. What did bother him was the way Taz's presence in the limousine made him feel guilty for the completely natural attraction he felt for his large companion. Storm rarely felt guilty for taking home casual lovers and the unwanted feeling was annoying to say the very least. In the past month since he'd hired Taz, he and the bodyguard had come to an understanding–he was there to provide him protection–and nothing more. *But, I do feel more for my bodyguard, don't I?*

Storm tucked the unbidden thoughts away to be examined later, and let himself return his thoughts to the way Petros was touching him. The big bear's hands were large, his body strong and needy judging from the moans he was making against his mouth, and all Storm wanted was to get to his place and get him naked. He reached up with both hands, placing them around the bear's broad shoulders, holding him close as the bear ripped his mouth away and began kissing

Storm's neck. Storm lifted his chin, turning his head to the side to give Petros easier access to the soft skin on his neck, and opened his eyes. He didn't expect to catch a glimpse of Taz's frown in the rearview mirror from the front seat of the limousine and when he did, irritation coursed through him. Petros lifted his mouth from Storm's neck and looked down at where he lay, staring at him with a lust-filled expression.

"I can't wait till I have you naked, Storm," he growled.

What should have been a phrase that turned Storm on, had the effect of solidifying his resolve to fuck the bear, whether his bodyguard objected to it or not. The last thing he expected was to have to feel strange for taking home a trick for the night, but he did and it angered him and cemented his resolve even further.

He gazed deeply into the bear's dark eyes. "And I can't wait to feel you inside me, lover," Storm said, focusing only on his date and shutting out any thoughts of the large bodyguard and his critical glances from the front seat. Petros looked down at him, raking over his features with his gaze and Storm shivered under the suggestive glance. He was ready to take this man to bed and there was nothing Taz or anyone else could have said to him at that very moment to change his mind. The car turned and slowed and Petros looked up before letting go of Storm and pulling away from him as he sat up. When Storm felt himself frown, Petros grinned at him.

"Don't fret, my love, we've arrived."

Petros reached out and took Storm's hand, drawing him up to sit beside him on the long bench seat as Storm got a look outside the darkened windows of the car. They were pulling up to a high-rise apartment building in a neighborhood in Beverly Hills' Miracle Mile district, an area filled with skyscraper apartment buildings and penthouses where Los Angeles's rich and famous made their homes. Storm had lived most of his life in southern California and he knew the landscape like the back of his hand. When the limo stopped at a building in the six thousand block of Wilshire Blvd, Storm recognized the address. It was a place he'd visited several times after he'd been signed by his agent. Alan had sent him there to be photographed for updated headshots and he'd continued to use Michael d'Alegra for his modeling shots once he'd become famous. As the car came to a stop, the front door opened and the driver and Petros's other guard got out followed by Taz, who was just getting out as Storm climbed out of the limo with his hand firmly held by his date.

"Thank you, Petros," Storm said to the tall bear who had his hand around his waist again. Storm glanced over at Taz, noting the unhappy look on his bodyguard's features as he stared at him, standing on the sidewalk. For the thousandth time he wished he could see the look in the handsome man's eyes, but they were hidden behind the dark glasses. Ignoring him, he intentionally pulled his gaze away from Taz and looked back at Petros. The man looked very pleased with himself as he ordered his guards around in a brusque manner. Something about the way the rich man spoke to his men set Storm's stomach fluttering and not in a good way. Petros seemed very full of himself and he barked out orders at his men like a general. Storm hoped he never talked to Taz like that and made a mental note to check himself if it ever came to that.

When Petros surrounded his shoulders with a huge, thick bicep, propelling him into the building's lobby and blocking Taz from his line of sight, Storm felt the first flutters of worry in his stomach. The truth was, as Taz had pointed out, he really shouldn't be alone with the man–he was a total stranger after all. For the first time that night, he was glad Taz had insisted on accompanying him. In reality, Storm had been jealous of the attention and easy banter Taz and Jules had shared. He was still uncertain whether his gorgeous bodyguard was gay or straight and the way he and his best friend had instantly connected like old friends bothered him to no small degree. Storm desperately hoped she and Taz weren't attracted to each other. He'd hate to have to feel the way he was at this moment if the two began dating; Storm knew he was going to be sick. *You're a lovesick puppy, you idiot!*

They entered the building after a liveried doorman opened the door for them with a small bow and walked to the elevator with the trio of guards following. In the double mirrored doors of the elevator, Storm noted his handsome bodyguard flanked by Petros's men several steps behind them. The look on Taz's face was frightening in its intensity and Storm guessed if he were to be asked to speak at that moment, a growl would come out from between the firmly-set lips. His jaw was set so hard, he looked as if he could chew nails and spit glass. Petros reached for Storm and he turned, looking up into the handsome man's face. The lascivious glint in the man's dark eyes was replaced by lust so fast Storm almost thought he'd imagined the hard expression for a second before it disappeared. The man reached out and drew him close, leaning down the couple of inches between them and kissed him hotly, forcing his tongue into his mouth so hard it took Storm by surprise and he reached between them, pushing at the bear's chest before the bear broke his hold on Storm, pulling away.

"I'm… I'm sorry," Storm said, apologetically. He heard an audible growl and glanced to the side, realizing that it came from Taz and not the bear as he'd first thought.

"Storm…," Taz began.

"You will back off now," Petros said, shooting Taz a murderous look.

Seeing that, Storm began to have second thoughts about the wisdom of going home with the bear. He reached out and touched Petros's chest with the palm of his hand even as he turned and admonished Taz with a helpless look in his eyes and a nod of his head.

"It's okay, Petros. Taz is only doing his job trying to protect me," Storm said. Turning to Taz, he lifted his chin, looking into the man's reflective glasses. "As for you, I am fine, Taz; I can take care of myself."

Taz frowned and visibly thinned his lips as he bit the inside of his cheek. Storm felt his stomach churn once again but he was determined to have sex with the bear, if for no other reason than to prove something to Taz as well as to himself. Besides that, the domineering style of Petros had him getting just a little hard. It was nice to be so very much wanted by someone who would be willing to antagonize a man as intimidating as Taz. Hell, Taz's very presence intimidated most people and Storm had no doubts their fears were well founded.

The elevator doors whooshed open and Storm found himself being pulled inside. He turned and backed up against the elevator wall beside Petros, watching Taz and the man's two bodyguards step in. Taz stood facing him, flanked by the two large men, seemingly watching Storm and his companion for the evening. The fluttering in his stomach still hadn't eased by the time they reached the penthouse. When the doors opened again, Taz and Petros's men stepped out. Petros said something to his men in a foreign language and then turned down the corridor, Storm's hand firmly in his until they approached the large penthouse double doors.

"This is as far as you go," Petros said, turning to Taz.

"Petros, I…" Storm began, suddenly wanting Taz inside the apartment very badly.

"They will remain outside," Petros said in a low voice, looking down at Storm.

"No. I will not," Taz said.

Before Storm knew what was happening, the door was opened and he was shoved through it, into a large living room. Petros managed to grab the door just as Storm witnessed Taz's arms being seized by the bear's two guards as he attempted to follow. When the door was slammed shut by Petros, Storm began to panic. He could hear shouting in the hallway and he knew Taz was in trouble of his own.

"This was a bad idea," Storm said, making a move toward the way out. Petros stepped in front of the thick door, blocking his exit as he smiled at Storm. The smile had none of the sexiness it had had in the club and Storm sensed danger almost immediately. *I should have listened to my instincts. I should have listened to Taz.* He almost managed to step around the bear, when he was pulled into the big man's embrace.

"Come now, my reluctant beauty. Petros wants you very much. Leave the boys alone to play," the bear said, trying to sound sexy as he grasped Storm's side of his neck with a large hand.

Unfortunately for Storm, all the fun had bled out of the evening and when Petros bent to kiss him again, Storm fought against the muscled man and the hands holding him. He realized almost immediately he was in trouble and no amount of strength was going to get him free of the sinewy bands that held him tight. Taz shouted from outside and something slammed forcefully against the portal, shaking the door and causing the hinges to creak.

"Let me go," Storm cried, close to panic.

Almost immediately the bear let go and stepped back, dropping his hand from the side of his neck. The angry look in his eyes was frightful. "I told you not to bring your bodyguard, Storm. My men are perfectly able to protect you but if you wish, you can let him in," Petros said, angrily.

"I want to leave," Storm said, hearing the shakiness of his own voice. He watched a dark look cross the large man's face before he smirked.

"You have cost me a night of fun, and you are not at all what they say," Petros growled. "I was expecting the whore the tabloids write about." Suddenly he stepped forward, reached up, and grabbed Storm's hair, yanking his head back so he was staring into the man's angry features. "You should not play games with powerful men, Storm."

To Storm's great relief, he let go as quickly as he'd grabbed him, shoving him back until he hit the door. He groaned, knowing he was going to be aching in the morning and not in a good way. At that moment, he heard Taz shout again and suddenly something slammed against the outside of the door. Storm's heart soared, knowing that Taz was fighting to get through the guards and then a moment later, he was consumed with guilt. He turned around and grabbed the doorknob, yanking the door open.

Petros's men had Taz pinned against the far wall of the hallway and he was looking quite worse for the wear. His mirrored glasses were missing and his lip was bloodied. His clothes were disheveled but when Storm got a look at Petros's two bodyguards, he was shocked to see them in worse condition than Taz. From behind him, Petros shouted something and the men instantly let Storm's bodyguard go. Taz struggled for his footing and shot a glance at Storm, letting his gaze run the length of his body from head to toe. When their gazes met, Storm nearly lost his legs. The look in Taz's silver-colored eyes was filled with concern, not fear of Petros or his guards, but for Storm's safety; he recognized it instantly.

"I'm fine," Storm said, stepping into the hall, a few feet from his disheveled bodyguard. "Taz... I'm..." The last part of what he wanted to say was abruptly cut off as Taz grabbed his upper arm and yanked him away from the three others, propelling him down the hall toward the elevator. "Taz... I..."

"Shut up, Storm," Taz barked.

Storm realized it was the first time he'd heard his bodyguard say his name but the anger behind it shut him up faster than the way he was being manhandled. They arrived at the elevator and Taz punched the button so forcefully Storm thought it'd break. When the doors dinged open, Taz pushed him inside and pressed the button to the lobby. Unthinking, Storm reached up and touched the side of his neck, gasping as he felt a bruise rising from where Petros had grabbed him with his big hand. In an instant, Taz stepped in front of him and reached around his waist, pulling him up against his body with one hand while reaching up to take Storm's jaw in his huge mitt. He relaxed as Taz looked down at him with worry in his stunning gray eyes.

"Did he hurt you?" Taz said softly, turning his chin gently with the fingers on his jaw as he looked down at his neck.

Storm closed his eyes, feeling Taz's breath huff over his cheek from his close proximity. "No, he… he let me go when he heard you fighting…" he began to say. Storm felt himself melt into Taz's body and only a second later, he felt a soft touch on the side of his neck. It took Storm a second more before he realized Taz was caressing the bruise Petros had left behind with his lips. A shudder went through Storm as he tilted his head to give the man who was rapidly becoming his fantasy better access. Storm savored the moment as it continued for a few seconds before he felt Taz lift his head. When he opened his eyes, Taz met his gaze as he pulled back. His frown was fierce but the look of anger in his eyes was fleeting and he felt Taz's grip on his waist ease. When he dropped his arm, letting him go as he stepped back, Storm instantly missed their contact.

"Don't ever disobey me again, Storm. It's my job to protect you and if I tell you something with regard to your safety, you will listen to me," he growled, angrily.

"Your job?" Storm said, feeling stupid he'd thought there was anything more to Taz's touches than his purpose in checking his well-being. *He kissed my neck.*

"It's my job to protect you, sir," the bodyguard repeated, the formality back in his voice, all the while staring at him with those amazing gray eyes. Storm opened his mouth to say something stupid when he was interrupted by the ding of the elevator as it reached the lobby of the expensive building. They stepped out.

"God dammit!" Taz cursed, "We have to call a cab."

Storm once again opened his mouth but then shut it quickly when Taz walked away from him toward the doorman who'd let them into the building earlier. He stood in the lobby, listening to Taz as he asked the doorman to call them a cab, feeling ridiculous that he'd so offhandedly agreed to going home in Petros's limo, leaving them stranded. He also felt like a shmuck for leaving Jules to get home alone. Even though they'd left each other in the care of Storm's driver when one of them found a date for the night many times before, he still kicked himself, regretting his choice of companion. Storm contemplated his own actions of the evening. Even though he'd gone home from clubs with men many times, they'd always ended up in a hotel room on his dime. The choice to go to Petros's place had been careless and now that he had the time to think about it, he wondered why he'd done it. Was there some reason he thought he'd be safe with the bear? Not really. Was he trying to push Taz's buttons by telling him to leave with Jules? *You wanted to see how far Taz would go to protect you… idiot!*

When Taz returned to where Storm was standing, his face wasn't relaxed in the least. He could feel the anger coming off the bodyguard and he kept his own mouth shut, standing off a few feet until the cab arrived a few minutes later. The doorman nodded at Taz when the car drove up and Taz glanced at Storm. He looked a lot calmer and it was only then Storm realized what a desperate and dangerous situation he'd put Taz in by choosing to go home with Petros and his two men. For all he knew, they were armed the way Taz was, and the situation Storm had placed himself in by trusting Petros rather than trusting Taz had been foolish to say the very least. If one of Petros's men had managed to disarm Taz… well, he didn't even want to think of what might have happened to his bodyguard. When Taz held out his arm to Storm, he walked past him and stepped into the back of the cab. Taz followed him in and gave Storm's address to the driver before settling back on the seat and turning his head to look out of the window, ignoring Storm as they pulled away from the curb.

When they arrived at the gated estate thirty minutes later, the driver stopped and Taz climbed out, paid the cabbie, and punched numbers into a keypad. Storm got out of the car, silently watched as the gate opened, and followed Taz into the house. By the time he'd locked the door to the house, he turned only to find the bodyguard heading off to his room without another word. *Well, I guess that went well… NOT!* Storm headed to the kitchen, pulling out his phone as he did so. There was a text from Jules. *"Call me as soon as you get home, baby."*

He swiped the screen, feeling like a total ass not only for putting Taz in the situation he put him in, but as he remembered the look of concern on his best friend's face, he felt really bad. Even though she hadn't said anything, she'd been uncomfortable, regardless of the fact that Taz was by his side. He set down the phone, opened the refrigerator, and made himself a sandwich at the large granite counter. After pouring himself a glass of milk, he sat at the long farm table in his dining room and picked up the phone, hitting speed dial. Jules picked up after a couple of rings.

"What happened?" she asked.

"I'm home, babe."

"That was fast," she said, sounding surprised.

"Yeah, it was a bad scene; Petros wouldn't let Taz into the apartment and then he got rough," he said around a bite of sandwich.

"Rough? Oh, Storm. Are you okay?" Worry laced her words.

"I'm fine. Petros's thugs fought with Taz though. He got a fat lip but they looked pretty much worse than he did." He shut up, feeling bad as the bite in his mouth began to feel bigger as his throat closed up with emotion.

"Oh, Storm," she sighed.

"I'm sorry I left you there, Jules," he said, quietly. "Can you forgive me?" Storm was feeling about two inches tall. He knew he'd fucked up and somehow saying it out loud was worse than just feeling it on the inside.

"Nothin' to forgive you for, Storm," she said. There was a minute's pause before she asked, "So how hot was Taz when he was fighting off those brutes for you?" The last was said with what he knew was a smile on her pretty face. He could almost see her eyes twinkle mischievously through the phone.

Storm smiled, grateful he had someone who knew him so well and loved him even when he was an idiot. "Yeah, how hot that would have been... I didn't get to see him. Petros opened the door to the apartment and shoved me through it, closing Taz outside with his men."

"Is the apartment door still there?" she laughed.

"Yeah, but just barely. I thought Taz was gonna knock it down."

"You said Petros got rough with you?" she asked, more serious than before.

Storm sighed. "Just a little. He didn't hurt me... really."

"What do you mean? Did he hurt you or didn't he?" she asked, her voice rising.

"Easy does it, Jules," Storm answered, chewing as he reached up and gingerly touched the side of his neck. He bit his lip as the ache from the bruise shot through him. *Motherfucker!* "He squeezed the side of my neck with one of his big paws."

"Storm, what the hell!" she practically yelled.

"I'm fine. Taz kissed it all better," he replied, remembering the warmth of the bodyguard's soft lips. He closed his eyes at the memory of it, savoring their brief contact.

"He kissed you?" she nearly shrieked.

"Not exactly. He just brushed his lips over the bruise," Storm said, before taking another bite and downing the sandwich with a few sips of milk.

"You have a bruise?" She sounded beside herself.

"Down girl! Dealing with one disapproving person at a time is all I can process." He heard her giggle.

"Serves you right, you ass. You tried to send him home!"

"I know. It was a huge mistake, Jules. I should have listened to him and my own instincts. I think Petros scared me a little more than I let on and I know his two thugs scared me." He examined his feelings a second before continuing. "I think knowing Taz was going to be there and that he would never let me go without him, made me take a risk. It was idiotic and I won't do that again. He could really have been hurt." He took another sip of milk and examined the crumbs left on his plate.

"Yeah, I was wondering why you chose that big bear anyway. He's not your type at all," she said. The factual truth was, bears usually were his thing but he'd never tried going home with one as big as Petros. There was something exotic about him and his accent was alluring. Storm liked all kinds of men, from the twink who'd sucked him off in the dressing room to the big bears; Storm wasn't picky, as long as they were good-looking. As he said it, Storm thought how shallow he sounded. He was twenty-five years old but he sure hadn't acted like it tonight. He'd put both him and Taz in a bad situation. As he thought about it, he realized Jules may not have seen him with a bear before, or at least a scary one like Petros. Most of the time, he chose smaller guys, bears included.

"Of course, Taz is a bear and he's big," Jules said, interrupting his musings.

"Jules!"

"Look, I know you're trying to act like you're not attracted to him and that's just so much shit. I know you like him. You should see how fluffed up you get whenever he's around."

"Fluffed up!" Storm laughed. "You need a therapist, sicko."

"Okay, well, it would be hard to describe you as fluffy anything, but you definitely get nervous as a cat when he's around," she said.

Storm was quiet as he pictured how angry Taz had been when he'd nearly been injured. At the time, he'd thought it was because Taz hadn't had control over the situation but as he thought back on it, he realized Taz probably did really care for his welfare. "How do you think Taz is around me, Jules?" he asked.

"You like him! I knew it! You just admitted it, Storm."

"Look," he said, knowing he sounded exasperated, "the fact is, I don't even know if Taz is gay, Jules."

"He kissed your neck, idiot!" she said.

"Yeah, I guess he did, at that." A flutter of excitement rose in Storm's stomach the same way it had when his bodyguard had brushed his beautiful mouth over the side of his neck. Lascivious thoughts crept in as he pictured those same lips wrapped around his cock and he began to harden in the tight leopard jeans he wore. He heard Jules yawn and glanced at the clock. It read one thirty am and he knew he had a workout scheduled with Guru Shamsa in the morning. "Look sweetie, it's late. I just wanted to check in." Storm stood up and picked up his plate and glass, balancing the phone between his shoulder and cheek as he walked to the kitchen to set the dishes in the sink.

"I love you babe. I'm glad you're safe," Jules said from the other end of the line. She yawned again.

"I love you too, angel. Goodnight, Jules," Storm said.

"Goodnight, Storm."

Storm swiped the phone closed and headed upstairs, determined to explore more of his attraction to his courageous bodyguard in the morning.

CHAPTER FIVE

Storm heard the front doorbell chime as he headed downstairs dressed in his yoga clothes. He hit the marble floor at the bottom of the stairs and walked across the foyer, heading toward the door.

"I've got it, Rebecca," Storm called out, then remembering it was the maid's day off just as he got to the door. He confirmed it was indeed the handsome tanned bald guru he'd been expecting when he pulled the door open. The guru smiled at him as he stepped aside to let him in. "Good morning, Guru."

"Namaste, Storm," the guru said, making the traditional bow with his hands folded in front of him.

"Namaste, Guru." Storm bowed back and then swept out an arm toward the workout room. "Ready for some yoga?"

"Always, Storm," the guru said.

Storm turned and led the way toward the workout room with the guru by his side. As he neared the closed door to his workout room, he heard the clang of barbells being placed back on a rack. His heart rate sped up, knowing there was only one person who would be working out in the room at that time of day. When he opened the door, he confirmed it. Across the room, Taz was lying face up on a weight bench, his huge arms bunched with muscle as he lifted the heavily-laden barbell from its perch, resting the bar on his chest for a second before he pushed it up above his chest until his straining arms were straight and his elbows locked. Taz was wearing headphones attached to an iPod and concentrating so hard he didn't notice the two enter. Storm stepped into the room and stopped dead in his tracks when he saw the stunning form of his gorgeous bodyguard. His mocha-colored skin was beaded with sweat and his sleeveless T-shirt was wet and clinging to his muscular form in several places. He wore basketball shorts and Storm was blown away by a massive package outlined in the damp material. *Jesus, the man is hung!*

"It seems we have company this morning," Guru Shamsa said from beside him.

Storm turned to find the guru openly appraising Taz and he was flooded with irritation at the way the man ogled his bodyguard. For some reason, Storm was feeling very territorial but he squelched the odd notion and walked toward a long counter in the room where he reached out and turned on music with the touch of a button. He hadn't realized the volume was turned way up and when the music blared out of the CD player, he jumped and reached out, instantly lowering the sound. When he turned back toward Taz, the bodyguard had replaced the barbells on their perch and was looking at him as he sat up.

"Sorry about that. I didn't realize the volume was so high, Taz," Storm said, apologetically.

Taz ignored him and swung a leg over the bench, reaching for a towel as he stood up. He glanced at Storm and his companion only a second before turning back, bending and wiping the bench clean of his sweat. Storm watched Taz bend, noting the way his damp shorts clung to his beautiful ass, outlining the crack. He really had a gorgeous form and when he straightened to his full height, he covered his face with the towel as he turned back. The fact Taz wouldn't meet his gaze wasn't lost on Storm and his face flushed with embarrassment, realizing Taz was still pissed from the night before.

Taz lowered the towel and finally met Storm's gaze. "No problem. I'm finished anyway," he said, walking toward them.

"Good morning," Guru Shamsa said, smiling at Taz, "Namaste." He bowed and Storm was suddenly annoyed as hell with his yoga partner.

"Good morning," Taz replied. "I'll see you later." He turned to leave.

"Don't leave on our account, Taz," Storm said. He hated the way his voice sounded like a lovesick puppy's. Just a week before, he'd been filled with self-confidence and bravado. He had no idea what made him feel like a pussy around Taz… well, it could be his gorgeous macho persona or maybe the aloof way he spoke to Storm.

Taz stopped wiping his shaved head with the towel and stared at Storm. His bright gray eyes were stunning and Storm suddenly felt weak in the knees.

"Will you be going out for lunch, sir?" the bodyguard asked.

So we're back to formalities, then. Fine. "Actually my agent will be here in an hour or so. We have a meeting in Beverly Hills with the producers of the movie they want me to make for them. You'll be accompanying us," Storm replied, trying to sound as businesslike as he could. Unfortunately, he heard the shakiness in his own voice.

"Very good, sir. I'll leave you to your workout then," Taz replied, courteously. Without waiting for another word from Storm, he nodded at Guru Shamsa before turning on his heel and walking out of the room. He closed the door to the hall with a snick.

A painful knot settled in Storm's stomach and at that moment he knew he'd fucked up big-time with his bodyguard. He looked over at Guru who was standing deathly still and threw him a forced smile. *This workout is going to be hell.*

****

Taz strode down the hallway away from Storm's workout room and across the foyer headed toward the other wing of the house where his room was located. He'd moved into the mansion at Alan Steinberg's insistence as well as part of his contract with the superstar, but Taz had kept his small Hollywood apartment, convinced he wouldn't be long on the job if Storm turned out to behave with his staff the same way his reputation indicated he did with everyone else. The tabloids had painted him as a spoiled, gay playboy with nothing but time on his hands between gigs to party, get drunk, and use drugs. He had a reputation for using guys, breaking hearts, and not taking any names.

In all honesty, Taz sometimes regretted going into the private security business after his time in the military. The fact is, most of his clients lived up to their reputations and they were all rich like Storm Ellison. His years in the Marine Corps had taught him three things… never leave a man behind, avoid hurting an innocent at all costs, and do what you were told, when you were told. Taz had been perfectly ready to hate Storm but the man had surprised him almost from the get-go. He hadn't expected to be able to control him but more importantly, he hadn't had to ask him to curb his behavior until last night. Storm asking him to leave him with Petros and his two thugs and fend for himself had been the ultimate in stupidity. Last night, when Taz had turned in, the last thing he thought of before falling asleep was the awkward conversation he was going to have the moment he had his client alone.

Taz opened his bedroom door and stepped into the room, closing and locking it behind him. He kept it locked when he was out but since he and Storm were the only ones living in the huge house and it was Rebecca's day off, he'd left it unlocked when he went to work out. Storm was the only other person in the house and he was pretty certain Storm wasn't going to violate his privacy by going through his belongings while he was doing his own workout. He walked across the bedroom, passing by the king-size bed in the middle of the room, and went into the ensuite bathroom where he turned on the shower before yanking the T-shirt over his head and dropping his shorts and jockstrap to his ankles. He sat down on the commode to pull off his shoes and socks, throwing them and his clothes into a pile on the floor against a far wall.

The shower was steaming as he stepped inside, and he let the spray pelt him for a few minutes as he placed both flat palms on the wall of the shower, letting his head fall forward so his chin was touching his chest as he waited for his sore muscles to loosen up. The spray from the shower worked magic on him as he thought about the day to come, accompanying his client around while he did his meeting with his agent. Taz smiled when he pictured David, the limousine driver, boldly asking him if he was gay and flirting outrageously with him as he checked out his muscles. He looked down at his limp cock hanging between his legs, halfway down his thigh. He wondered what it would feel like to fuck a guy like David and then he realized that as bold as he was, the sex would most likely be off the charts hot. David would probably try everything once and then again if he even remotely liked it.

Taz reached down and took his cock in hand, slicking it with soap from the bar in the dish as he pictured David kneeling in front of him and wrapping his lips around the foreskin on his long, uncut cock. Taz wasn't circumcised and he'd realized he was richly endowed the first time his high school boyfriend wrapped both hands around his dick to jack him off. The water coursed down his body, dripping off the end of his dick as he began to stroke it. Thoughts of the handsome limo driver hardened him and he closed his eyes as he pictured the man pushing back the foreskin of his dick, exposing the head of it with his lips as he teased his slit. Taz stroked harder as he thought of David's handsome face, his cheeks hollowed as he sucked, and then suddenly, David's face transformed to Storm's. *He reached down and took Storm's light hair in his hand, guiding his head closer to him as his sweet sucking mouth did nasty things to his cock.*

"Yeah, Storm, like that…" *he groaned out loud as he pictured the man of his fantasies sliding his lips over the shaft in the futile attempt to swallow the whole thing. Taz thrust his hips forward as his hand sped over the slick shaft of his cock, picturing Storm's slender neck as he swallowed, squeezing the head of his dick with his throat as he milked it, preparing for Taz's orgasm.*

"You're gonna get a mouthful of my come, Storm. You gonna swallow for me?"

The image of the star nodded as he smiled around Taz's dick, hollowing his cheeks as he sucked harder and moaned. The vibrations of Storm's moans sent Taz over and he began to come.

"Suck it! Swallow! Swallow!" he cried out in the shower as his climax erupted, spewing spunk all over the wall of the enclosed space. He opened his eyes and looked down, picturing Storm's open mouth and waiting tongue as he emptied his balls over it and then painted his stunning face with thick, creamy ropes.

Taz felt his entire body shudder as he came and when he was spent, he let go of his dick, supporting himself as he dropped his forehead against the wall in front of him, concentrating on slowing his breathing.

"Jesus!" His knees were shaking as his climax ended and he flattened one palm on the shower wall while he ran the other up his front, feeling the planes of muscle beginning at his abdomen all the way up to his chest. Taz had very little hair on his chest, a natural state of being, though he did manscape down below, shaving his balls and clipping the rest of his bush short. His daily workouts and years of physical conditioning exercises had turned Taz's body into a mass of muscle, hard planes, and the picture of health. Taz knew he looked good and was proportionate for his height which was well over six feet; he didn't overwork his muscles like some of the bodybuilders he found so unattractive.

Taz shut off the water, stepped out of the shower, and grabbed a towel, drying his body as he stood in front of the fogged mirror. He reached out and wiped the glass, catching a glimpse of his naked form in the reflection. *You just had the greatest orgasm of your life from thinking of your boss. This is so not good.* He couldn't believe he'd let himself fall into the trap of Storm Ellison's charms. Hell, the man hadn't even come on to him and he was having all kinds of nasty thoughts about him. Taz knew he was playing with fire. It would be so easy to just fuck David and put all thoughts of the boss out of his mind but the truth was, ever since he'd met the star in person, he was having a really difficult time imagining doing that. If Storm were the man Taz had expected him to be, it would have been so easy to think of him only as a boss but the fact was, Taz genuinely liked the star. Even last night when he'd put himself in very real danger, Storm hadn't been the one responsible for it; Taz had. *You have no business blaming him for something that was your own damn fault. The man deserves an apology.* Fuck! Taz knew he was going to have to find Storm and speak with him before they left the house. He dressed quickly, closed and locked his bedroom door, and went in search of Storm, determined to make things right or offer his resignation.

****

Storm was sweating like crazy. He couldn't remember the last time he'd worked out this hard. People who didn't practice yoga didn't realize how much effort it took. Most people who had never done yoga would never understand how focused one must be to get the most out of the exercises. As Storm attempted a particularly aggressive stretch, his muscles suddenly groaned with agony. He gasped and relaxed, sinking to the mat in a puddle of his own perspiration.

"Storm," Guru Shamsa said, gracefully sitting beside him, "Your mind is not on your stretches today."

Yeah, no kidding. Since the moment Taz had walked out of the room, refusing to acknowledge him, Storm had been off his game.

"I'm sorry, Guru. You're right. I had a bad evening and my mind really isn't into the exercises." He looked over at the man, feeling guilty. After all, he'd come all the way out to his place just to lead Storm through the stretches. On any other morning it would have been easy to go through the paces; he knew all the routines by heart, but thoughts of Taz and his skimpy workout clothes clinging to his beautiful body with sweat, had his mind in another place entirely.

"Storm, part of the reason you do this yoga with me is to help you to get out of your own head and concentrate on going to a higher plane. You defeat the purpose entirely if you don't focus on what we're doing here."

He sounded angry and that was unusual for the guru. Storm was suddenly ashamed, feeling as though he was letting down everyone who counted on him. He looked over at Guru Shamsa. The man would be considered handsome to some, tall, with a shaved head, and his body was toned from years of working out the way they had this morning. Storm appreciated the way Guru Shamsa always seemed like he had his act together. He was the epitome of inner peace, something Storm never claimed to have. One of the reasons he'd started doing yoga with the guru was to try to capture that inner peace. So many of the people in his life expected something from Storm. All he was trying to do was please him and he hadn't even been able to do that this morning.

"I'm really sorry. You're right of course, Guru. I will try not to bring outside contradictions into our yoga sessions. I always feel better when I free my mind of all the things that bother me."

"You must unburden yourself, Storm, and you know money and wealth stand in the way of your growth. If, for only a little while, you are able to put aside all the worldly things which tend to bother you, your life will improve by leaps and bounds. Once the temple is completed, many of my followers will be able to experience this peace."

Guru Shamsa was building a temple in the Griffith Park area of Los Angeles. When he'd first been introduced to the guru at the opening of an art gallery, Storm had eagerly offered to contribute to the building of the temple. Though the amount of his commitment was staggering to the average person, Guru Shamsa had accepted the generous offer of the gift and the contractor had broken ground on the project with money from Storm's first check. The project was well under way and the guru had been eager to share the progress his builder was making on the compound. From what Storm could determine, Guru Shamsa intended the refuge to be an even larger temple than the large Scientology compound on Sunset Blvd in Hollywood. Millions of dollars in tax deductible donations had been gathered by the guru and Storm had been responsible for much of them, asking wealthy friends to contribute to a cause close to his heart. After all, the guru had done so much for people who were less fortunate, at least that's what he'd been told when he'd gone to meet with the guru's business manager. The fact Storm's previous business manager had freaked out when Storm had asked him for a huge check to begin Guru's project, was just another annoyance Storm wished he didn't have to deal with. Having tons of money was fun but it wasn't why Storm worked so hard at the television show which took up much of his time. He wanted to give back and rack up good Karma; it was as simple as that.

"Of course, Guru, you are right. I need to be able to give back as much as I can to stay karmically balanced."

Guru Shamsa smiled at him, showing his shining white teeth in his handsome tanned face. He was the epitome of what Storm wished to be. Free of the trappings of earthly possessions, though Storm hadn't thought much about the neighborhood where he resided or the mansion he lived in, other than how throwing large parties with a comfortable place to hold them would help to move Guru's agenda forward. He'd held a couple of high-profile parties on Guru's behalf, helping to collect donations from the rich and powerful on behalf of the guru's temple project. It was all Karma after all, wasn't it?

Guru stood up and reached out a hand. Storm looked into his eyes, noting that he was smiling, his whole being filled with an aura of peace. He took the guru's hand and stood up. He was wet with sweat and he bowed to his counselor.

"Namaste," he said. He turned and walked over to the counter and pressed a button on his CD player, shutting off the meditation music. When he turned back to speak to the guru, Taz was standing in the room. He had showered and was dressed in the black suit he wore every day. He was looking luscious.

"Sorry to bother you, sir," the large man said, "I wanted to have a word with you when you're done with your workout." His rumbling voice made Storm weak in the knees and he had a fleeting need to feel the beautiful man speak again just so he could hear it.

"I am finished here, Storm," Guru Shamsa said. "Namaste." He bowed to Storm and smiled before turning and walking toward the doorway where Taz stood.

Storm noticed the expression on Taz's face as he looked at the guru. *You don't like him... huh.*

"Goodbye, Guru," Storm said, not wanting Taz to notice how flustered he was now the bodyguard had returned. He followed his guru, needing to walk right past Taz who stepped aside. When Storm passed by, he noted the crisp spicy smell of Taz's aftershave and he had the inexplicable urge to lean in and sniff him. He walked the guru to his front door and after a few pleasantries, let him out, closing the door behind him, and turning around. Butch was in the backyard barking like crazy from the other side of the screen and Storm realized he must have seen his guru whom apparently his dog hated. Taz was standing a few feet behind him, cloaked in the suit and sunglasses, looking good enough to eat. Storm walked up to him, determined to apologize for the way he'd behaved the night before.

"I wanted to say I'm sorry for the way I behaved last night, Taz," Storm began. Before he could say anything else, Taz lifted a large hand, stopping the rest of what he had to say.

"Please, sir, I must apologize for my behavior. I just wanted you to know I was out of line when I spoke to you last night," he said, matter of fact.

Storm's stomach did a little flip-flop and he got a sinking feeling, hoping he wasn't right about what Taz was about to do.

"I am tendering my resignation, effective now. I've already called Herman Morrow. He will be sending over candidates for you to interview for my replacement, Mr. Ellison," the bodyguard said.

Storm looked at him, wishing he'd been wrong about what he'd already guessed. Taz was resigning because of his own shitty behavior with the bear the night before. Well, that was the last thing Storm was going to allow. He certainly had become accustomed to having Taz at his back and the thought of not having him there was unacceptable. "I refuse your resignation. You can just call Mr. Morrow back and tell him I'm only interested in one bodyguard, Taz… you."

"Mr. Ellison, if you recall, I was unable to protect you last night. You could have been raped, sir, and I take that very seriously." Taz's voice was monotone and Storm hated how businesslike he sounded. He wished he could get the emotion back the way he had the night before… *when he'd held me and kissed my neck.*

"Taz, it was my fault. I'm not letting you resign for my own stupid behavior," Storm said, frustrated as hell. Sweat rolled down between his shoulder blades, tickling his back. The bodyguard's face was serious and Storm couldn't see any expression due to the hated mirrored sunglasses and he had the urge to reach up and yank them off his face. It was frustrating not knowing what the man was thinking. When Taz's beautiful full lips turned up just the slightest hint at the corners, Storm's heart soared. Maybe the bodyguard would give up his foolish ideas about resigning and agree to stay after all.

"Mr. Ellison, I…"

"Oh, for Christ's sake, can you call me Storm? You did last night!" Storm blurted. He couldn't stand that they'd become so formal.

"Mr. Ellison… ah, Storm, I think I have no choice but to resign," Taz said. The pitch of his voice had dropped and the sound of it was having a disconcerting effect on parts of Storm's anatomy. Seeing Taz big and beautiful and smelling so good standing in front of him had Storm heating up all over again just as his body was cooling off from his workout. "You won't listen to me and you put yourself in dangerous situations where I am unable to do my job. You must let me do my job the way I tell you because I can't be responsible for your safety if you don't."

Storm found himself getting more and more aggravated with the hunky bodyguard but he was sticky and hot and horny and all he wanted to do was end the conversation. He was close to getting the man to agree not to quit and for now, that's what mattered.

"Fine. You're right. Like I said, Taz. I'll listen to you. Now, I'm off for a shower. Alan is going to be here any minute to take me to Beverly Hills for a meeting with the movie people. After that, Jules and I will be going out clubbing. I promise to listen to you and do whatever you say, Taz." Storm knew he sounded petulant and he hated it.

"Very good, sir," Taz said. His face was once more devoid of any emotion at all.

"Call me Storm or I'll fire you myself," Storm growled before brushing past the tall bodyguard, headed for the stairs. As he climbed the curving staircase, he thought he detected laughter from the foyer. *Fuckin' bodyguards!*

****

Taz accompanied Storm and Alan to his meeting in Beverly Hills. He listened to the conversation between the two men from his perch in the front passenger seat. Ever since Storm had returned from his shower, he'd been in a terrible mood. As he'd come sailing down the curved staircase to the foyer where Taz and his agent waited, he'd been frowning. Taz couldn't help but believe it had something to do with the new rules he'd insisted upon and though he felt a little guilty about the way he'd spoken to Storm, the last thing he was willing to accept was the very real possibility that his client was going to put himself in danger again… at least knowingly.

As Alan Silverstein fawned all over Storm, telling him how good he looked and what a great opportunity the movie deal was for him, Storm stomped petulantly out to the sleek black limo where David awaited with an open door. Storm nodded to David at his greeting and ducked into the car, followed by his agent. David smiled brilliantly, winking at Taz before climbing into the car, and memories of masturbating to the thoughts of having sex with the stunning driver crept into his thoughts. Of course, the memory of finishing himself off with a vision of Storm's lips around his cock were clear as day and Taz climbed into the front of the car with a semi hard-on, thinking about Storm's strongly sucking mouth.

****

Taz was waiting outside the producer's office when Storm and Alan left it after their meeting. Alan was grinning and Storm was rather somber for someone who, judging from the agent's demeanor, had just agreed to do the movie. When Storm's gaze met his own, his blue eyes were sparkling and Taz once again realized just how beautiful the superstar really was. Storm glanced away almost immediately, turning his head to look at his agent as the man babbled his happiness at the great deal they'd made, going over some of the details. Taz noted Storm wasn't really listening very closely because his replies were mostly nods and an occasional affirmative grunt as Alan rambled on.

"So, have you given anymore thought to going out with me?" David asked, drawing Taz's gaze away from the rearview mirror as he realized he'd been watching Storm in the back of the car again. David was looking extraordinarily handsome in his uniform and Taz wondered how his body would look beneath it… better yet, beneath him as he fucked him silly.

Taz smiled. "Look, man, I'm flattered, but like I told you. I don't date guys I work with. It's a bad idea," he told David, reluctantly.

"Why?" David asked, reaching across to touch Taz's knee. "I think we'd be amazing together and I've been fantasizing about you fucking me into the bed since the moment I saw you." He waggled his eyebrows suggestively causing Taz to laugh.

As he did, he glanced into the rearview mirror, realizing Storm must have overheard their conversation. The privacy screen between the back of the limo and the front seat was open, allowing Storm to hear what was going on between him and David the same way he could hear the conversation between the star and his agent. Storm was glaring at Taz, sending him a dirty look and for just a second, Taz was certain the superstar had been intentionally eavesdropping on David's remarks. Taz wondered why it bothered him for Storm to think that he and the driver were going out together.

"I can't, David," he said, reaching down and brushing the chauffer's hand off his knee. Taz realized if it had been any other time or place, he would have enjoyed having the handsome man's hands all over him but the timing was off. With Storm in such close proximity, all thoughts of other men fled his brain and Taz found himself at sea. Since high school, Taz hadn't had any serious lovers except for Gregor and when the need came, he found himself picking up guys at gay bars to satisfy the urge. He'd spent the occasional long weekend in bed with stunningly handsome lovers but Taz hadn't committed to any one guy since he'd had his heart broken as a very young man. Besides that, he didn't like the way most men fawned over his body. The only way to describe it was that he felt as though he was treated like a piece of meat. That had been great in his younger days, but after leaving the military and beginning his adult life as a civilian, Taz had come to want something more out of his relationships and he knew he wasn't ready to settle down in his late twenties. A quickie blowjob in a bathroom stall or up against a wall at a gay club and Taz was happy. He certainly didn't need ties or commitments at his age.

David seemed to lightheartedly accept Taz's rebuff and they continued the drive to Alan's apartment where they dropped him off. Taz was surprised to see Alan was living in a modest apartment in the Valley Village area of the San Fernando Valley, a bedroom community in the northernmost suburb of Los Angeles. He wondered whether Alan Steinberg's gambling addiction kept him from better digs on the west side of LA, a more affluent and expensive part of town where most of the Hollywood elite resided. After dropping the agent off, Storm remained seated in the back, quietly looking out of the windows and checking his cell phone as they drove to Jules's place. She lived in Culver City, in an upscale apartment. Taz wondered how a girl her age could afford a place like that but he figured her wealthy and well-connected parents probably footed the bills. Once again, Taz contrasted his life growing up in a house with multiple generations all under one roof with the way the rich and famous of Los Angeles lived. It was nearly impossible for a young person to afford the pricy real estate in the busy metropolitan area unless they settled for a neighborhood that was less than desirable or shared their place with multiple roommates.

Storm had explained to Taz that Jules lived alone and as far as he knew, she was a merely a student and had no paying job. Jules had told Taz she was studying international law, though her real desire was to work in diplomacy, following in her father's footsteps. She interned as an interpreter at the Federal building adjacent to the 405 Freeway on Wilshire Blvd and though it didn't pay anything, it counted for college work credits. Jules had confessed wanting to move to New York and find her dream job at the United Nations where she was convinced she'd meet a handsome member of royalty who would sweep her off her feet someday to live in a foreign land. He genuinely liked the girl and he wished he had the opportunity to speak to her more often. As it was, their conversations had been mostly conducted at the VIP tables in the various clubs Storm enjoyed going to while they both watched Storm dance with one pretty boy after another.

David slowed the limo to a stop in front of her building and Storm told Taz he'd run up and get her. He'd just exited the car when David once again reached across the bench seat and put his hand on Taz's leg. Taz looked over in surprise as David leaned in, reaching out and taking Taz's jaw in one hand as he swooped in for a kiss. When the man's lips touched his, Taz was taken by surprise. David groaned as his lips plied Taz's for a second when he didn't pull back. The man tasted of mint and smelled even better, wearing some kind of designer perfume. He'd just begun kissing David back when there was a violent tap at his passenger window. Taz ripped his mouth away from David's and turned his head only to find Storm standing on the outside of the car shooting him a look filled with daggers. *Shit.* He instantly rolled down the window and looked up, happy for the glasses that shielded his expression to some small degree.

"I'm locked out," Storm spit, angrily. "Give me your phone."

Taz reached inside his coat for his cell, punched in his unlock code, and handed it out the window to the star who grabbed it, putting it to his ear before walking away from the car. Taz heard Storm as he began to bark into it and then a moment later, he spun back, walked to the car, and handed the phone back through the open window to Taz.

"She's on her way down," he said nastily, glaring first at Taz and then at David.

The only thing Taz could figure was that Storm was either profoundly put out by being locked out of Jules's apartment or he was pissed at catching Taz in a lip lock with the chauffer. He hoped it was the former because the last thing he wanted was more drama when it came to David. The kiss had been unprovoked and he had only responded to it because David tasted so good. After all, the chauffer was handsome as hell, he was gay, he'd made it absolutely crystal clear he wanted Taz, and Taz had no responsibility to explain his actions to Storm. If it hadn't felt very wrong to be caught by Storm, which the butterflies in his stomach attested to, he would have probably enjoyed the attention the younger man was giving him. As it was, he felt guilty for kissing the driver for other reasons. *You wish it was Storm.*

Jules came out of the apartment a few minutes later, grinning and filled with what Taz could only describe as enthusiasm for the night ahead. Storm, who'd been pacing outside the limo since handing back the phone, looped his arm around his best friend and planted a kiss on her surprised mouth. She pulled back from the kiss and grinned as he opened the door for her and climbed in after her. They relaxed back on the seat as David started the car and pulled the limo away from the curb.

"Where to, Mr. Ellison?" David asked.

"Take us to The Cellar," Storm said before Jules had a second to respond.

Taz watched the pair in the rearview mirror.

"You hate The Cellar, Storm," Jules said almost immediately. "You said the place is full of skanks."

"I need a skank tonight, Jules. I intend on getting laid, more than once, hopefully," Storm said, staring straight at Taz. The look on his face was so petulant, Taz expected the superstar to stick out his tongue at him and blow raspberries. Taz bit his lower lip to keep from smiling. *Someone's in a hell of a mood.*

"Storm!" Jules said, smiling slightly. "What's gotten into you tonight?"

"Nothing, Jules. I'm going to get fucked and then fucked again and then maybe I'll get drunk," Storm said, again glaring at Taz one more time before he turned back to his friend.

"Yes, sir, Mr. Ellison," David replied, checking the side view mirror to the left of him, before turning the car into traffic and heading on their way.

Stay on your toes tonight, Taz. The boy is looking for trouble in the worst way. A lump settled in the pit of his stomach and Taz was certain by the end of the night, he'd be wishing he was anywhere but where he was... taking care of a self-indulgent child who was determined to get into as much trouble as he possibly could.

CHAPTER SIX

The Cellar was a small, dark club located in one of the seedier sections of Hollywood. As soon as Taz learned of their destination, he'd pulled out his phone and called the establishment, arranging for a VIP table. He hadn't been to the venue before and had no idea what to expect, but if Jules's judgment was anything to go by, it was going to be a difficult evening. It seemed Storm had made up his mind on getting laid and though Taz's job wasn't to vet his tricks, it was a bold pronouncement when he hadn't even seen what fare was on the menu. Taz just hoped he didn't have to get between Storm and another bad choice as the evening wore on. In truth, the fact Storm wanted to get laid at all, had him angry and he wasn't exactly sure why. Taz had been attracted to Storm's good looks from the outset but he wasn't foolish enough to believe having a relationship with the star other than as someone who worked for him would be a good idea at all. Having made the decision to come to work for such a high profile client, Taz was determined to keep their relationship purely professional.

David pulled the limo up to the valet in front of the club and Taz was almost immediately distressed when he perused the neighborhood and the dark look of the place. The outside of the old brick building was painted black, there were no visible windows on the front of it, and only one small pink neon sign lit the place with the name of the club. A large bouncer stood at the door checking IDs as he let club-goers into the establishment where a short line had formed in the front on the narrow sidewalk. Wads of trash littered the street and a small parking lot with an asphalt driveway seemed to be the only parking on the entire block. A sign at the front of the lot read "Lot Full" and a club employee stood in front of it, directing cars away when they pulled up. Where they went to park, Taz had no idea. As he stepped out of the limo, he glanced upward to the top of the two-story building where barbed wire was looped in coils along the roofline. The club was located on a block of ancient buildings in downtown Hollywood and Taz judged the area to have been built in the 1920s or 30s.

Taz walked to the back of the car and opened the door on Storm's side, standing off to the side as the superstar exited, pulling Jules out of the car by the hand. Storm was wearing skintight black pants and purple crocodile ankle boots with zippered closures that must have cost a month of Taz's salary. His purple silk shirt flowed around his chest and was unbuttoned from the neck nearly to his bellybutton, affording admirers an unobstructed view of his hairless pecs and nipple rings. Storm's hair was gelled into a fauxhawk and his eyes were encircled with black kohl liner. He looked good enough to eat and as Taz looked him over, he noted Storm's eyes on him. They glimmered with something Taz couldn't identify and if he were asked to, he would have said mischief but that would have been incorrect. The expression was more like determination and confidence. *Oh yes, the boy is out to stir up more than a little trouble tonight.*

Surprisingly, the star wasn't met with paparazzi as he usually was and Taz wondered whether no one expected a man as famous as Storm to come out to such a lowbrow establishment. Whatever the reason, the lack of onlookers made it easy for Taz to clear a path past the short line after speaking to the bouncer who craned his neck, eager to get a glance at such a famous man and his companion. The moment he recognized Storm, he let them through the door, no questions asked.

They entered the club and Taz's senses were immediately hit with the scent of sweat and cloying aftershave as the throbbing throng gyrated on the dance floor to a grinding beat. A DJ was up front on an elevated stage and Taz was surprised to note that the inside of the packed club was a lot nicer than what he'd expected. In fact, it seemed rather upscale and they were greeted at the door by a hostess who stared boldly at Storm and his companions before leading them back to a roped-off bottle service area. The couches were white leather, very posh, and Taz was pleasantly surprised at the comfort afforded them. As they settled into their seats for the evening and drinks were ordered, Taz surveyed the room. The weight of his gun was comforting to him as he noted some less than savory types. Storm was garnering a lot of attention as he was recognized and without the seclusion of their usual half-moon booth.

Taz was seated as usual, with his back against the wall, Jules beside him and Storm beside her. Storm laughed and Jules giggled along with him and Taz was reminded how young they were, filled with vibrancy, and making the most of their night out. When their drinks were delivered, Storm picked up his shot of 1800 Tequila and downed it, ordering another before the waitress even had time to walk away. He glanced over at Taz, and Taz found himself having to blank his features so his disapproval wouldn't show. The waitress arrived only a minute later with a second double shot of 1800, which Storm downed again, slamming the glass down onto the table. When a good-looking twink approached the table and asked Storm to dance, he immediately stood up with Jules's encouragement and followed the man out onto the dance floor. Taz watched them closely for a few moments before he felt Jules's gaze on him.

"What is it?" he asked, glancing her way.

She grinned widely. "Why don't you just admit you like him?" she asked innocently.

Taz blinked, not really certain if he'd heard her correctly over the thumping beat of the loud music. He leaned closer. "What?"

Jules grinned again. "You like Storm, Taz. You LIKE like him!" she raised her voice and Taz looked around to see who else could have overheard her.

"I like him fine, Jules. I work for the guy," he replied, intentionally misunderstanding her.

"No, Taz, you are 'in like' with Storm," she reiterated. She reached up and took hold of his sunglasses, dragging them off his face. "Look me in the eyes and tell me you don't like Storm like that, big guy. Whoa, those are some dreamy eyes," she sighed.

Taz felt embarrassed and exposed without his shades and hated the fact she could see the very real truth in his eyes when all he wanted to do was deny it. He averted his gaze, staring out onto the dance floor only to regret it immediately when he noted Storm's arms wrapped around the twink, his lips being plied by the smaller man's as their lower bodies ground against each other to the beat of the music. The moment he saw them, he frowned.

"See? That's what I'm talkin' about, Taz. You can't stand the way that other man touches Storm. You want him for yourself," she said emphatically.

How fuckin' transparent am I? He dragged his gaze away from Storm, forcing himself to look over at Jules. She was looking smugly satisfied. "I don't LIKE like him," he said, making air quotes with his fingers. "I have to keep track of him because it's my job, Jules," he said, sounding insincere even to himself as the lie slid off his tongue. He'd never been a good liar, even when he was asked to cover an illicit affair of a CO while he was stationed overseas. The man had asked Taz to lie for him, knowing he was inferior lower-ranked officer who would probably be forced to oblige, and when Taz had been questioned later, the truth came out. He couldn't lie nor would he... usually. It was very hard not confessing his attraction to Storm though he knew Jules meant no harm. Taz was not, however, going to come clean about his feelings for Storm, especially when it could compromise his ability to protect his client.

He glanced back out onto the dance floor, picking up his ginger ale and sipping it, wishing for something stronger. Thankfully, a man approached the table just then and Taz was relieved when he asked Jules to dance, even though he winked at Taz before escorting her out to the floor. Taz glanced out at the dance floor, once again locating Storm and the man he'd been dancing with, only now another twink had moved in behind Storm, sandwiching him between them. The man in back of Storm had his hands on

Storm's hips and he was rubbing his cock up and down along the crease of his tight ass. Irritation flooded through Taz and he wished he was anywhere but where he was at that very moment. Storm's eyes were closed as he once again held the man in front of him and kissed him deeply. When he finally broke the kiss and leaned back, he turned his head and his gaze met Taz's across the room. Butterflies filled Taz's stomach as he recognized the lust in Storm's eyes. He picked up the ginger ale and lifted it, knocking it back, blocking the star's face with his hand and the glass. When he replaced the glass to the table and looked back again, Storm was approaching the table with a man on each side of him. Both twinks held on to Storm's arms, making their claims on him and Taz found himself scooting back and sitting up, not realizing until then how slumped he'd been in the booth. Jules walked up right then and Taz quickly diverted his gaze toward her, relieved he didn't have to acknowledge Storm by looking into his face.

"Taz, we're ready to leave now," Storm announced.

"I need to use the restroom," one of the men slurred. Taz looked into his eyes and now that he was closer, he could clearly make out the fact he was under the influence of some sort of drug or a lot of alcohol. Taz glanced over at Storm who smiled at the man.

"I'd join you, baby, but I'm afraid we'd get busy and miss out on something much better," he told the man.

Taz watched as the man looked up at Storm and smiled drunkenly. "Miss out on going home with you, Storm... no way," the man slurred. Storm leaned down and kissed the man deeply, standing only inches from where Taz sat.

"Hey, I wanna piece of that too, Storm," the other man pouted from Storm's other side. He reached around Storm and the star turned with a smile, letting go of the first man who walked off. Within seconds, the man had his arms locked around Storm's middle and the star began kissing him as well.

"Mm, you taste like sex," the second man slurred as Storm finally lifted his head.

Taz dragged his gaze away from the pair when he felt Jules's eyes on him. She had retaken her seat across from Taz and was watching him with more than a little interest. Taz knew she couldn't see the expression in his eyes or his own frown behind the glasses on his face and he was relieved. *This is bullshit!*

Taz was sliding out of the booth and standing to his full height as the first man returned to their table.

"Wow, you gonna join us, sugar?" the man asked, raking Taz's form from head to toe. "I bet you got a great big cock under there." He reached out to grab Taz's package and just as Storm opened his mouth to warn him, Taz had the man's wrist in his hand, squeezing it hard.

"Ow!" the man cried, pulling back as Taz let him go.

"Keep your hands to yourself, sugarpants," Taz growled.

"Stop manhandling my dates, Taz," Storm dared to say.

Taz stared at him as anger coursed through him. "I thought we talked about this, sir," Taz said through gritted teeth.

"Oh, a Dom," Storm's second date said, breathlessly.

Storm threw a filthy look at Taz and for a fleeting second, he thought he saw an apology in his eyes, before it instantly disappeared.

"Can you call for David?" Storm asked as the twinks blanketed him on either side, not sounding apologetic in the least.

"Follow me," Taz growled, reaching out a hand to help Jules out of the booth before escorting her in front of him with a hand on the small of her back. He could hear Storm and the men giggling behind him as he cleared a path through the crowd. As patrons of the bar recognized Storm, a few approached.

"You go ahead, Jules. I'll get behind Storm and his friends and clear these people away," he said to the girl.

"Okay, Taz," the girl replied pleasantly as Taz let her walk in front of him, watching the three men as they passed by him, moving quickly toward the exit. When it was in sight, Taz felt relief wash through him. He wanted to get out of there before more people realized their favorite superstar was in their club. They reached the door in no time and Taz followed the group out through the exit just before the crowd closed in on them. He reached into his pocket and pulled out a ten, handing it to the bouncer and telling him to call the limo.

He was relieved that David was parked only twenty feet down the block, standing beside the car, smoking a cigarette. David spotted them immediately and dropped the lit cig to the ground, stomped it out, and ran around to the driver's side. In less than a minute, Storm and his two companions had piled into the back of the car and Taz had climbed into the front with Jules situated between him and David. David steered the car away from the curb as flash bulbs began going off and Taz glanced over at Jules who was looking slightly put out. His heart went out to her. She could have had a really good time because she had just been asked to dance by a third guy when Storm and the two men walked up to the table. Storm certainly hadn't scored any points in Taz's book tonight and to say he was pissed would have been putting it lightly. Just when he'd begun to think there was more to Storm than what he'd expected, he'd been proven wrong by his selfish behavior.

As they headed off toward Storm's mansion, Taz's anger diminished somewhat. *At least this hellish night is nearly over.*

****

Storm couldn't believe what a dick he was being to Taz. The fact was he wasn't feeling ultra charitable toward his gorgeous bodyguard at the moment and if the shoe were on the other foot, he knew he'd be pissed if he were the bodyguard. It had begun in the morning when Taz had been so stoic and judgmental when it came to the way he looked at Guru Shamsa. The man had been a confidant over the last several months since their meeting and regardless of the fact Butch didn't care for his guru, there was nothing the man hadn't done for him. He'd taught Storm to be unselfish, shared his positive energy with him, taught him the healing ways of eating the proper foods, and brought him a world of normalcy by teaching him his exercises and about Karma.

Storm didn't care that there was a major part of the world who looked down at "Hollywood Types" like Storm because of their ideals and their money, but Storm hadn't come from money. His adoptive parents had been very middle class and very kind to him growing up. They'd given him a set of principles to live by and he was grateful he'd learned from a young age not to hurt people, be unkind, and work hard, understanding the importance of earning a day's pay for his work. Storm had never taken handouts and he took pride in that. He was kind to those who were less fortunate, and he had a family who'd loved him before they passed away. Those were great qualities in him and if he wanted to go out and party every night, as long as he showed up at the studio or set and did a good day's worth of work, he felt justified living the way he lived and being the person he was. No one could tell Storm he was a mistake because he was gay either. His parents had taught him to be independent and a self-starter, accepting the person he was. Who cared what his sexual preference was? Certainly not Storm.

He'd listened to Taz's resignation knowing he wasn't going to accept it. The fact was, not only did he need a bodyguard now that his stardom was probably going to increase with the movie deal, he wanted to keep Taz around, and Storm was unbelievably attracted to the man and he felt extremely safe in his presence. Jules had given her stamp of approval almost from the moment she met him and that was a huge bonus. Jules had an innate ability to see the good in people and she'd been championing Taz to him since meeting the gorgeous man. He trusted Jules because he knew she loved him like a brother and wanted only the best for him. She didn't pretend to like Storm because he was rich and famous; she was his best friend and she spoke her mind around him.

The thing was, tonight, Storm had started out the evening in a great mood but when Jules had taken longer than he'd wanted, well, he was just itching for a fight. He was more than a little pissed at himself tonight though he wouldn't admit to it when he picked out the place they'd ended up at. When she commented on the skanks they'd surely find there, Storm had heartily agreed. He was on a mission to show both Jules and Taz that he ran his own life and if he wanted a skank, well he'd have one. Why he'd ended up promising himself to two at once was a bit of a mystery even to himself, but once he'd done it, he had to live with it.

As it was, he was already regretting his decision. The moment he'd climbed into the back of the limousine with the two men, and they'd begun groping him, he'd pushed them off onto the floor telling them he wanted to watch them together. Even though he'd ordered David to close the privacy screen, he'd known Taz and Jules were sitting in the front with David most likely thinking all kinds of things were going on between the three of them in the back. Storm couldn't for the life of him remember the names of the men, and he honestly didn't want to.

When he'd caught David kissing Taz and Taz enjoying it, he'd made up his mind to show the big burly bodyguard that he wasn't going to take any judgments on his part lying down. To his credit, Taz had looked embarrassed by being caught kissing his

driver but it had solidified one thing in Storm's mind…
Taz was gay and there was no doubt about how much
he loved men. He'd caught a glimpse of lust in the
driver's eyes but Taz's had been hidden behind those
damned glasses. The one time he had seen the
bodyguard's amazing eyes, after he'd lost his glasses,
Storm had hoped he didn't have a replacement pair.
The fact was, Storm wished he'd be able to stare into
that beautiful dark face and actually know what Taz
was thinking without having to drag it out of him.
Storm knew Taz had a military background and he
held his cards close to his chest but seeing the emotions
in his eyes was something he was missing when he
looked at him. Taz was good at hiding behind the
mirrored glasses and it pissed Storm off.

The two men on the floor had their cocks out,
giving each other head as they moaned while
performing a sixty-nine for him. He reached down and
touched his cock, noting with distress he wasn't even
getting the least bit turned on by their show. He was
soft in his tight jeans, only watching. Maybe he'd had
too much alcohol, he thought absently, though the two
double shots of tequila shouldn't have made him
drunk. One of the guys on the floor opened his eyes
and glanced up at where Storm sat. He pulled off the
head of the other twink's cock and smiled drunkenly at
Storm. He was the one who'd used the bathroom in the
club before they'd left The Cellar.

"Hey, Storm, you won't join us here so you can
have some fun?" he asked, drunkenly. Before Storm
could answer, he reached into his jeans and pulled out
a glass vial and a tiny spoon. "I got some crank," he
said. "It'll keep you up so we can party." He proceeded

to unscrew the top of the vial and dip the spoon inside, lifting out the white powder and holding it out as he sat up. The other guy sat up as well, fingering his slick semi hard cock as he watched with a grin.

Storm cursed himself for bringing the guys into the car with him. He didn't do drugs no matter what the tabloids reported. He shook his head. "Nah, I'm good. You guys have fun," he said through gritted teeth.

The moment he'd seen the drugs, he'd prayed Taz wouldn't open the privacy screen. He didn't care what his fans thought about him; the tabloids were going to report whatever the hell they wanted about him, including painting him as a druggie, but he certainly didn't want his driver, his bodyguard, or God forbid, Jules, looking into the back of the car and seeing him snorting crank or anything else.

"You sure? Okay." The guy lifted the spoon to one nostril and snorted the drugs, repeating it with the other nostril.

Storm watched as he handed the drug laden spoon to the second guy who greedily snorted the drugs as well. *Okay, I'm finished with these two.*

"Guys, sorry to break up the party, but suddenly, I'm not feeling so good. Let me have my driver take you home," Storm said.

The men looked at him and Storm could have sworn they were both cross-eyed as they shrugged, tucking their cocks back into their pants. He reached over and hit a button on the door of the car.

"David, drop these guys off, please," he said into the intercom.

The privacy screen slid open as the men got up off the floor and proceeded to climb onto the seat on either side of Storm. With all of the fun gone out of the evening, Storm could barely stand the heat of their bodies pressed up against his. Taz turned his head and looked to the back of the car the very moment one of the men began kissing his neck. His lips firmed and he looked extremely unhappy, though Storm couldn't see his eyes. Storm leaned away from the guy who was kissing him and looked over at him.

"Give my bodyguard your address," he said, feeling extremely irritated he'd been caught in a compromising position once again.

The guy rattled it off, still sounding drunk and Taz nodded before slamming the privacy screen closed again.

Fifteen minutes later, they'd pulled up to the address in the San Fernando Valley. They'd agreed to stay the night with each other and Storm was relieved they only had one stop to make. After the men kissed Storm goodnight and got out of the car, Jules climbed into the back with Storm for the ride to her house. She shot him a look as she settled into the seat beside him.

"Please don't say I told you so, Jules. I can't stand to hear it," Storm growled.

She looked hurt. "Hey, what's your problem anyway?" she asked.

He didn't really know why he was annoyed with Jules. She hadn't said or done anything to him to make him feel bad. It was probably his own guilt about having invited the guys home and making him look like a real jerk to Taz that had him disappointed with himself, but there was no reason for him to take it out

126

on her. She wasn't the one being the tool; he was. He softened his features and smiled at her.

"I'm sorry, babe. It's all my fault. I'm just completely off my game these days. They started using drugs back here and the fact is, I was really happy that they seemed to be more into each other than into me anyway."

She looked over at him with a look of sympathy on her face. "You were showing off for your bodyguard, Storm. Trying to look like you don't give a damn when you really do," she said. "Damn, sometimes I think I know you better than you do."

He reached around her shoulders and hugged her close so she couldn't see the truth in his eyes. "I don't know why he affects me that way. I just want to show him that I don't care what he thinks."

She pulled out of his hug so she could look at him in the eyes. "Why?"

That one threw Storm for a loop and for a second, he didn't know how to answer. "I don't know. I want to be a good person, Jules and everyone thinks I'm not."

"Are we having a major pity party now or what?" she asked with a smile. She'd nailed it right on the head.

"No, I'm not feeling sorry for myself." It sounded like bullshit which it was.

"Yeah, sure tell it to someone who doesn't know you, Storm. You're a good guy. Why do you want Taz to think you're a selfish dick?"

"Maybe I do like him," Storm admitted, sighing deeply and closing his eyes, as he leaned his head back against the seat. He wanted to crawl right into a hole and bury himself. He hated being wrong, especially when it mattered and it mattered with Jules. He loved and respected her like no one else he knew. He felt a squeeze on his knee and he opened his eyes, staring into her pretty almond-shaped ones, feeling miserable and not even trying to hide it.

"I know you do, baby. And you know what? He's a keeper, Storm."

I know. That's why he doesn't deserve a guy like me.

CHAPTER SEVEN

Taz walked through the dark house, making his final rounds, checking to make certain all the doors were locked before he turned on the alarm he'd installed when he'd first come to work for Storm. He got to the back of the house and looked out through the double French doors to the yard. Storm's pool was lit with a pink glow and the sky looked dark. Taz opened the doors and stepped out, letting the cool breeze wash over him. He'd changed into casual clothes after the tumultuous night at the club. He wore dark blue sweats, flip-flops and his favorite black muscle tee. He took a deep breath, appreciating the clean scent of the Pacific Ocean. He'd been born and raised in the southland and to Taz, there was nothing more refreshing than Los Angeles in the fall, too early to bundle up for winter and too late in the season for the sweltering heat that had California in the worst drought they'd experienced in twenty years. He stepped farther out onto the patio and lifted his face, staring up at the stars and a very dark moon framed by a bright pink aura.

"It's a total eclipse tonight," Storm said, from his spot on a chaise lounge beside Taz. He nearly jumped out of his skin, not realizing that the star was lying out on a patio lounger enjoying the night air. He'd expected Storm had gone to bed once they'd arrived home after dropping off the two young men they'd met in the club as well as taking Jules home to her apartment. "Did you know that the next lunar eclipse visible in our hemisphere isn't going to happen until next spring?"

Taz stared down at Storm who was petting Butch. The dog looked up at Taz from where he was lying in Storm's lap and began wagging his stubby tail.

"That's a good boy, Butch. Taz has come out to watch the moon turn pink, just like me. Hey, he's not wearing his glasses for once."

Taz couldn't help but chuckle when he looked down at the ugly little mutt; his curled tongue lolled out of his mouth and Butch appeared to be smiling at him. He watched as Storm picked up a glass filled with something red, and sipped it. "You've had a busy night, Storm. You needed just one more nightcap before saying sayonara?"

This time he heard Storm's low laugh. "Yeah. Ya gotta love the healing powers of tomato juice. Butch told me that every good star-gazer needs sustenance." Storm picked up a bowl of water which had been sitting on a low table beside him, and placed it on the ground at the dog's feet. He set down the dog and he waddled up and eagerly drank from the dish.

Taz looked back up at the dark sky and the amazing pink-rimmed moon. One side of it had started glowing brighter and he knew the eclipse would be finished in only a few more minutes. The stars were even brighter than usual in the darkened sky. He didn't know much about stars but he could make out the Orion constellation. That and the Big Dipper were the only ones he could name. He absently wondered whether it was possible that Earth looked like a star to other civilizations living on their own planet far away. He shook his head. "It's really beautiful out here. You're lucky, Storm," he said. When the star said nothing, he looked over where he was relaxing on the chaise lounge. His arms were crossed over his chest as he lay back on the lounger and stared into the sky.

"Taz, do you think there is life somewhere else in our universe?" Storm asked. He turned his head and raised his chin, looking up and staring at Taz with the most beautiful blue eyes he'd ever seen. They were still framed with black kohl making his light eyes stand out. *You're breathtaking.*

"I think we're stupid to think we're the only life in the whole vast universe or the universes beyond," Taz said, honestly. He was rewarded when Storm's face lit with a smile that went all the way to his eyes.

"Thanks, Taz. Really. Sometimes I think no one realizes I have a brain in my head. The truth is, I have a pretty huge imagination. When I was a younger, after my parents died, I used to sit out and stare at the stars. I had all these posters on my wall that showed the universe and the planets orbiting the sun. I was enthralled with things like that. Did you know it takes Pluto 248 years to orbit the sun and that since it was discovered in 1930, it hasn't even completed a third of an orbit?" Storm stopped and smiled a tiny smile. He actually looked embarrassed. "Sorry if I'm boring you. I just find little things like that to be fascinating."

Taz smiled at him and walked over to the chaise lounge beside Storm. Butch had finished his water and was lying between the two chairs. He looked up when Taz sat down and then wagged his stump of a tail when Taz started petting his head. Taz smiled at the little guy for a minute and then looked over at Storm. "You know, I think it's really neat that you know things like that, Storm. It makes you interesting, not boring at all," he said. He meant every word of it and somehow, seeing Storm out here in the yard, lying down in cargo shorts and a tank top made him very sexy to Taz.

Storm signed and looked up at the sky again, chuffing a little. "Yeah, well, you're in the minority there, Taz. Most people would think it's pretty nerdy if they knew I thought things like that. Alan wouldn't approve. He thinks my image of a vapid selfish star is sexy." He looked back at Taz and he had an almost sad expression on his beautiful face.

"I don't think it's nerdy. I think it's really cool but I also think the people you hang out with, with the exception of Jules, wouldn't realize you thought about the stars."

"Yeah, that was a mistake tonight. Honestly, when they pulled out drugs, I realized what a huge mistake I'd made," Storm said, looking away shyly.

"They offered you drugs?" Taz asked, suddenly regretting stepping outside. He really didn't know why it bugged him that Storm was a partier but it did.

"I didn't use them. I don't do drugs and never have; hell, the two doubles I had tonight will give me a killer headache tomorrow morning," he said with a frown. "I bet you don't believe me."

Taz suddenly felt very sad. It was hard to put into words because the truth was he had believed what he'd read about Storm and after his behavior tonight, he'd felt justified in it. "The tabloids paint you very differently, Storm," he said.

Storm sighed again, and he turned back to look at Taz, his expression sad. "Alan says all publicity is good publicity. I don't have parents or brothers or sisters for them to attack and I guess it doesn't really matter what people think of me. Alan would have been happy to see the paparazzi catch me getting into the limo with the two twinks."

"Give the drooling masses a reason to jack off for a few minutes," Taz chuckled. He watched Storm's pretty face transform as he smiled sexily. He looked young and happy when he smiled like that. Suddenly, Taz had the overwhelming urge to kiss the star.

"I do have that effect on some people, Taz," he said, growing serious as he dropped his gaze to Taz's lips.

"I can see why. You're very sexy," Taz said. He knew he was going to regret it but he reached out a hand and lightly touched Storm's cheek with his fingers. Storm lowered his lashes, closing his beautiful eyes as Taz trailed his fingers downward before firming them on his chin. He knew he was most likely going to regret kissing Storm, but the urge was overwhelming. When he leaned forward and touched Storm's lips with his own, they were soft and pliable, and deliciously kissable. Storm let out a small groan, and when he began kissing Taz back, arousal shot through his veins, lighting him up inside.

Taz scooted to the edge of the lounger, reaching out with his other hand to frame Storm's face, holding it in place as he plied Storm's soft lips, deepening the kiss. He felt Storm's hands on his shoulders as the man reached up and wrapped his fingers around them. Taz loved kissing, especially when he was kissing a man as sweet and beautiful as Storm was. He let all thoughts of the disparity between them wash away as he was drawn deeper and deeper into the moment. Taz opened his mouth and felt Storm's relax. The sweep of his tongue, flavored with the tart tomato juice, was intoxicating. Their tongues began to dance as the kiss deepened. Storm flexed his fingers on Taz's shoulders and suddenly, Taz desperately wanted to make love to the smaller man. It had been a while since he'd taken a lover and in this place and at this time, all he wanted to do was to pick him up and carry him upstairs to his bed, laying him out, and peeling off his sexy clothes one layer at a time. When Storm began to moan again, Taz knew he couldn't let the kiss go on unless he was going to take action; the most difficult thing he'd ever done was letting go of Storm's face and pulling back, slowly separating them. When he opened his eyes, he was staring into the most beautiful light blue gaze he'd ever seen.

"My God, your eyes are beautiful, Taz. I want you to make love to me," Storm said, shakily. His voice was throaty and low and everything in Taz made him want to growl out loud, grab Storm, and take him the way he wanted him.

"You know I can't do that, Storm," Taz said sadly. "I work for you and even kissing you… as wonderful as it felt, was wrong."

Storm reached out and laid a hand on Taz's leg. He reveled in the warmth of the way it felt and he reached to cover it with his other larger hand. Storm looked down at their connection for just a second before looking up again. His beautiful kohl-rimmed eyes were pleading and alluring in the moonlight. "But how can you say that it's wrong when it feels like this, Taz?"

Taz sighed and looked upward. The eclipse had moved across the moon and all but a sliver of it was showing. The pink had faded away, leaving the sky bright with a nearly full moon again. "You know why, Storm," he replied, wishing very badly he'd met the beautiful man in another time and another place. He let his hand fall away and slowly stood up, not breaking his gaze with Storm's. His cock was hard and throbbing and he couldn't believe he was about to walk away, knowing he must. "It wouldn't be right, Storm."

Butch whimpered and stood also, wagging his little stump of a tail as he stared up at Taz. The dog was so sweet, Taz smiled.

Storm stood also and suddenly they were face-to-face again. It would have been so easy for Taz to just forget he worked for the star. He leaned in and kissed Storm softly, pulling away as he felt Storm's need. Their gazes connected again. "Goodnight, Storm," he said.

Before he could say another word, Storm nodded slowly. "Goodnight, Taz. We would have been good together."

Don't I know it… don't I know it.
****

Taz walked through the house the next morning. He knew Storm had an early appointment with his masseuse because Rebecca had let him in earlier. The two were in the workout room. But as he walked into the living room headed for the kitchen, he was surprised to hear salsa music blaring out of the sound system in the backyard so he went to investigate. The culprit turned out to be none other than Jules who was lying on a lounger in the middle of the pool, looking scrumptious in her string bikini. Taz walked through the double French doors which Rebecca had most likely left open. He kicked himself for not knowing Jules was even in the house. *Some bodyguard you are!* She must have arrived when he was busy elsewhere in the huge mansion or possibly when he'd been out checking the perimeter earlier. The moment he walked outside, she saw him and grinned widely, lifting her hand as she waved.

"Hey, Taz! Good morning," she called, good-naturedly.

"Hello beautiful," he said, walking up to the edge of the pool with a wide smile.

"Storm's getting a massage so I just thought I'd get some rays. We have a salon appointment in the mall at noon but a girl can never have enough sun."

Jules's skin was already golden brown, kissed by the sun. He suspected that was mostly from her Puerto Rican heritage but he didn't really know for sure.

"So, you guys are going out to the mall," Taz said. "You know, I gave Storm a calendar and asked him to fill in his plans for the week. It's really important that I know where you guys are going and when. He writes certain things down, like today's massage appointment, but half the time, he leaves stuff off."

"Well, it's partially my fault, good-lookin'. I broke a nail and I begged him to go with me," she said, holding up her index finger to show him the broken nail.

She was so sweet and bubbly, Taz couldn't be upset with her and he really didn't want to be. "So what mall are you going to?" he asked.

Her mouth opened and closed a couple of times as a look of surprise washed over her features before she began grinning. "Seriously? Aside from Rodeo Drive, there is no other mall but the Century City Mall, Taz."

Taz laughed. "Rodeo Drive isn't a mall; it's a street, Jules, or should I call it your mother ship?" he teased.

She reached over the side of the lounger and splashed him with an arc of water. It landed on his shoes and the bottom of his suit pants before he could step back. She burst into giggles as he stumbled backward.

"Jules! What are you doing to Taz's shoes?" Storm called out. He'd walked into the yard behind Taz wearing nothing but a white Speedo with a diagonal red racing stripe right over the bulge in front. *Holy shit.* Taz's mouth fell open and he gulped as he got a look at the star's swimsuit. When he was finally able to drag his eyes away from Storm's groin and up to his face, Storm was flashing him a killer sexy smile. He was wearing sunglasses but if he hadn't been, Taz knew he would have seen a teasing glint in his beautiful light eyes. "See anything you like?" Storm asked, sauntering up. He was swinging a towel and wearing flip-flops. When he got close he smelled like cocoanut.

Taz was speechless and he knew he'd been caught staring. Even behind the mirrored sunglasses he wore to disguise where he was looking, he knew the expression on his face must have given away the fact he'd been openly staring at Storm's package. "Sorry, Storm, I…" Taz stopped and cleared his throat as the star came to a stop right in front of him. The scent of his tanning lotion filled Taz's senses. "I understand you are going to the mall," he finished lamely, completely ignoring Storm's question.

Storm grinned even wider and then looked over Taz's large shoulder at his friend. "We're going to the mall?" he asked as Taz turned sideways to look back at Jules who was grinning herself.

She held up her index finger. "I broke a nail."

"Dear God, call the President," Storm said with a snicker, brushing past Taz where he threw his towel onto a lounge chair. He stood at the edge of the pool and looked back over his shoulder to see if Taz was watching him before diving in. A huge splash covered Jules and she squealed before starting to laugh.

When Storm came up for air, Taz turned away from the pair and started walking to the house. The sun was hot and he was beginning to sweat in the late morning heat. "I'm going to change my shoes," he said.

"What's wrong with wet shoes?" Storm asked playfully, and Taz lifted his hand and waved without turning as he continued into the house, ignoring the star. He knew Storm was more confident about their relationship since the kiss the night before. He was feeling kind of happy himself, even though he knew their relationship was going to have to stay on strictly professional terms, regardless of how attracted they were to each other.

****

Storm swam laps for about fifteen minutes before he came to rest, holding on to the side of the pool. He was breathing hard, refreshed from the vigorous exercise as he watched Jules paddle her float over to him. She had flipped over to lie on her stomach and her skin was glistening with sweat; he had the overwhelming urge to topple her into the water but she saved herself when she opened her mouth to speak.

"I like him a lot, Storm. He's perfect for you," she said.

Actually, Storm couldn't argue with that. There were only two things standing between them, the fact Taz worked for him, and the fact he knew Taz had a hard time coping with his lifestyle. "You said that before, Jules," he replied, reaching out and brushing a stray curl out of her pretty face. Her amazing eyes were filled with mischief and he realized once again how much he loved his best friend. He honestly hoped she'd find the perfect guy someday.

"No, Storm, I think he's the one. You should go for that man, honey. He's a lot better than those skanks you picked up last night. Most of the time, I try to stay out of your business and I don't say anything but… what were you thinking anyway?"

Storm looked over at her. She wasn't being judgmental; she was just being Jules and he knew she loved him. The question was a good one. *Maybe I don't have the confidence I should or maybe I was just being an idiot.*

"Babe, I don't know," he said, hoping she would drop it and knowing she wouldn't.

"I call bullshit," she said, frowning at him. "You know you are so much better than that. You deserve a man like Taz."

"You don't even know Taz," Storm said. "What you've had a couple conversations with him and now he's your best friend?"

"No, but I do know a good man when I see one and he's a keeper, love," she said.

Of course he already knew that. He'd not only read Taz's resume which included the honors he'd earned in the service, but he'd had a good feeling about the big man since the moment he'd first talked to him.

"He kissed me last night," Storm blurted.

Her mouth flew open in surprise and then her face transformed as she smiled. She reached out and punched Storm on his arm, hard. "What the fuck happened? You're waiting till now to tell me?" she shrieked.

Storm's eyes darted to the back of the house, worried Taz may have heard her. The French doors were closed and Taz was still inside.

"Geez! Keep it down, brat," Storm said with a smile.

Jules reached out and circled his neck with both of her hands pretending to shake him. "Tell me now or I shall kill you... bwahahahahaha."

Storm started laughing, dunking his head to get her to stop choking him. He came up shaking water off his head, spraying her. She squealed and he loved the sound. "I was sitting out on the patio with Butch watching the lunar eclipse when he came out for some air. He came over to me and we started talking and then he kissed me. That's it."

"Okay, now you're just being mean," she said with a frown. "I want to hear every horny little detail, right now, Storm!"

He finally relented and told her the whole conversation, remembering Taz's kisses with great relish. When he thought about the way Taz's beautiful mouth tasted, he began to get hard and he knew he'd better take a few more laps before he got out of the pool. The last thing he needed was for Jules to see him with a hard-on and the Speedo would do little to hide it from view.

"Well, that's a great start, babe. Maybe there's hope for you after all," Jules said, touching him on the side of his face. His beard and goatee was trimmed to a designer stubble and he liked the look on him.

"I think so. Well, I hope so. Taz thinks we can't kiss again, although he was tempted to take me to bed last night," Storm said.

"Did he say that?" she asked. Her eyes were bugging out of her head, making her look hilarious.

He grinned. "No. I actually made a pass at him, but he turned me down telling me it's a bad idea for him to get involved with a client… shame though, I could only imagine the man in bed," Storm replied.

"I told you he was a man with integrity," she said. "Now as for the imagining him in bed part, sigh… Holy Moly, that ass, those thighs, that package… I'll bet he's packin'," she said with a grin.

Storm laughed. He loved her. "You have a dirty mind, Jules."

"Oh you bet I do," she replied. "So, we'd better get out of the pool. My salon appointment is at noon."

"Okay, go get your shower. I'm gonna do a few more laps and then come inside." He watched her climb out of the pool. He began doing laps as he thought about his best friend. He loved Jules like a sister and she was the very best friend in the world. She was forever patient with him and had never been even the least bit critical about the way he picked up guys at clubs and bars, bringing them home with few questions asked. She was good about telling him if a guy seemed nice or if she thought he was simply out to get something from hanging out with Storm. She had a great head on her shoulders and she was wise beyond her years. She was fiercely loyal to him and he just knew he'd lay down his life for her if needed. That's just what you did for people you loved. Storm finished his laps and got out of the pool, anxious to get showered and have more time to spend ogling his bodyguard.

****

"What do you think of getting Taz a present?" Storm said, leaning close to Jules who walked beside him and then glanced over his shoulder at the bodyguard who walked ten feet behind them.

"Oh, I love surprises. What's the occasion?" she whispered conspiratorially.

"Well, none that I know of. His birthday isn't until July but I was thinking he's been with me for thirty days. Doesn't that count for something?" Storm asked.

"Um… yeah, if you're in AA," she replied, "Oh, is he a drinker?" she said.

He burst into laughter and slapped her on the shoulder. "Stop it. I just thought it might be nice to get him something… I don't know… just something."

"Oh look, there's Bloomies. I know we'll be able to find something there," she said, suddenly veering off in the direction of Bloomingdale's. Storm and Taz had to practically run to keep up with her.

"What's up with you today? How much coffee did you drink before your nail appointment, Jules?" Storm asked with a grin as he caught up to her with Taz on his tail. He didn't mind walking fast; he wore sunglasses and a hat when he was out so there was less chance of him getting recognized but if she was darting through the outdoor mall like a frickin' gazelle and he had to chase after her, it was going to call attention to them, especially with a very HUGE bodyguard following them.

"I had a Starbucks, that's all," she replied. "Well, it did have a double pump of espresso in it."

"Okay, you're not allowed off your leash for the rest of the day," Storm said. He turned and looked back at Taz. "Did you bring Jules's harness?"

Taz smiled, "No, sir."

"Fuck," Storm said, turning back to her. "You'd better behave yourself or you won't get any Cold Stones." Cold Stones made the best ice cream on the planet and Storm knew it was Jules favorite.

"You're mean," she said, throwing him a pouty moue. "Oh, look, sparkly!" She said before darting away to the men's department.

Storm laughed and followed her. They browsed through the department for about a half hour, checking out some of the newest clothes. Storm tried on several pairs of jeans and decided on two pair, while Jules picked out a dress shirt she wanted to see him in when he went to meetings. Taz stood off to the side about eight feet away from them, trying to look inconspicuous and failing badly. The black suit, white shirt, black tie, and mirrored sun glasses had him either looking like a G-man, a bodyguard, or a follower of Malcolm X. Storm smiled at the thought but tried to hurry as best he could; he wanted to get out of the store before he was recognized.

A table of folded sweaters was on the way to the wrap desk so he and Jules stopped to check them out. When he held up a gorgeous gray sweater and admired the soft cashmere blend, he looked over at Jules and mouthed the words *For Taz.* She grinned and nodded madly, glancing over at him before looking back at Storm. She walked over to Storm's side of the table and helped him pick out one they thought would fit the tall man and put it with the rest of the items Storm had chosen before going to the register to pay for the pile. Jules was practically bouncing out of her shoes as they walked out to the car. They'd taken Jules's red Mustang in order to look less conspicuous. He only took the limo when he went out at night or was expecting paparazzi would follow him. Alan told him he must allow himself to be photographed sometimes but he resented being molested everywhere he went so during a quick shopping trip like this one, Storm wanted privacy. Some days he missed the times when he was just allowed anonymity.

With Jules behind the wheel, they made it to Storm's mansion in record time. Taz sat in the backseat behind him and he could barely stop the urge to turn around and talk to him. Storm realized he was beginning to have a desperate crush on the bodyguard and he felt giddy. He couldn't wait to give him the present and he began to stress about when and where they'd have time alone. He glanced at the digital clock on Jules's dashboard only to realize he'd forgotten he had a yoga workout scheduled with Guru Shamsa in only half an hour. That would barely give him time to wrap the gift and get changed before he arrived. With regret, he pushed away the excitement of giving Taz his gift, knowing it was going to have to be later. As soon as they drove through the electronic gates to Storm's house, he saw Guru's car there. *He's early, dammit.* Jules dropped off him and Taz, promising to call Storm later and they went into the house. The guru was standing inside, looking tanned and fit. When he saw Storm he smiled and Storm remembered how peaceful the man seemed.

"Namaste," he said, bowing as Storm bowed back. "Your maid let me in, Storm. I was a little early," Guru explained.

Storm opened his mouth to say something when he heard Butch from the backyard. He was going crazy, barking so loudly, Storm craned his neck to look outside.

"Oh, for some reason, that dog hates me," Guru said. The look on his face was stern and unhappy. "Your maid put him outside to keep him from eating me."

Storm looked back at Guru. Butch liked everyone but he did seem to have a negative reaction to his yoga partner every time he saw him. *Huh.* "Sorry about that, Guru," Storm said, holding up the bags

145

from their shopping trip. "Let me just put these away and get changed for our workout."

"No problem, Storm. I will wait here with…" He looked over at Taz.

"Taz," Taz said. "And I'd love to wait with you, but I have to check my e-mail. I'll be in the library if either of you need me," the bodyguard said. He hesitated a second, looked back at Storm and then walked off toward the library.

"I'll be just a minute," Storm said and then ran upstairs. Storm had caught a look on Taz's face, firming his lips when he looked over at Guru. He had a feeling Taz didn't like the man but then he didn't think Taz liked his agent either. Taz held his cards close to his chest and for the thousandth time Storm wished he could look Taz in the eyes to read what he could possibly be thinking, but he was unable to with the damned glasses. He'd only seen his eyes after Petros's men tussled with him and last night when he'd thought he'd be alone outside. Every time he looked at them, he wanted to cream his jeans, they were so beautiful. He got to his bedroom, only then remembering he'd forgotten to let in Butch. He dropped his things on the bed, promising himself to put the dog in the kitchen while they worked out. It just wouldn't be right to lock him out of his own house just because of Guru Shamsa.

CHAPTER EIGHT

Storm was distracted as he finished the last of his stretching exercises once the workout was done. The fact is, he'd been more than a little distracted throughout the entire workout while he thought of giving Taz his present. He couldn't wait to get a glimpse of his eyes again and he planned on insisting Taz take off his glasses while he was in the house. The fact he couldn't tell what his gorgeous bodyguard was thinking was unnerving in the very least. Besides, Storm was desperate to see if Taz had any interest in him as well. He did his last stretch, looking over to see Guru Shamsa sitting in the lotus position, his eyes closed, seeming completely serene as his chest moved ever so slightly with his controlled breathing. He hoped that someday, he'd have the same kind of serenity as his guru did. The yogi opened his eyes and looked over at Storm, smiling.

"Well, that was nice. How are you feeling, Storm? You look healthy. Have you been eating well?"

"I have… as well as I can. I'm at the point now where eating meat is not important to me and my diet is mostly vegan. I admit, I do feel better," Storm said.

"This is good," the guru said, unfolding his legs as he began his stretches. "As you know, the body is the temple of the spirit. How about your colonic regimen?"

"I'm building up to that. I have booked an appointment with your colon hydrotherapist."

"Very good. It is important that you see a professional. It would be dangerous to develop an electrolyte imbalance."

The idea of having a colonic scared Storm a little. He pictured someone putting a large hose up his rectum and then pumping water and herbs into his colon and the idea wasn't pleasant but so far, the advice Guru had given him had been solid. He'd seen an increase in his energy since seeing the massage therapist the guru had referred him to and that was good. Overall, Storm felt better. Besides, so much had been written about the benefits of colonics to remove parasites, Storm felt compelled to trust Guru and take the next step. Storm's thoughts were interrupted by a knock at the door of the workout room. Rebecca stuck her head in a few seconds later.

"Meester Storm, ju lunch... she is ready. Ju want to eat some lunch, Meester goo?" she asked in her thick accent.

Storm had to cover his mouth with his hand to keep from grinning and embarrassing Guru.

Guru Shamsa looked downright irritated as he looked over at the innocently blinking maid waiting by the door. "No thank you, madam," he said tersely. He looked back at Storm and Storm noted how he carefully schooled his annoyed features and replaced them with a smile which didn't go all the way to his eyes. In fact, Guru Shamsa looked as though he could use a colonic of his own at that moment. Storm wished Jules was around so he could look at her and share a secret smile with her. He watched Guru get to his feet and then did the same himself. Storm's cell phone rang as he was getting up and he ran over to the counter where he'd left it.

"Just a second, Guru Shamsa," he said, picking up the call and swiping the screen.

"Mr. Ellison, this is Anthony Kinkaid. I am glad I caught you, sir. I wanted to schedule an appointment with you. I've been going over the figures your guru sent over."

"Figures my guru sent over?" Storm asked looking over to where Guru stood. The man's ears perked up as he met Storm's eyes.

"Yes, sir. Something's come to my attention and I must see you," the young man said.

"Oh, okay, no problem. Perhaps next week," Storm replied, still looking at the bald man who listened with interest.

"Yes, sir. I had some questions about your investment in the temple, sir, and as I studied the numbers, I had some even deeper questions."

"Well, that sounds ominous," Storm said with a laugh.

Guru wasn't looking terribly happy.

"Yes, sir. It may be. But, I'd really like to meet with you before… well, as soon as possible, sir."

"Of course, Anthony. Wednesday at noon here at the house then."

"Very good, sir." Storm swiped the phone as Anthony hung up.

Guru Shamsa was looking very uncomfortable.

"Is something wrong, Storm?" Guru asked.

"Nothing important, Guru. My business manager was looking over some paperwork and wants a meeting with me that's all," Storm said, knowing it would be just formalities. Even though he paid his people well, everyone had questions.

"I see, well, I will leave you to your lunch, Storm. Namaste." He bowed with his hands pressed together and Storm did the same.

"Namaste, Guru." He followed the man out of the workout room, passing by the living room. Butch was once again at the back screen jumping up and down in the yard and barking like crazy as soon as he saw Guru. Rebecca must have put him back outside. Storm and the yogi looked over to him and then as a pained expression spread across Guru's face, Storm ignored his dog and saw the guru to his front door. As soon as he was gone, Storm turned; Rebecca was standing there, looking at him with a frustrated expression of her own.

"Ju don't let me give ju food, Meester Storm. Ju make me geeve ju weeds," she said, shaking her head as she handed him a cold bottle of water. "Ju need meat. Ju die weeth no meat." She looked quite disgusted with Storm's food choices and actually distressed by the fact Storm had explained to her that he was giving up meat.

Storm grinned and walked over to her, taking the bottle and putting his arm around her shoulders as he walked with her to the kitchen.

"Rebecca you take very good care of me. Vegetables are good for me and salad after a workout is important."

"Ju need meat. Meat she ees good for ju!" she said emphatically, doing her best to frown severely at him. All Storm could do was laugh. "An… ju need a man… no a man like thees guru man… he's a skeenny… ju need a man like Meester Taz," she made a humming sound as Storm sat at the farm table where

Rebecca had laid out a huge salad for him. On top of it were cut up cubes of chicken and hard boiled eggs. He smiled and began picking them out of the greens. When he looked up again, Rebecca's face was pinched and she was standing with her arms crossed, frowning at him. He smiled at her and she opened her mouth to argue when she was interrupted as Taz walked in. He stopped as soon as he walked in and seemed surprised to see Storm in the kitchen.

"Oh, I'm sorry. I thought you were with your trainer," he said from the doorway. "I just came to get a sandwich. I'll come back."

"Don't be silly. Sit down," Storm said, holding out his hand to an empty chair. "Rebecca, will you get Taz something?"

Rebecca shot Storm an ear to ear grin and ran away to the stove where she had something that smelled really good in a large pot.

"Si, si. I have somtheen good for Meester Taz. Ju love thees Meester Taz," she said, enthusiastically.

Storm watched Taz's face light up as he walked over to the table and pulled out a chair. When he reached up and removed his glasses to set on the table, Storm nearly drooled. His eyes were not gray at all; they were light silver and they were as breathtaking as anything Storm had ever seen before. With his dark features, they sparkled like two stunning beacons.

"Jesus, why aren't you a model with those eyes?" Storm asked, feeling silly but unable to help himself.

Rebecca took that moment to walk up to the table and set down a plate of the most delectable looking homemade tamales in front of Taz. Steam rose from the plate and Taz looked down at the feast without answering. Storm immediately felt stupid for blurting out what he'd been thinking.

Taz looked up at Rebecca. "Thank you, Rebecca. This looks delicious," he said appreciatively, ignoring Storm's observation.

Rebecca beamed at him and Storm's stomach growled. He looked down at his own bowl and picked up his fork, stabbing into his salad, feeling like he was missing something delicious. He stuffed the salad into his mouth and chewed, hoping he'd be satisfied. The mixed greens did nothing for him except make him angry at himself for missing out on Rebecca's amazing tamales. *I'm an idiot.*

"Thank ju, Meester Taz," Rebecca said, walking back to the counter where she picked up a bowl of salsa before returning to the table. Storm watched as Taz spooned a heaping amount onto his plate beside the tamales before digging into the meal. As Taz chewed, the expression on his face transformed into a mask of utter joy.

"Oh my God, Rebecca," Taz said, "these are amazing." He looked over at Storm and then pointed his fork at his bowl. "Is that all you're eating? These are delicious."

"Guru has me on a probiotic diet. I'm vegan," Storm said defensively.

"Vegan? That's no meat or something?" Taz asked, forking another bite of the great-smelling food into his mouth.

"No meat, eggs, cheese, dairy…" Storm replied.

Taz stopped chewing for a second. "Seriously? So, no food, basically."

Storm felt the frown as it crossed his own face when Rebecca chuckled. "It's food. It's just healthy food," he said.

Taz stuffed another bite of the tamales in his mouth and looked back at Storm. "Okay, if you say so, but this stuff is the bomb." He chewed and Storm's stomach growled again. *Hell.*

"Guru says the body is the temple of the spirit and in order to keep it healthy, one must rid it of toxins and parasites," Storm said, chewing the tasteless greens. "I'm getting a colonic too."

Taz's brow furrowed as he looked over at Storm. "A colonic? You mean like an enema?"

Storm knew he wasn't being judgmental, just curious, but the thought of it bugged him. He'd had the identical conversation with Jules.

"It's similar to an enema but it's not, Guru says," Storm replied, feeling a little like a snob, something he'd been accused of by the tabloids. "It's more of a colon cleansing." He watched as Taz stuffed another bite of the delicious smelling food into his mouth.

"So, it's like an enema but you have a fancy name for it," the infernal bodyguard said.

Storm had the idea he was being mocked but he was serious about his regimen so it didn't bother him so much... okay, it bothered him a little. "It's like an enema if you must know, but it's performed by a colon hydrotherapist." It even sounded stupid to him when he said it and Storm was getting upset. He knew he must sound like some health food whack job.

"A colon hydrotherapist?" Taz asked. He looked serious, but a smile threatened around the corners of his mouth.

"Yes, a colon hydrotherapist," he pouted, stabbing into his salad again. He petulantly chewed and remained silent.

"I'm teasing you, Storm. If that's your thing, it's great," Taz said. "Does it make you feel better?" he asked, once again pointing to the bowl of greens in front of Storm.

Storm sighed, silent as he looked down at the salad. He glanced over at Rebecca who stood looking hopeful in front of the pot of delicious smelling tamales and sighed. "Aw hell, give me a tamale, Rebecca," he said.

The woman nearly jumped for joy as she squealed, instantly turning to the stove and reaching for a plate and spoon. When she placed a dish in front of Storm, the amazing scented steam rose straight into his nose. Storm leaned down and took a huge whiff of the food and then, feeling eyes on him, looked up to see Taz's pretty eyes twinkling in front of him. His face was split with a wide grin and his white teeth shone brightly in his stunning face.

"Atta boy," he said, before returning his attention to his own plate where he began eating again. Storm's mouth watered and he lifted his fork, stabbing into the salsa covered tamale. He lifted it and stuffed it into his mouth. The flavor of the delicious food burst on his tongue as he began to chew.

"Holy hell this rocks! What's in here?" Storm mumbled around the huge bite in his mouth.

"Ees peenapple an goat sheese, no meat. Ees good for ju," Rebecca replied with a grin. She patted Storm on his shoulder. "Ju gonna feel better now, Meester Storm."

"It's fantastic, Rebecca, thank you," Taz said, finishing off the last piece on his plate. He glanced over at Storm who was shoveling the food into his mouth. "Told you it was good," he said with a smile.

Storm looked over at him as he chewed. "I'm gonna regret it but fortunately I have a pool and I'll just swim another hundred laps."

"You have nothing to be worried about, Storm. You have a fantastic body," Taz said.

Storm stopped chewing mid bite as he lit up with tingles all over. "Really?"

Taz rolled his eyes at him and then pinned him with a serious look. "You're kidding, right?"

"Well, I try but then, look at those models on the catwalk," Storm said.

"Those skinny bitches?" Taz asked. Storm laughed. "I'd be afraid to take them to bed and break them."

Storm loved the fact Taz was friendlier with him than he had been and was excited they seemed to be having their first real conversation aside from their usual short exchanges. The other thing Storm liked was how he shivered with lust, imagining Taz attempting to break a man in bed. Storm was versatile, both a top and a bottom, depending on the partner, but imagining being topped by a man like Taz had him nearly squirming in the chair and horny as hell.

"Well, anyway, I'm definitely trying to look my best," Storm said, flirtatiously. He really hoped Taz would make a pass at him. He couldn't get over the kiss with Taz and the thought of moving their relationship into sexy territory excited him.

"I think you look pretty amazing, Storm," Taz said. Suddenly, as if he remembered something, he rose.

Rebecca scooted up to the table and began clearing away their dishes.

Storm couldn't help but smile and then suddenly, he remembered the present he wanted to give Taz. "Um, do you mind waiting here, Taz. I have something to give you."

"Me?" Taz asked, frowning just a little.

Storm felt only slightly embarrassed. He hoped the bodyguard would take the gesture the right way and even help make him think differently about him than he clearly wanted to... only professional. "Yeah, I... well, I'll only be a minute if you don't mind. Let me run upstairs. I'll be right back." He'd cooled off but he was still sweaty from his workout but he was too excited to wait. He was dying to give Taz the sweater he'd picked out with Jules.

"No problem," Taz said. "I'll be right here."

"Great."

He started to walk out of the room when Rebecca said, "Oh, Meester Storm. I am feenish for today. I leave food for ju and Meester Taz een refreegerator. I go home. I leave food for Butchy-boy een the keechen, okay?"

"No problem, Rebecca. I'll see you tomorrow," Storm said, before turning to walk briskly out of the kitchen. Once he got upstairs, he reached into his closet, pulling out the white box he'd wrapped for Taz.

It had a simple gold ribbon and bow on it and, happy with himself, he practically skipped down the stairs.

When he got to the foyer, Rebecca had her purse and she was just walking out the front door. Butch was wagging his tail as he met her at the bottom of the stairs. The maid had probably let him in from the backyard after the guru's departure. Once again, he pondered the reason his dog didn't like his guru but he thought no more about it as he reached down and chucked his happy dog under the chin, cooing at him before running off to the kitchen. Butch followed and when Storm walked in, the dog padded in behind him running off to his bowl where he began gobbling over it loudly. Taz was standing beside the table, waiting for him. Their attention was drawn to the cute little dog for a few seconds and when Taz finally looked back, Storm had moved to stand a few feet from him.

****

Storm looked absolutely edible standing in front of him holding a white box with a gold ribbon. In addition, he smelled of clean sweat, even better than the food they'd just eaten. In truth, when he'd come to work for Storm, Taz definitely had preconceived notions about the person Storm was, but he had surprised him. Storm was as wealthy and famous and gorgeous as he had expected him to be. What he hadn't expected was the way Storm made him laugh or how decent and humble Storm really seemed to be. On the outside, the star exuded confidence and sexual sureness in a way few men did. But Taz had seen another side to Storm. He had been excited to go home with Petros but when he'd felt threatened, he'd cried out for Taz. It had been easy for Taz to rescue him.

When he'd known Storm was in danger, he'd swept in to save Storm which he'd told himself was only a part of his job. At the time that might have been but he'd gotten to know Storm and he genuinely liked him. Taz had watched Storm with Jules and Rebecca and he saw the humorous side in him as well as the kind and caring character the man possessed. On the serious side, he'd heard his conversations with Anthony Kincaid and Alan Steinberg and Storm had treated both of the men who worked with him with respect, completely destroying the ideas he'd had about Storm before coming to work for the star.

"Here, Taz. I picked this up at the mall for you," Storm said, holding out the box to him.

Taz hesitated for a second, unsure of what to do. An employer had never given him something before so he was a little bit surprised but he reached out and took the box. "Thank you, but I don't really think…"

"It's just something small to thank you for your work with Petros the other night. The fact is, I was pretty embarrassed by that whole thing after your warning, but… well… ah hell, just open it before I lose my nerve," Storm said, looking down shyly, refusing to meet Taz's eyes.

"Okay, Storm but you know, I was just doing my job."

"Yeah, I knew you would say that which is why it's something small," Storm said, looking up at him. "Please open it."

Taz looked down at the package and then nodded. "Okay, Storm." He removed the bow and set the box down on the table. When he opened the lid, the scent of new clothes and department store hit his senses. Tissue paper fluttered up at him and he took the sides of it, spreading it. Beneath the tissue lay a beautiful gray sweater with a vee neck. It looked soft and very expensive and judging by the Bloomingdale's box, it was. His heart rate sped up a little as he lifted the sweater by the shoulders, noting the extra-large size on the label sewn into the neck. He held up the sweater, feeling the silky soft fabric in his fingers, knowing it was not the inexpensive gift Storm had said it was. He glanced up to see Storm looking at him with a childlike glee glittering in his beautiful blue eyes. He was biting his lower lip and practically bouncing with excitement on the balls of his feet.

"Well, what do you think? I thought it would match your eyes and" —Storm leaned forward, touching the neck of the sweater with a shaky hand— "I thought the fabric would be soft against your skin," he said rapidly.

Taz thought his voice shook a little. "I don't know what to say, Storm. You didn't have to give me anything. I was just doing my job," he said, feeling a little embarrassed himself.

Storm smiled widely. "Do you like the fabric?" His face was so open and questioning, Taz realized Storm was genuinely hopeful Taz liked his present. He found it utterly endearing but he still felt uncomfortable about the gift. He looked down at the gray sweater and rubbed the fabric between his thumbs and forefingers. It felt amazing. He lifted the sweater to his face, taking a deep sniff of it and then touched it against his cheek where he felt its softness. Taz knew it was going to feel amazing against his body. He looked over at Storm who'd moved a step closer. The star was staring at him so intensely that Taz could nearly feel the electricity as it buzzed between them. When Storm's gaze dropped to his lips, Taz felt the electricity move lower to his groin and arousal began. He lowered his hand, pulling the sweater away from his face.

"I love the fabric. I can imagine how it's gonna feel on my skin," he said, quietly.

Storm moved a step closer until there was only eight or ten inches between them. He had to look down a few inches as Storm raised his face to meet his eyes. When the star lifted his hands and touched his jacket, the urge to kiss him was strong.

"Put it on for me, Taz. I want to see it on you, please," Storm pleaded softly.

"Now?"

"Please," Storm breathed.

Their eyes were locked and when Storm reached between them and unbuttoned his suit jacket, Taz was more than a little startled. He stood stock still, unable to move, afraid that if he did so, he'd reach out and grab Storm and drag him into another embarrassing kiss. He looked down as Storm's fingers smoothed over his belly, separating the sides of his jacket and he unconsciously felt his shoulders relax, letting his suit coat slide toward his elbows. He twisted, placing the sweater on the table as the jacket slid farther. His cock hardened and he hoped against all hope Storm wouldn't move even closer and let their bodies touch.

"Try the sweater on for me, Taz," Storm said. His voice was silken and thick and for a moment he let himself picture the two of them in the bedroom.

"I..."

"Please, Taz." Storm's gaze dropped to his chest, openly staring at him with admiration sparking in his pretty eyes.

Taz finally gave in, stepping back and letting the jacket slide off completely. He placed it on the table and before he could reach for his tie, Storm's fingers were there, tugging on the knot as he loosened it. Taz reached up and placed his hands over Storm's, bringing his gaze back up to his own from where it had been focused. Storm's gaze was filled with lust as his fingers stilled. They felt warm against his skin through the fabric of his shirt.

They stood as still as statues for a few seconds and finally he felt Storm's fingers relax as he dropped his hands. As if they had a mind of their own Taz's own hands finished the job of opening the tie and he yanked it over his head. He reached up and began unbuttoning his shirt as Storm's gaze was riveted on his chest. His eyes were heavily lidded and sparkling with desire. He finished unbuttoning his shirt, pulling it out of his waistband and he watched as Storm admired his chest for a second before looking back up to his face.

Taz was breathing deeply now, his cock fully hard and pounding against his zipper as he pulled off his shirt and reached for the sweater. He could feel the heat of Storm's gaze on him but he closed his eyes and reached up, threading his arms through the sleeves of the sweater and then pulling it down over his head and wiggling it over his shoulders. He opened his eyes as Storm reached out and placed both hands on his bare pecs, stopping the sweater's decent.

"Please let me touch you, Taz," Storm said, his voice a quiet as a whisper.

Taz stared at him, and sucked in a breath, almost unconsciously expanding his chest. Suddenly, Taz felt sexy as hell with the way Storm regarded him and touched him. He wanted his hands on him, as warm and wonderful as they felt just at that moment and in fact, he realized he wanted Storm's hands all over him. The unexpected kiss on the patio had been one thing, but this was entirely different. They'd crossed the line between employer and employee the night before, but this intimate touch was bringing them into a sexual territory Taz wasn't certain he could run from. He knew if he didn't stop it immediately, he'd find himself unable to and he knew that would compromise Storm's safety. When Storm's fingers brushed over his nipples, he felt his cock jump and he squeezed his eyes shut.

"No," he said suddenly, stepping back as he opened his eyes again. Storm was staring at him with a devastated and unbearably sad expression. "I can't, Storm," he ground out, gruffer than he'd meant. His gut roiled in agony when he saw the abject pain on Storm's face. The skin of his face reddened as two bright spots appeared on his cheeks.

"I'm sorry," the star said miserably. "Honestly, I don't know what I was thinking." Storm stepped back and turned away, walking quickly toward the kitchen doorway.

The sweater made its final decent down Taz's body, covering his belly. The fabric felt soft and perfect and Taz hated what he'd forced himself to say. The very real hurt in Storm's voice sent a bolt of shame and self-loathing through Taz and he realized he'd never felt like such a jerk in his life. The very real fact was, he'd turned Storm down the night before and now he'd done something vastly worse… he'd led him on before turning him down. The night before had been spontaneous and Taz had known Storm still had alcohol in his system, explaining the spontaneity, but this had come after a nice shared meal. He'd practically asked Storm to react this way and he'd been shameless letting him beg Taz to try on the sweater. He'd deliberately allowed Storm to undo his coat and had taken off his own tie and shirt. *You're the lowest of low.*

"You don't have anything to be sorry for, Taz. You set the boundaries before; I crossed them," Storm said. His gorgeous blue eyes were bright with hurt and Taz's heart did a little flip-flop. He was a total ass. "By the way, I won't be taking your resignation, so don't offer it," Storm said, thickly.

"Storm…," Taz said.

"Butch!" Storm called, deliberately talking over Taz. The little dog padded to Storm's feet where he bent and picked him up. "I'm off to take a shower," he said, walking out through the door without another word.

Taz watched him go, feeling like a real jerk.

CHAPTER NINE

Storm stood under the shower spray, letting it pelt down on his shoulders as he beat himself up for coming on to Taz the way he had… again. He'd felt so stupid for having gone out and bought Taz a present like a schoolgirl with a crush. He should have known from the way Taz turned him down when he'd come on to him the first time, that doing it again would be the ultimate in stupidity. He was only setting himself up for failure by chasing a man like Taz. It wasn't that he hadn't slept with men like the bodyguard before. If it was possible, he might have slept with men even more beautiful and worldly than his bodyguard, but having a long lasting relationship with a man as good and decent as Taz seemed out of reach for a man like Storm. He turned off the shower spray and looked down onto his wrists. The scars from cutting were visible even though they were white and silvery. In truth, unless someone looked very close or knew better, no one would ever know Storm had once been a cutter. As he stared at the scars and the old self-doubt crept in, the urge to go to the medicine cabinet and pull out a blade was strong. Maybe the pain of the blade on his skin would take away his pain as it had so many times before. *Bullshit.*

Storm knew he was one of the most sought after stars out there… in fact, many of the tabloids had called him a superstar, though he didn't buy in to the good things they said about him, lest he be forced to buy in to the bad things and utter lies they said about him as well. They'd called him talentless and overrated and as much as he knew those things weren't true, his visceral reaction was always to believe they had some basis in fact. Maybe because his birth parents had given him up, Storm had believed the lies the tabloids told about him. As much as his adoptive parents had impressed upon him how much he was wanted, he'd always had a niggling worry that he wasn't worthy after all.

When his father had passed away leaving him parentless while in acting school, Storm had begun to believe all the things he feared most... he wasn't ever going to be good enough to land a good role without having to give it up on the casting couch and no one was going to cast him if he was openly gay. Those fears had haunted him for a long time and he'd begun to cut to remove the pain. Ironically, he'd never been forced to have sex to land a role and he'd decided to come out publically the moment an interviewer had asked him if he had a girlfriend. The admission had the opposite effect. It had helped him secure the role on the hit show "Trapped on an Island" and now he'd been asked to star in "Silver Bullets", a gay part in a major motion picture. His phone was ringing as he was drying off. He threw down the towel and walked into his bedroom to pick up the phone. He swiped it, answering the call.

"Clive is that you?" Storm said recognizing one of his best friends as his name came up on the screen.

"Storm, it's Devon," Clive's wife said.

"Devon, how are you?" Storm was surprised. The last time he spoke to Clive, he'd told Storm that he had separated from his wife of almost twenty years, moving into an apartment a few months ago. Clive had been a friend of his father's and Storm had known him since childhood.

"Storm, I'm at Clive's apartment," she sobbed.

"What are you doing there?" Storm asked, holding his phone between his cheek and shoulder while he was yanking on his sweatpants . He could hear the pain in Devon's voice. Though much older than him, Storm loved her dearly and he knew her moods very well.

"Clive's off his medication and he's threatening to kill himself, Storm," she said frantically.

"He's not armed or anything, right?" Storm asked, grabbing a shirt and a pair of flip-flops as he ran out of the bedroom, headed downstairs. He saw Taz at the bottom of the stairs and the bodyguard looked up at him as he began running down. He must have looked worried because Taz frowned immediately.

"No, Storm. Clive got rid of his gun. I insisted. He's been drinking and he's crying. I can't leave him. Can you pick up his medicine? It's at the Chinese herbalist you referred me to."

He held the phone away from his ear and spoke to Taz as soon as he got to the bottom of the stairs. "We need to leave now. My friend is threatening to kill himself and his wife is beside herself," he said, grabbing his car keys from a hook on the wall near the door.

"Did I hear you say he's armed?" Taz asked, scowling.

"No, but we need to go." Storm flew out the door and ran toward his Land Rover, parked in the driveway. "Devon, stay right there. We're on our way." He swiped the phone and jumped into the car as

Taz piled into the passenger seat beside him. He started the car and peeled down the circular driveway, waited for the electronic gate to open, and then drove through it, making a right turn at the bottom of the drive.

"Who was on the phone?" Taz asked, glancing over at him.

Storm looked over at Taz, feeling slightly awkward after the abrupt end to their conversation in the kitchen. "That was Devon, my close friend Clive's wife. They're separated and she's at his apartment in Studio City. He's a manic depressive and he's been really good about taking an herbal medicine from the Chinese herb shop where Guru sent us, but Devon called last week and told me she was worried he wasn't taking his meds since the separation. He's been drinking heavily too." Storm got onto PCH headed toward the 10 Freeway and drove smack-dab into heavy afternoon traffic. On a good day, it was a twenty-five minute drive to Studio City but with the drive time traffic, it would take them much longer.

"It's gonna take an hour or more at this rate," Taz said.

"We still have to stop at the herbalist and pick up the medicine," Storm said, checking the clock on the dashboard.

"You said Clive might be armed?" the bodyguard asked.

Storm threw him a worried look. "I said no, he's not, but in the past, I know he had a gun. Devon told him to get rid of it." Storm began to worry and he threw Taz a look. "Well, she thinks he did." Storm watched as Taz pulled out his own phone and dialed.

"Hello, this is Balthazar Grant…"

Storm listened as Taz spoke to the 911 operator, then gave the bodyguard Clive's address as he called in a domestic disturbance call. He bit his lip, concerned that maybe Devon was wrong and that Clive actually had kept his gun. *She may be in danger right now.* When Taz hung up the phone, he glanced over at Storm and gave him a serious look.

"The police are on their way to Clive's house," he said as Storm swallowed hard. "Storm," he said, reaching across the console and taking his hand, "don't worry. The police will be there soon. Devon and Clive are going to be okay."

Storm looked over at him, seeing the honesty in his eyes and as he gripped Taz's hand, he felt oddly safe, connected the way they were. He squeezed Taz's hand.

"Why do you think he would go off his meds, Storm?" Taz asked.

Storm thought about that. Clive had been on medication for many years but he'd switched to the Chinese herbal meds when Guru had lauded holistic medicines to Storm and Storm had passed on the advice to Clive, telling him that he'd be much healthier if he took a natural approach to his health. The problem was, since he'd first begun taking the herbal medications, Clive had complained to Storm they didn't work, his mood swings had returned and he was having suicidal thoughts.

"He told me the medications that he'd begun taking were making him sick and he wasn't able to work. He's a screenwriter. He said he was throwing up and his old suicidal thoughts had returned," Storm answered.

"So he switched to a Chinese herbal medication to manage his depression?" Taz asked.

Storm looked down to where their hands were joined and sighed. "I know; it sounded crazy to me when Guru Shamsa told me the herbal drugs were doing great things for his client's health. He's the one who referred me to the shop. Clive was reluctant to take the new medicine, Taz." Storm felt the tears fill his eyes, blurring his vision as he steered the Land Rover through rush hour traffic on the 10 Freeway. "Clive didn't want to take the meds and I forced him to try them. I was trying to help him get off the mind-altering chemicals he was taking. You know the huge pharmaceutical companies make billions every year off of Americans. It's my fault." Storm was beside himself with grief. *What if Clive kills himself?*

"There is so much wrong with what you just said, Storm. I don't know where to begin," Taz said.

Storm glanced over at Taz who glowered. "What do you mean?"

"First of all, I assume you didn't hold a gun to his head to get him to try the herbal medication."

Storm blinked the tears away. "Of course not but he wouldn't have changed medications if I hadn't encouraged him to try something herbal."

"Fine, I will come back to that," Taz continued. "Secondly, I won't even touch on the evils of pharmaceutical companies making big money. Considering that I personally hold them responsible for the continued spread of AIDS in Africa because a week's supply of their medications can cost some

Africans a year's wages, yeah, they haven't earned any points with me." He glanced over at Storm whose jaw had dropped.

Then Taz continued. "Finally, psychiatric drugs *are* by virtue of their very nature, 'mind-altering drugs'. That's the whole point. They take the body's chemistry and alter it. In the case of schizophrenia, bi-polar disorder, chronic depression, and other psychotic disorders, these drugs have changed lives, vastly improving them and letting patients formerly relegated to living their entire lives in mental institutions or worse yet, asylums, lead seminormal lives. That is, as long as they take them," he finished. "How you think you are to blame for that, I have no idea."

Storm looked over, still staring, shocked at the concise argument. "How did you learn all that stuff... about AIDS I mean?" he asked, keeping his eyes on afternoon traffic.

"I read. A lot," Taz said. "My mother was also an AIDS hospice nurse for years. She was a very smart lady who made sure we all went to school, got As, and went to college. My dad was a university professor at USC. Both of my sisters have their master's degrees, one in education and the other in organic chemistry. My brothers went to college too. My oldest brother Phillip has a PhD in biophysics and works at UCLA, my younger brother Thomas has a bachelor's degree in biology and he's working on his master's in kinesiology. He wants to become a medical doctor eventually. He's applied to medical school, but his toughest choice has been which one."

"Holy shit. That's an accomplished family," Storm said.

"Yeah," Taz laughed. "They are impressive. I'm the black sheep. I barely finished my bachelor's in Criminal Justice before upping for the Marines."

"Your parents must have been very proud of you," Storm said.

"They were when I earned my degree, though my very opinionated father wasn't thrilled with my major. It was my choice to go into the military that they didn't like," he said.

Storm looked over and Taz was staring out of the front window, looking serious. "Did they have something against the military?" he asked.

"No, they had something against the bullets the enemy was firing at me." Taz chuckled and glanced over at Storm, smiling. "Actually, they didn't like me going into the private security business after my discharge. They wanted me to go back to school and get an advanced degree, go to work for the FBI or teach at a university, and marry well."

"I guess that last part didn't work out so well, huh?" Storm asked.

"Yeah, not so well. I had no desire to go back to school after I got back; I loved working security and carrying a gun, and well…"

"You're gay," Storm laughed.

"I'm gay."

"They didn't have a hard time with the gay part?" Storm asked.

"Hello? My mom worked in an AIDS hospice for many years and had no prejudices, my dad was an academic and very open-minded. The kids pretty much fell in line. Not a one of us was raised to hate."

Storm was totally floored and he felt as though his eyes had been opened a lot. Not only was Taz gorgeous, he was educated, and it seemed like he came from good stock. It made him even more attractive in Storm's eyes. They had driven onto the 405 Freeway, transitioning onto the 101while Taz talked, and Storm saw his Laurel Canyon Blvd exit approaching where he would find the herbal shop a few blocks from Clive's. He glanced at the dashboard clock. They'd been in the car nearly an hour. Storm's phone rang. He reached down and swiped it, pressing the speaker button.

"Storm?"

"I'm driving so I put you on speaker, Devon. What's going on?" Storm asked.

"The police are here," she said.

"Yes, I... well, Taz, my bodyguard, called them just in case Clive still had his gun," Storm explained.

"Okay, Storm. The paramedics are loading Clive into an ambulance. He began to have an asthma attack when the police showed up. They said you can't give him the medicine you were bringing him. The doctors at the hospital will want to evaluate him and they don't want him on anything so maybe you shouldn't come here."

"Well, I was stuck in traffic so I'm just a half a block away," Storm said. "We didn't even have time to stop at the herbalist. Besides, I want to talk to him before he goes to the hospital if I can."

"Storm, you don't want to do that," she said.

"Why?" Storm was perplexed.

"Because there's a bunch of photographers here. They must have been listening to the police radio. They know the address because of the last time you were here."

"Son of a bitch!" Storm said, growing angry.

"What happened the last time you were there?" Taz asked.

Storm looked over at him, hesitant to tell him.

"Who's that, Storm?" Devon asked.

"That's my bodyguard, Taz. Devon meet Taz. Taz meet Devon."

"Hey, Taz. Glad you're with him. If he comes here, he's gonna need you."

"Hello, Devon. What happened the last time you were there, Storm?" Taz asked. Storm looked over at him. His happy face of a moment before had darkened and he wasn't smiling.

"Clive and Devon had a very public fight in the street and the neighbors called the police. I came over and I didn't know the paparazzi were following me so…"

"So, now they know you might show up if another police incident is called in," Taz finished.

"Yeah, so sorry, Devon. I didn't even think," Storm said.

"Don't worry about me, Storm. I can deal with anything but if you want, you should probably leave," his friend said. The sadness in her voice said otherwise.

"No, we're here," he said. Up ahead he saw a squad car, an ambulance, and a fire truck. Flashing lights lit up the narrow street in the old neighborhood of Studio City. "We'll see you in a minute, Dev."

"Okay, love."

Storm disconnected the phone, parked the car, and then cringed when he recognized the vehicles of two of the paparazzi he really despised. They'd sold pictures of him to two of the tabloids he hated. "Shit."

"What?" Taz said.

"I hope you're ready. We're about to be recognized." He pointed to the two men who seemed to have spotted his car. They were holding cameras and running across the street toward them, already snapping photos.

"I'd say that's a good bet," Taz growled. "Let's go."

Storm got out of the car just as the photographers ran up. In a flurry of activity, he heard the camera shutters going off as Taz exited the vehicle and rounded the car from the other side, setting his bulk between Storm and the men as quickly as he could. Storm rushed across the street toward the gurney being wheeled out of the building as he ignored the paparazzi and spotted Devon. She'd been crying and was very distraught. She smiled when she saw Storm and flew into his arms.

"I'm so glad you're here," the petite woman said as he kissed the top of her head.

"Storm! Storm Ellison!" someone yelled.

"Back off!" he heard Taz yell. He glanced over to see him frowning down at a photographer as he held out his arms to keep them back.

"Why are you here, Storm?" a woman yelled.

"Oh, Storm, don't they have any decency?" Devon cried.

"I'm sorry, darlin'," Storm said, putting his arms around her shoulders as he walked her to the gurney. "Hey!" he said to one of the paramedics, "A second please."

The paramedic looked up at him. "Hey, you're Storm Ellison. I love your show," the paramedic said.

"Thanks," Storm replied, looking at the tall fireman. "You mind if I talk to my friend a moment?" A flashbulb went off in their face. "Hey, back the fuck away!" Storm said in utter frustration.

Taz once again got in between, blocking the paparazzi.

"Sure, Storm," the second paramedic said. "Make it quick though."

"Thanks." Storm looked down at Clive who was lying on the gurney, looking pale and crazed. He reached out and took his hand. An IV line was already hanging from his other arm. "Hey, man. What happened?" Storm asked.

"Bloody well famous now aren't you, luv?" Clive rasped in his thick British accent as he tried to smile, squeezing Storm's hand. Another flashbulb went off as Storm heard Taz swearing.

"Get the fuck back, buddy. You wanna lose that camera?" the bodyguard growled.

"Who's the big bloke?" Clive asked, forcing a smile. He looked sickly, his skin sallow and pale. Storm hoped he hadn't been drinking. Clive was an alcoholic and with the medication, he'd been even sicker than was normal when he drank. He'd been pretty good about staying off the bottle, even to the point of being able to write, but since he'd begun taking the herbal medications and complaining they made him sick, Storm had suspected he'd gone back to drinking again… at least Devon thought after they separated, he'd gone off the wagon.

"That's Taz, my bodyguard. I told you about him," Storm answered, standing beside the gurney.

"Yes, yes, you told me. Things are a bit muddy, you know," Clive said.

"I know, Clive," Storm said.

"We need to get going, Mr. Ellison," the paramedic who'd recognized him said.

Storm looked up at the handsome paramedic. "Okay, thank you. I'll see you at the hospital."

"Storm! I love you, Storm!" a man called.

"Don't think that's an option, Storm," Clive said as the paramedic began wheeling him into the ambulance.

"Back off!" Storm heard Taz say, from behind him as more flashbulbs went off.

"Storm, call us from home; these folks will just follow you to the hospital and wait for you to come out," Devon said, kissing him on the cheek as he reached out and squeezed her hand.

He looked down into the pleading eyes of his friend, realizing she was right. "Okay, love." He let her hand go, watching her climb into the ambulance.

"Let's go, Storm," Taz said from beside him.

A second later, his bodyguard's strong arm had circled his shoulder and he was being propelled through the throng of onlookers and fans who had begun to crowd around the ambulance. Storm relented and the two of them broke into a run as Storm clicked the key fob, unlocking the Land Rover. Taz held out his hands for the keys and Storm tossed them to him before running around to the passenger's side and climbing in. Taz locked the doors as soon as he was behind the wheel. Taz honked the horn in the face of a photographer who was standing in front of the car, blocking him from pulling out. The man jumped to the side and Taz turned on the powerful engine, gunning it with a roar. Within minutes, they had pulled out of the neighborhood and onto the side streets, headed for the 101 Freeway. Taz outraced the paparazzi, taking shortcuts to the freeway and finally Storm was able to relax back in his seat, checking the rearview mirrors, satisfied they'd lost the paparazzi.

"Thanks, Taz," he said, blowing out a long sigh. "They're like leeches. I can't even come to a friend's aid without the vultures swooping in."

"It's the life you signed up for," Taz said, glancing over at him as he took his eyes off the road for a split second.

"Yeah, not really," Storm replied, grimly.

"Why not?" Taz asked.

"I never expected this level of fame to be honest," Storm said honestly.

"Well, it's only going to get worse once you make that movie," Taz said.

Storm gritted his teeth, knowing his bodyguard was probably right. "Well, I'm really happy you were there tonight, Taz. Without you, I never would have been able to get out of the car. I'm glad I hired you." He looked over at Taz who'd begun to smile.

"I'm glad you did, Storm," he said.

"Really?" he asked.

"You know, this is the part of my job I like the best," he said.

When Storm looked back at him, the bodyguard was still smiling. *God you're so handsome.*

"Somehow that doesn't surprise me, Taz." Storm said. "Not one little bit." He sat there pondering the conversation they'd had before they were interrupted. Storm had been surprised to find out Taz had a degree in criminology. Anthony Kincaid had hired Taz so he had no knowledge about his prior careers except that Anthony had bragged about the bodyguard's military accomplishments. As they drove up to the electronic gate in front of his house, Storm made up his mind to find out more about Balthazar Grant.

CHAPTER TEN

As soon as Storm and Taz walked into the house, Taz punched the keypad at the front door, disengaging the alarm. Storm was wound up from the encounter with the paparazzi at Clive's apartment and still fuming from having whatever privacy he cherished ripped away from him at such a critical time in his friends' lives. He was feeling guilty as hell that Devon and Clive had been drawn into a confrontation in front of the apartment when all they were trying to do was live their lives, and he regretted bringing the drama of his life to their door. He turned and looked back at Taz, noting how handsome he looked in his black suit but longing to see him in something besides that.

"Taz, do you have a minute to talk? I mean, I could really use a glass of wine about now but I want to change clothes," he said.

Taz removed his glasses and stared at him with those magnificent eyes. "Um… sure, I was just going to pick out a book from the library, so no, I don't mind," he said.

Storm realized if he was feeling keyed up, Taz probably could use a glass of wine himself. "Do you want to change out of that penguin suit?" he smiled, going for a little levity, hoping to change the energy coming off of his handsome bodyguard.

"Actually, yeah," Taz replied with a smirk, "give me a minute and I'll join you in the living room."

"Good, be right back." Storm turned to the curving staircase and ascended, taking two steps at a time. When he got to his bedroom, he went into the

179

closet, pulled out sweatpants and a soft cotton T-shirt, and walked back into the bedroom. A few minutes later, he was headed downstairs, barefooted and a hell of a lot more comfortable already. He was surprised to hear classical music playing softly from the entertainment center in the living room. He wouldn't have guessed Taz to be a lover of classic music to be honest. The bodyguard was nowhere in sight. Storm walked into the family room, behind the bar, and pulled down two wine glasses. He was bent over, checking out the wine fridge, when he heard Taz enter the room from behind him. When he stood up and turned, his jaw nearly dropped. Taz was in navy blue sweats and a tight muscle T-shirt, also barefooted, and he carried a bottle of red wine.

"Well, you look much more relaxed," Storm said with a smile. His inner gay man growled as Taz walked closer and he got a view of his nipples outlined under the soft fabric of the tee. Taz smiled back and Storm was reminded just how beautiful his bodyguard really was.

"Yeah, those duds are nice but the gun is heavy and the tie is more than a little bit confining. This feels better," Taz said.

Storm placed the glasses on the long bar and nodded to the bottle in Taz's hand. "You bring your own red?"

Taz lifted the bottle and put it on the bar. "My friend Rome sent me this from Texas. He says it's from a vineyard out there in the Texas wine country."

Storm was intrigued as he reached for the bottle, turning it so he could read the label. It was a merlot from a winery called the Lazy E Vineyards. "I didn't even realize Texas had a wine country," he chuckled.

Taz grinned. "I didn't either. You have a corkscrew back there somewhere?"

"One sec," Storm said, suddenly feeling giddy as he bent behind the bar. When he straightened with the corkscrew, he was surprised to see Taz staring at him. His eyes were dancing with something resembling mirth and he looked handsome and relaxed. He handed the corkscrew back over to the bar. "Open please."

Taz smiled and took the corkscrew from Storm, plunging it into the cork and twisting. He looked back up at Storm as he opened the bottle. "You know, you clean up pretty well."

Storm snorted. "Ha ha, thanks," he said, coming back around the bar as Taz filled the bottoms of the glasses. Storm walked up beside him as the bodyguard picked up one of them and handed it to him. Storm sniffed it. "This looks great." He put the drink to his lips, taking a sip as he watched Taz do the same. "Oh wow," he said, holding out the glass as he looked at the burgundy-colored liquid. "This is amazing."

"Yeah, Rome has good taste," Taz agreed. He picked up the bottle and looked harder at the label. "Maybe these Texans know what the hell they're doing after all."

"Come on; let's go sit in the living room. I really like the music you put on," Storm said. "Bring the bottle along. Lord knows, after tonight, I may need more than one glass."

Taz followed him out of the room and into Storm's huge living room. The music had changed to an opera and the soft aria sung by a soprano was relaxing and gorgeous. Storm's living room was a two-story space with soaring twenty foot ceilings and wall to wall windows looking out on to the lighted infinity pool and view of the ocean beyond. The furniture was built for comfort with soft micro fabric couches in a muted tan shade with comfortable club chairs set around a huge iron and glass coffee table. Storm sat on the sofa and took another sip of his wine, watching as Taz set down the bottle and sat beside him, folding one bare foot beneath him as he got comfortable. Storm turned to face him, pulling up both feet and moving to sit in the lotus position. Taz watched him as well and then tilted his glass indicating Storm's position.

"Seriously, is that comfortable?" he asked, sipping the wine.

Storm took another sip, savoring the warm heat spreading through him. The wine and the company were both delicious. "I know, it's surprising, right? I thought the same thing when I first got into the lotus position but once I got used to it, I sit like this all the time... especially when I meditate."

"You do that a lot... meditation?" Taz asked, sipping wine.

"Every day. It really helps," he replied. "Have you ever tried it?"

Taz shook his head. "Not really but then again, I was never one for prayer when my grandma tried to drag us kids to church."

"Are your parents religious?" Storm asked, happy they were talking about anything other than his career which was all anyone besides Jules ever wanted to talk about.

Taz chuckled. "Religious? No." He shook his head. "My grandma tried to get Mom and Dad to go to church but after my mom grew up and got married, she told my grandma she had no interest in it, much to Grandma's horror."

Storm smiled. "So you never had a great interest in church?" he asked, suddenly wanting to know everything about Taz's intriguing family.

"Uh, no, ever since I heard an impassioned sermon on Leviticus, I have pretty much steered clear of church," Taz admitted.

"The whole man lying with man thing?" Storm asked.

"Well, the actual verse reads, '*Do not have sexual relations with a man as one does with a woman; that is detestable,*'" Taz said. "Some gay Christians believe that verse was meant to be interpreted as lustful behavior instead of behavior in a committed relationship such as boyfriends or gay marriage."

"You know, your brain is very sexy," Storm said with a grin.

Taz grinned back. "Thanks."

Storm sipped the last of his wine and realized he was becoming a little tipsy but he wasn't lying when he said Taz being intelligent was sexy. He was so tired of having conversations with his contemporaries that focused solely on sex, how to get it and where to find it. He realized he'd grown up a lot since landing his TV role and taking on the responsibility of a rigorous schedule, but relaxing this way with someone who had a brilliant mind was so much more enjoyable than going to bars all the time.

"Actually, you surprise me, Storm. You're not the kind of man I thought you'd be at all," Taz said conversationally, picking up the bottle from the table and refilling both of their glasses. He set the bottle back down and leaned one elbow on the couch, facing Storm while he sipped the delicious red wine.

"How so?" Storm asked.

"Well, I thought you'd be just another pretty face, really wrapped up in yourself and selfish."

"Because I'm a star or because I'm rich, or what?" Storm was very anxious to know.

"Well, at first, I believed everything the tabloids said about you. I suppose that's human nature," he said. "Then I came here and of course, one of the first major events was the Emmys."

Storm cringed, remembering how he'd let the twink named Coke suck him off with Taz in the room. He was suddenly so ashamed of his behavior.

"Then I saw you try to go home with that shitty bear," Taz said, drinking more of his wine.

"Please say no more," Storm said, "I know I made some really poor decisions and you probably think I'm a jerk…" He stopped when Taz reached out and took his hand, instantly bringing his attention to his beautiful gaze. Taz's silver eyes sparkled.

"You didn't let me finish. I was going to say, that was before I saw how you acted with Jules and how Rebecca loves you and cares about your diet," he said, "how concerned you were with Clive and Devon tonight."

Storm was humbled by what Taz said. He'd always known what was in his heart but it was sometimes hard to know if he was able to get across the person he really was deep down inside. He felt his throat close up as a giant lump formed there. Taz smoothed over the back of his hand with the pad of his thumb. The gesture was small but it felt so good to be connected this way.

"I don't know what to say," Storm said, quietly.

"I'm beginning to think you're as beautiful inside as you are outside," Taz said, quietly. His voice had a growly quality that turned Storm on. He took a long sip of the delicious wine, blaming the tingling in his groin on the alcohol and enjoying the hell out of it. Even if Taz insisted on keeping their relationship completely professional, he was sure enjoying their newfound connection. The sound of the music relaxed him the way no yoga or meditation could and he felt himself drifting on a wave of peace he rarely experienced in any man's presence. He couldn't remember feeling the way he felt with the gorgeous bodyguard... so exposed and yet so safe.

"I find myself surprised too," Storm admitted, gazing into Taz's eyes.

"How so?" Taz asked, squeezing his smaller hand gently.

Storm took one more sip of the wine and leaned off to the side, unwinding his legs from the lotus position. He let go of Taz's hand to put his wine glass on the table, turning back to see the man following his movements with interest. Storm inched closer, closing the distance between them as the music began a crescendo. Very slowly, he lifted his hand, reaching out as he touched the bodyguard's cheek with his fingers. The gesture was a risk but he couldn't help himself.

"I find myself baffled by how I've been able to resist touching you." He was terrified Taz would reject him again and he had no idea how he'd react to that. When Taz leaned sideways, putting his glass on the table before scooting closer to him, his heart skipped a beat. Storm let his fingers trail down Taz's cheek and then as he moved to pull them away, Taz captured his hand, tugging him closer. His breathing sped up at the look in the bodyguard's eyes. They were filled with desire.

"Come here," he said softly, pulling Storm forward ever-so-gently as he leaned in until only a few inches separated their faces. Taz's breath ghosted over his lips as his intense gaze took his breath away. "I'm going to kiss you, Storm," he murmured.

Storm swallowed hard and he felt his heart rate increase. Taz let his lashes fall, shuttering his silver eyes as he tilted his head and closed the tiny gap between them. The bodyguard's lips were softer than Storm remembered and they sent shivers through him as they touched. Arousal washed through Storm as Taz firmed his lips and deepened the kiss. He'd waited so long for this, he closed his eyes, held his breath, and relaxed into the moment, opening his mouth just a tiny bit, letting Taz take over.

****

Taz felt the tentative touch of Storm's tongue and he responded with his own, breathing deeply and letting out the low, soft groan he'd been holding in. Storm's answering moan was all Taz needed to hear as he let himself fall deeper into the kiss, relaxing his jaw and opening fully to the kiss he'd waited to steal for so long. Taz didn't even realize he'd laid Storm backward along the length of the sofa until he felt Storm's legs relax as he stretched out beneath him, and Taz lifted himself, covering Storm's smaller body with his own. As Storm reached up and wound his arms around Taz's neck, he felt a delicious tingle begin in his groin where he was already hard as a rock. He couldn't believe he'd allowed himself to be captured in Storm's net... the same one he'd been avoiding for days now. Somehow, some way, Storm had wormed his way into Taz's heart, whether he liked it or not. He'd already admitted to himself that he genuinely liked the man but even then, he'd avoided showing any interest other than professional until he'd cracked open that damned bottle of wine and let it heat his blood like crazy.

Whatever the reason, Taz had let down his barriers or Storm had crashed the gates to his heart — he wasn't certain which — but then again, he really couldn't care less, not with the way Storm was holding him and moaning beneath him, moving just the right way against his body and working him into a frenzy. Taz realized he was going to make love to Storm tonight... they both wanted it desperately and the truth was he'd begun to think there would never be an end to his monkish existence under the star's roof. He tried to recall all the reasons why this was a bad idea and how important it was to remain a professional and then Storm groaned and arched his back, driving his rock hard cock into his, setting up a grinding motion between them. Any thoughts of stopping what was happening flew right out of his head and he heard himself growling as if he were detached from what was happening and watching it all from outside his own body. Taz pulled his mouth away from Storm's and looked down at his lips; they were swollen from his brutal kisses and ever so beautiful and he'd been the cause. His inner beast roared and he set out to claim his prize.

Taz's mouth came crashing down on Storm's and he slid his tongue inside, forcing his mouth even wider, devouring him as he sucked on his tongue, biting at his lips gently, and kissing him with a desperate need to taste every last bit of him. Storm moaned and wiggled beneath him and Taz felt electric shocks going through his body; he knew if he didn't stop now, he was going to embarrass himself right here on the couch. He pulled his mouth away and looked down. Storm gazed up at him with his sky-blue eyes surrounded by that sexy as hell guyliner and Taz was struck by why men desired the star so desperately… he was the most stunning man he'd ever seen. In the throes of passion, Storm radiated sensuousness like no one he'd ever met and as Taz sat back, reaching down and taking Storm's hand, he couldn't look away.

"I need you, Storm. Will you let me make love to you?" His entire body quaked as he waited the split second before the star answered.

"I desperately want you, Taz," he whispered.

Taz knew those were the sweetest words he'd ever heard and he climbed off the couch backward, drawing Storm to his feet in front of him, not letting go of him or dragging his gaze from his, terrified that if he so much as blinked, his lover would disappear as if he'd never been. A heartbeat passed as he swept his gaze down the length of Storm's body. His sweatpants were tented with his erection and without conscious thought, Taz let his hand slide between them, taking Storm's cock in his grip through the fabric, squeezing it. Storm's pants were damp with his precome or Taz's precome… he didn't care. The only thing that mattered as he stroked Storm's cock was the fact they were standing in a room that was miles too far away from his bed.

Taz let go of Storm's thick erection and bent down, reaching behind his knees and lifting him from the ground as Storm gasped out an adorable "Oof" and instantly wrapped his arms back around Taz's neck, holding on as if for dear life.

He took two steps toward his room and then came to a complete standstill, looking down at Storm and then up the stairs leading to his bedroom. An instant later, making up his mind, he began walking again, striding toward the stairs as he pictured himself laying Storm out on his massive four-poster bed and stripping every last stitch of clothing from his body. *Shredding it is more like it.* He got to the foot of the curving staircase and began ascending two at a time, holding Storm's body close in the cradle of his arms as Storm's eyes never left his. Taz tore his gaze away and looked at the stairs in front of him, if only to keep from tripping, and in what seemed like moments, he was at the top, striding down the carpeted hallway toward the star's bedroom. When he got to the closed door, he hesitated only a second before making up his mind and with a swift kick, he smashed his bare foot into the door, slamming it backward, splintering the molding as it crashed open.

"My God!" Storm cried and the joy in his voice emboldened Taz further as he strode to the bed, tossing the six foot tall man onto it as if he weighed nothing more than a feather. Storm grunted, landing on his back with a laugh, his gorgeous face luminous in the darkness of the room.

"Something funny?" Taz growled.

Storm giggled. "Not funny, no. I just always knew you'd be a tiger in bed," Storm said. He was grinning from ear to ear.

"Rawr," Taz growled with a grin.

The fireplace had been lit but when or how it had been done only mattered to Taz because of the magnificent way the glow danced over Storm's face and body... a body covered by way too many clothes. Storm must have known what was coming because he grabbed the hem of his shirt and ripped it over his head, sailing it off to some distant corner, revealing the clearly defined muscles of his abs. It was only then Taz spotted the glistening rings piercing Storm's beautiful nipples which pebbled on his chest like two playthings begging to be tugged by his teeth.

"My God, look at you," Taz heard himself say, reaching down and yanking his own shirt over his head before wadding it into a ball so he could throw the infernal fabric as far away as he could from the half-naked man on the bed. Taz wanted nothing between them and he wanted it now. He stalked up to the bed like a predator and crawled onto it as Storm crab-walked backward toward the pillows piled high against the headboard. When Taz crawled over Storm, the smaller man laughed again, grabbing his upper arms and the look on his face was so happy, Taz knew nothing on earth could possibly be wrong with what was happening between them at this very moment. In Storm's bed, Taz ceased to be a bodyguard and the superstar ceased to be his client… they were just two men, hot and horny and deliciously turned on by each other. The fact they were meant to share each other's bodies should have been a given from the moment they'd met. *Irresistible force meets immovable object*. Taz should have known Storm would prove the paradox the moment he met him.

"Look at these biceps, Taz. God, you're beautiful," Storm said, staring at his body as he stroked up his arms, squeezing his muscles as if to test their strength. Taz felt ten feet tall as Storm admired him openly.

"Look at yourself, Storm. Talk about beautiful. No wonder every man on earth worships you," Taz said, reaching for Storm's waistband as he straddled his shins. He hooked his fingers in the sweats and yanked them clear to his knees. Storm gasped and his engorged cock sprang up and out toward him and Taz's mouth began to water. Storm's body was completely manscaped, leaving only a tiny rectangle of closely clipped hair above his bobbing cock. Taz fixed his gaze on Storm's dick as he scooted back, dragging the sweatpants the rest of the way off his feet, and tossing them off into the darkness as he appraised Storm's form. He climbed back up the length of his body and reached out, taking his lover's circumcised cock in hand before looking back at his face. Storm's gaze met his glance with a heated one of his own.

"Suck me, Taz," Storm whimpered.

He didn't have to ask because Taz's mouth had been watering since the moment he'd seen the nipple rings. "There's something I need to do first," he said. His voice came out so thick and deep, he almost didn't recognize it himself.

Storm grinned and lifted his hands, putting them behind his head as he bucked his groin. "Do your worst."

Taz grinned back. "And then some." He held on to Storm's cock, circling its girth with his fist and pumping it as he leaned over him, balancing himself with his other hand on the bed beside Storm's chest, opening his mouth and engulfing one pierced nipple with his lips as he sucked hard. When Storm cried out, grabbing the back of Taz's head and holding it in place at his chest, Taz slipped his tongue through the nipple ring and tugged with it, sucking on the nipple at the same time.

"Oh my God! Oh my God!" Storm begged, bucking his hips upward, as Taz's hand squeezed and stroked his cock. "Suck my nipples… suck them… oh God!" Storm cried.

He's a screamer! How fuckin' sexy. Taz gave in to Storm's pleas, teasing the first nipple, tugging on the ring before pulling off and moving to the other one, all the while jacking Storm as hard as he dared. His dick was slick with precome and the last thing Taz wanted to do was to get him off before he had a chance to take the head of his cock in his mouth and catch Storm's climax on his tongue. Storm was wiggling and moaning like a wanton slut as he continued to buck his hips off the bed. *I love the way he moves when I touch him.* As Taz looked up, he spied the long corded column of

Storm's neck as he bared it for him, like an animal waiting for the kill.

Taz let go of the second nipple with a pop and then released Storm's cock, scooting back down the bed and off the edge. He hooked his thumbs into the sides of his own waistband and dragged down his sweats. They were damp with precome and as he pulled them over his own engorged cock, he heard Storm gasp. Taz glanced up at his lover who was now propped up on both elbows, staring at his dick as it stood proudly from its nest of clipped short curls. He straightened, using the bottom of one foot to pull the elastic off one ankle and then off his foot, repeating the action on the other side as he wrapped his own dick with his hand, stroking it up and down, showing Storm just how much he wanted him. Precome slicked the length of his long cock and he watched as Storm's gaze stayed riveted on it while the tip of his tongue snaked out from between his lips and licked over his puffy bottom lip. Storm blinked and raised his gaze to meet Taz's. Lust and want and need were all mirrored back at him. *I've never seen someone so beautiful.*

"Suck me Taz… suck me before I come right here," Storm whimpered. His expression had become serious and he'd lowered one hand to his own dick, circling it and pumping it as the other hand remained behind his head.

Taz had every intention of tasting Storm's cock but there was one more thing he needed to do first. He got back on the bed and threw one bare leg over Storm, straddling him again before leaning down and nuzzling Storm's armpit. His lover's hand instantly went to the back of Taz's head, again holding him in

193

place as Taz licked, reveling in the spicy scent and taste so unique to the smaller man.

Storm began making a thrumming sound in his throat, and Taz felt it on his tongue as the vibrations made their way down to his chest. "Ah… ah… ah, keep it up, Taz and I'm gonna come," he groaned, his eyes squeezed tightly shut.

He looked down and saw Storm furiously jacking his own cock with his fist and he reached out, placing his own hand over the star's, stilling his motions.

"Leave that to me," Taz growled as he lifted his face and moved lower on the bed.

Storm stretched back, gazing sweetly up at him, lust shadowing his eyes as the firelight played over the planes of his body and muscles of his chest. Storm's pecs were smooth, free of any hair, and Taz wondered if he waxed or shaved. Only a boy could be so naturally smooth but Storm was most definitely not a boy. His abdomen was cut with muscle and Taz tried not to count how many individual muscles he saw as he let his gaze travel farther south, down the treasure trail of soft light brown hair that began just below his bellybutton and led all the way to his groin. The urge to lick him was too hard to take and Taz lowered his head, licking into Storm's bellybutton as his lover groaned. Taz felt Storm's hands on either side of his head encouraging him as he licked his way downward, teasing the tiny hairs of his treasure trail with his tongue. Storm's spicy scent rose from his body and the smell of hot horny man tickled Taz's senses until he was painfully hard.

Storm widened his legs, bending them at the knees, arching upward as he planted his feet on the bed, and Taz moved between them until his face was level with Storm's groin. He glanced up and into Storm's sexy eyes, took his cock in hand, and lowered his mouth. Taz licked the tip of Storm's wet cock, lapping gently at the slit beading with precome as the taste of Storm's cock exploded on his tongue. Taz growled his pleasure from deep in his throat and he tasted the spongy head of Storm's dick, sucking hard before firming his lips and sliding them down his meaty shaft, engulfing his entire length until the crown hit the back of his throat where he swallowed. Precome slid down Taz's throat as Storm cried out again, bucking off the bed as Taz swallowed again, milking more tiny droplets from his lover.

****

Storm was on fire. He wasn't certain if the merlot had lowered his gorgeous bodyguard's inhibitions or if it was the fact they'd spent a roller coaster few weeks getting to really know each other, but whatever reason Taz had for letting his guard down, Storm was just happy it had finally happened. In truth, he wasn't sure Taz would have ever decided to give in and take him to bed but here he was sprawled out with the amazing man giving him the blowjob of his life.

Taz sucked him harder, moving his mouth up and down the shaft of his cock with abandon and Storm had never felt anything like it in his life. He'd had a slew of lovers, something he wasn't particularly proud of and the fact was, he'd gone through life up to this point needing nothing more. He would go to a club, meet a man, and end up in a bathroom stall or pushed up against a wall taking what he wanted from them and leaving them, always, like the twink in the dressing room, without the promise of any further contact. The spontaneous sex had always filled a need in Storm, but never the one he'd always dreamed of… a deep connection with someone he truly cared about.

Balthazar Grant was different… he was a good man whom Storm had formed a bond with, and whether it was a good thing or a bad thing he was a man who worked for him really wasn't important. Keeping Taz around after this night was all said and done would be the test of whether they'd make it as a couple… and that's what Storm wanted. The bond he imagined true lovers shared was what he desperately needed, but for now, as Taz growled around his cock once again, Storm was enjoying the moment for what it was… one of the hottest sexual encounters he'd ever had.

Storm looked down to where Taz was working his cock with his huge paw and his talented mouth, feeling tiny little electric shockwaves in his groin, his balls tight against his body as they prepared for what Storm could only imagine would be the orgasm of his life. He reached down, gripping the top of Taz's beautiful smooth head with one hand as he propped himself up with the other elbow, and watched his bodyguard bob up and down at his groin as he sucked him like a vacuum. If he'd gone out and found the most amazing, highest paid gigolo on the planet, Storm knew he'd never get sex like this and he desperately wanted it to last, unsure of whether he'd be able to repeat the night. Taz looked up at him and Storm gasped at the sight of him; his dark shoulders were as broad as the side of a barn and muscles rippled over his arms; his gorgeous light silver eyes gazed at him lustfully, squinting adorably as Storm noticed the tiny crow's feet at the corners for the first time. He watched Taz's glistening lips as they moved up and down over his engorged cock, his hollowed cheeks as he pulled back, and when he groaned, it sent vibrations t right down to Storm's balls, lighting him up.

A tingle began in the small of Storm's back and he knew he was going to come. "Yeah, baby, that's right… ugh… I'm gonna come, Taz," he gasped, thrusting up, burying the shaft of his dick in Taz's mouth as he felt the man swallow around it.

Taz groaned again, closing his eyes and at that moment Storm knew Taz was gonna suck him through it. The thought of the man swallowing everything he had to give was intense and electrifying as he began to face fuck Taz. "Yeah, baby, yeah…," he whimpered, fucking his face harder as he held Taz's head hard against his groin. "I have a load for you, Taz," he gasped. "You're gonna get a mouth full of my come if you don't pull off now," Storm warned.

Taz nodded, blinking up at him and Storm knew that was his hearty approval.

"Suck me, Taz… here it comes," he warned. His orgasm began and Storm screamed. "Yes! Yes! Taz, I'm coming! I'm coming, baby!"

Storm's orgasm hit him full force as he felt the come roil in his balls for a second before he convulsed, feeling the come blast up his shaft and into Taz's strongly sucking mouth. Storm squeezed shut his eyes as the first shudders racked his body and then he opened them, looking down. Taz's face was awash with ecstasy as he sucked and swallowed over and over. Storm gasped as another spasm rolled through him before he finally relaxed, letting go of his lover's head.

Taz looked up and him, sucked on the head of his cock one last time, and pulled off with a pop. His face split in a broad, white smile and Storm's heart soared. He couldn't remember ever seeing a man as beautiful as Taz before.

He held out his hands and wiggled his fingers. "Come up here. It's my turn," he said softly.

"With pleasure," Taz said, crawling up Storm's body to lie down over him. His enormous erection poked into his stomach and Storm could feel it slick and burning hot between them as he lay flat beneath his large body. Storm snaked his arms around Taz's neck, bringing his face down to his as he reached for a kiss. Taz's mouth was hot and demanding as he kissed Storm deeply. Storm tasted himself on his lips and tongue as Taz moaned. Taz's kisses grew more and more demanding as he rubbed himself on Storm.

"Want you, baby…," Taz moaned between kisses. "Want you."

"Yes, Taz," Storm groaned, feeling blindly between them for Taz's cock with his hand. It was pretty hard to miss, as in… the thing was so big it nearly needed its own zip code. He giggled, burying his head in Taz's massive shoulder as the thought struck him funny. Taz lifted his head and looked down at Storm, reaching up and framing his cheeks with the long fingers of both hands. His silver eyes twinkled with amusement.

"What's so funny?" he asked, cracking that sideways smirk Storm was beginning to anticipate.

Storm firmed his lips, trying his best not to laugh as he circled Taz's dick with the palm of his hand. It was so thick, his fingers and thumb weren't even touching.

"Nothing, Taz; I just never had a python in my hands before." He couldn't help but grin.

"A python, huh?" Taz asked, smiling.

His dark face was radiant in the firelight. Storm was glad he'd taken a moment to flip the gas switch on the wall, turning on the fireplace when he'd come up to change. He certainly couldn't have managed it whilst being carried into the bedroom like Scarlett O'Hara. He grinned again. He nodded. "You're a well-built man, Balthazar Grant."

"I know how to use it, too," Taz said.

Storm pumped Taz's dick in his hand again. "We'll see," he said, "but first…" Storm wiggled a little bit and then pushed up and sideways, rolling Taz to his back and quickly moving over him until he was in the position he wanted. He glanced up the muscled length of the huge man, still holding on to his erection. While Taz watched, Storm glanced down, noting the wet head of the bodyguard's cock, peeking out from beneath the fold of foreskin Storm had pulled back. He loved uncut men and there was something about the size and shape of Taz that had his own dick growing hard all over again as he anticipated going down on him.

Storm kept his gaze locked with Taz's as he opened his mouth and took the head of his cock inside. Taz hissed as Storm managed to fit the very tip of his tongue under the foreskin, circling the head as he tasted his lover for the first time. The flavor of tangy precome exploded on his tongue like a deliciously decadent honey and Storm felt his mouth water as he sucked as much into his mouth as he could. Taz groaned loudly and as Storm reached for a nipple and squeezed, the man opened his mouth and began to pant. The same way Storm had, Taz took the back of his head and held it in place, while he did his best to slide his lips partway down his shaft. When the head of Taz's cock hit the back of his throat, Storm realized he'd only taken half of the big man's cock.

"Oh, like that, Storm," Taz growled. His hips bucked off of the bed, taking Storm right along for the ride.

Storm glanced back up to find Taz watching him intently, the lines in his face hard and his jaw set. Storm concentrated on sucking hard on his cock as he pulled back and was rewarded as another wash of precome filled his mouth.

"Oh, my God, I'm gonna come, Storm… I can't…" Taz suddenly shouted as come filled Storm's mouth.

He was so unprepared for Taz's orgasm, he nearly choked on it. He was barely able to swallow and take a breath before his mouth was filled again. Taz's climax must have gone on a full minute as Storm felt his whole body ripple with convulsions. When Taz finally stopped shuddering, Storm looked up at him, swallowed again, and pulled off with one more sucking pop. Taz's entire body glistened with sweat and in the firelight, he was beautiful. His skin glowed and Storm likened his body to a Roman gladiator, so perfectly cut with muscle and hard planes everywhere he looked.

He let go of Taz's cock and smoothed both hands up his muscled thighs, past his hips and belly, resting them on his pecs as he stretched out over Taz. Taz looked down at him and reached around, circling Storm's own slick back with his huge arms, grabbing his waist and hefting him upward, sliding their bodies together until they were face-to-face.

Storm smiled and leaned down, kissing him softly as Taz lowered his lashes and opened his mouth. Storm couldn't get over how soft the bodyguard's lips and tongue were. He kissed him gently and deeply, and Storm realized he'd never made out with a lover after they'd gotten off. His encounters had always lasted as long as they needed to until they'd both ejaculated, but once that was accomplished, Storm was pretty much done with them and was already wishing them well and away in his head. He'd always done his utmost to get them gone and out of his sight as soon as he possibly could.

This encounter, in stark contrast, couldn't last long enough. They kissed for several minutes, Storm reveling in the attention Taz was giving him until they finally broke their kiss. Storm held Taz's gaze as he finally rolled off him to his back, almost immediately scrambling back to the big man's side and curling into it. Exhaustion washed over him as Taz threw his arm around him and without another word from either of them, Storm slipped into a peaceful sleep.

CHAPTER ELEVEN

Storm woke the next morning with a smile on his face. At first, opening his eyes in his own bed, he wasn't certain why, until he sat up and looked over at the crease in the pillow beside him. When he heard the shower running, memories of the night past came back to him. He stretched out as he sniffed the air in the room and picked up the scent of sex hanging heavily in the air. The shower turned off as he grinned to himself. *Taz spent the whole night here.* They'd made passionate love not once but twice; first exchanging mutual blowjobs and then after a few fumbles of trying and failing to bottom for Taz, the bodyguard had rolled over onto all fours and offered up a feast Storm couldn't refuse. A rim job that had Taz groaning into the pillow from Storm's tongue had been followed by the greatest anal sex he could remember. It turned out, Taz had grown accustomed to bottoming for his lovers, but at some point Storm had promised himself he was going to change all that. It just hadn't happened last night.

Storm looked across the room when the bathroom door opened and Taz stepped into the bedroom, a white towel hanging precariously low on his hips. He smiled sweetly at Storm and walked up to the bed. His upper body was as huge as Storm remembered and was beaded with water from the shower.

"There you are… looking sexy, superstar," the big man said, leaning down so he could kiss Storm.

His lips were softer than Storm remembered and he was transported by how amazing it felt to be kissed by a lover in his own bed, something that had happened only infrequently before then, and never with someone he really cared about.

"How do you feel?" Taz asked, straightening again. He was so tall, he towered over Storm and it made Storm feel sexy to be the lover of such a big, beautiful man.

Storm unconsciously reached down to the sheet that covered the lower half of his body and he squeezed his growing erection through the thin fabric as he looked up to Taz. "Starving," he said, staring at the giant bulge in the towel in front of him before looking up at the bodyguard. Taz's gaze was fixed on Storm's hand for a minute before he glanced at the clock beside the bed.

"Holy shit, is that the time? We slept late." Taz asked, looking suddenly serious.

Storm looked over to the clock. It read twelve noon. *Dammit.* Storm remembered he had promised to call back his business manager, Anthony.

"I need to take a quick shower and call my business manager," Storm said, standing up and reaching for the sweats Taz had ripped off him the night before.

Taz walked to the bedroom door near where his T-shirt lay in a heaping pile and he had just stooped to pick it up when the already broken door flew open and Rebecca walked in, balancing a silver tray on one hand with her other hand on the doorknob.

"Ayee! Dios mio!" she screamed, catching sight of the huge man in front of her as she carried the tray piled high with pancakes, syrup, a bud vase, and orange juice. Her forward momentum would prove to be both their undoing because she probably couldn't have stopped if she wanted to.

As if in slow motion, Storm watched as Taz straightened to his full height, holding the towel in place with one hand and his sweats with the other. As the tray holding Storm's breakfast began to topple, Taz let go of the towel and reached out with both hands trying to catch the tray before it fell from the screaming maid's hands. Somehow she must have hooked the towel with the rosebud vase on the tray because it, along with the towel, went crashing to the floor a second later, leaving a stunned Taz standing naked as the day he was born only a foot in front of Rebecca. The look on the maid's face was priceless as she got a full frontal look at Storm's huge lover in all his naked glory.

Her mouth flew open and her eyes bugged out as she looked down to see Taz struggle in vain to hide his long, flaccid cock with two hands. She stared for a few seconds in the utterly silent room and then looked up and began grinning.

"Aye, Dios mio," she whispered into the now silent room as Taz's feet were bathed in the syrup and juice which puddled on the carpet.

Storm, from his position beside the bed, had only managed to pull his sweats up a second before Taz was bared before his maid, not that it would have made any difference at all, judging by the look on her face. The silver budvase mocked the silence as it swung in an arc back and forth on the metal tray, making a clicking sound and but for that, Storm could have heard a pin drop. That was, before he started to giggle. Taz turned and shot him a dirty look as Rebecca continued to grin and that only caused Storm to laugh harder. Within seconds, Taz had spun back around and was addressing Rebecca, apologizing profusely.

"Oh, sorry ma'am," Taz said, bending in half as he scrambled for his towel, lying on the floor covered in orange juice. Storm got an amazing view of the most beautiful high bubble butt he'd ever seen. All Storm could think was how fortunate he was to have a lover as amazing as Taz.

"Meester Taz... ju are... MEESTER Taz!" Rebecca exclaimed, causing another burst of giggles to spring from Storm as he wholeheartedly agreed with whatever she was trying to say.

Taz managed to straighten to his full six and a half foot height with the dripping towel in his hand, slapping it in a circle back around his middle as fast as he could. Storm could hear the wetness hitting his skin from the sticky syrup and orange juice and he was pretty certain there would be another shower in the bodyguard's near future.

"Are you okay, Rebecca?" Taz asked the maid, reaching out to touch her elbow, once he'd tucked the offending cloth back around his waist, hiding his finest feature.

"Oh, jess, Meester Taz... ju are... okay, Meester Taz," she said, waggling her eyebrows as she cocked her head to the side, grinning and nodding at his crotch.

Oh to be able to sell tickets. Storm was dying inside with laughter but he knew Taz was highly embarrassed at being caught not only in his room but *flagrante delicto* to boot, and he also knew if he bit his lower lip any harder, he was gonna draw blood. He stepped forward and did his best to rescue Taz.

"It's okay, Rebecca. Let us get dressed and you can clean up when we go downstairs," he said, holding out his hand to take hers as she stooped to start picking up the sticky mess on the floor. Pancakes, syrup, silverware, and juice were scattered all over the carpet. Rebecca straightened and quickly made her exit. It wasn't until the door was shut that Storm heard her burst into giggles of her own, adding one more, "Dios mio" as her laughter drifted down the hall. As soon as she was gone, Taz wheeled on Storm and stared him down. A smile threatened at the corners of his beautiful mouth as he stalked over to where Storm was standing.

"Haha, very funny," he growled in a voice between disgust and humor.

Storm had been holding in his laughter but for the occasional giggle, and it finally bubbled up and burst forth as he doubled over. He laughed so hard, tears filled his eyes and when he was finally able to straighten, the moment he looked at Taz's face, he began laughing again. Taz reached out and grabbed him, tackling him to the floor, crawled right on top of him, wet towel and all, and began kissing him. It went on until Storm stopped laughing and he began getting hot and horny again and just as he heated up, Taz stopped, rolling off him and holding out a giant paw to give Storm a hand up.

"Come on. I need another shower," Taz said dragging him along into the bathroom. It was a good half hour, and mutual blowjobs before they were dressed and ready to leave.

****

As they walked out of the bedroom, Butch came running over. Storm leaned down to pick up the dog but he instead jumped up on Taz's leg, begging to be lifted. Taz bent and scooped the dog into his arms where Butch proceeded to lick his face. Taz glanced over at Storm who looked stricken.

"Hey, Butchy boy? You don't love me anymore?" Storm said, reaching over and petting the dog. Butch began licking Storm's hand and his expression lit with joy as he smiled at the dog. He held out his hands and Taz gladly handed the little dog over to his owner. Butch began covering his face with puppy kisses and Taz could tell from the way he laughed that all was good in Storm's world again. As they walked toward the head of the stairs, Taz could hear the thumping beat of the newest Nicki Minaj song playing loudly from the sound system in the living room. He glanced over at Storm the moment he heard the lyrics.

"My anaconda don't… My anaconda don't… My anaconda don't want none unless you got buns, hun…"

"Oh my gosh… look at her butt…"
"Oh my gosh… look at her butt…"
"Oh my gosh… look at her butt…"
"Look at her butt…"

"Look at her… look at her… Look… at… her butt…"

"This dude named Michael… used to ride motorcycles…"

"Dick bigger than a tower… I ain't talkin' 'bout Eiffel's…"

"Real country-ass nigga… let me play with his rifle…"

Taz and Storm stopped at the bottom of the stairs. Rebecca was swinging her butt in time to the music, a feather duster in her hand with her back to them as she dusted the furniture in the living room. When she started to twerk, Taz turned to look at Storm. Storm had one hand over his mouth and he was silently cracking up laughing as he stared back.

"You have got to be shitting me!" Taz growled, feeling completely at a loss for any intelligent thing to say.

Storm burst into laughter and doubled over as Rebecca spun around with a gigantic grin on her face, the feather duster held high in one hand pointing to the kitchen as she walked up to them. Nicki and some dude with a very deep voice continued their assault on Taz's eardrums.

"Meester Storm. Meester Taz. Ju meesed ju breakfast," she said. "I make ju lunch."

"Good, we're starving," Storm squeaked and then cleared his throat, looking over at Taz and pleading for sympathy with his gorgeous blue eyes, lit with mirth as much as he tried to hide it. Storm deliberately dragged his gaze away from Taz's eyes and turned to the maid again. "What's for lunch, Rebecca?"

The maid looked entirely too pleased with herself for Taz's peace of mind.

"I make ju a twelve eench meat, Meester Taz," the maid announced proudly. "And ju, Meester Storm… I make you a twelve eench veggie," she said, scrunching up her face.

Taz assumed she was talking about sub sandwiches but anything the woman said or did now would have been suspicious. "Unless ju like a twelve eench meat, Meester Storm?" she asked, turning to Storm with a look of such unutterable innocence, if Taz didn't know better, he would have laughed. "Meester Storm… a twelve eench meat is sooo good for ju, Meester Storm."

"That's it. Let's go," Taz said, taking Storm's arm and dragging him away from the maid, toward the kitchen. Storm was laughing again as Nicki continued the stupid lyrics.

"Bang bang bang… I let him hit it 'cause he slang co… caine…"

"He tossed my salad like his name… Romaine…"

They walked into the kitchen as the song continued. Sure enough as promised, Rebecca had two foot long subs waiting for them on plates in the kitchen. Taz was embarrassed as he sat across the table to eat but he could see Storm was doing his very best to try to hold it together so he did the same, keeping his dirty looks at bay. When he bit into the sandwich, it was delicious. He watched Storm open the bun of his sandwich and pick out the egg which Rebecca had put in, probably with the intent of getting Storm to eat something healthy. It seemed she couldn't accept the fact Storm was vegan. Hell, she probably equated a no-meat diet with blasphemy. *She should have known better. That boy ain't gonna eat anything he don't wanna eat.*

Taz chewed his food and watched his lover. He couldn't really put a finger on when he'd started thinking of Storm as his lover but he knew it was definitely sometime around when he'd set down his glass of wine and pulled the superstar into his arms, and when Storm had tried so hard to bottom for Taz the night before. If it hadn't happened to Taz many times before, he would have been really upset by it. The fact is, he knew he was a well-built man and that had always served him. Men were crazy to see what he had in his pants. It just simply came with the territory.

This, though… crossing the line the way he did with Storm wasn't something that was supposed to happen. Bodyguards weren't supposed to give in to the stereotype portrayed in the famous Whitney Houston movie with Kevin Costner. They weren't supposed to become personally involved with the people they were charged with protecting. It was true; up to this point, there hadn't been any serious threat to Storm's safety. A few paparazzi at his friend Devon's house and a few overzealous fans at the clubs Storm liked to hang out in… those were all easy to handle. Taz knew his size alone was intimidating to anyone trying to go through him and get to Storm. It was only one of the things that made him good at his job. Forget his military training, his complex knowledge of hand to hand combat, whether it was using Krav Maga techniques or his KA-BAR knife, Taz was a skilled former Marine. At this point, he was so keyed up, he almost welcomed a confrontation.

As they were finishing their sandwiches, Taz's new nemesis came into the kitchen. They both looked up and saw Rebecca entering the kitchen. She was smiling as she walked up to the farm table where they were both sitting.

"Meester Storm. I forgot to tell ju that Meester Goo was here. He bring ju thees and he say eat thees and ju be strong." Rebecca handed Storm a small brown bottle and Taz watched as he opened it, tipping it on its side so a handful of small gel caps rolled out into his palm. They looked like vitamin E pills which Taz had used to reduce scarring for the wound on his thigh.

Storm examined the pills and looked back at the maid. "That's all he said, Rebecca?"

"Jess, Meester Storm. He just say, ju take thees and ju be beeg and strong like Meester Taz…" She looked over at Taz and grinned. "Very very beeg and strong like Meester Taz." When she looked down at Taz's crotch and nodded, looking back at Storm with a sideways cocking of her head, he'd had enough.

I'm never gonna live it down. To his credit, when Taz looked over at Storm, he had the most innocent face Taz had ever seen. He knew what Storm was thinking but he masked it well as he schooled his features into a disinterested face. *He has better acting skills than I give him credit for.*

"Thank you, Rebecca," Storm said. She walked out of the room and Storm poured the little pills back into the bottle, closing the top.

"How do you know what it is?" Taz asked. He was honestly curious about what Storm was taking. He knew little about the guru other than the fact Storm liked to do yoga with him. From a purely professional point of view, Taz knew he should look into all the people Storm was associating with. He already knew Alan Steinberg had a gambling habit and he suspected it was probably an addiction. Judging by the fact Alan had laid bets before Storm had signed the movie deal, there was always the possibility he could somehow be ripping Storm off. Taz made a mental note to check into that ASAP.

"Guru has given me vitamins before," Storm said. He opened his mouth to say something else when Butch began gagging. Their attention was drawn to the little dog who was standing next to his food bowl near the kitchen sink. He had thrown up a pile of undigested dry dog food and he was gagging again, probably trying to bring up more of the foul stuff in his stomach. Storm leaped up from the table and ran over to the dog, bending down to speak to him.

"Butch, what's wrong, sweetie?" he asked. The dog looked up at him for a second and then looked down at the floor and threw up another pile of the food. Storm glanced over to Taz who was still sitting at the table in front of their empty plates. "He eats this food all the time," Storm said, indicating the half-empty bowl on the floor. "I don't understand it."

Taz got up from the table and walked over to Storm. "Could he have gotten into something here in the house?" Taz asked, looking down at the little guy.

The dog had stopped throwing up and Storm picked him up, petting his head. "Probably, but that doesn't look like anything but food." He held out a hand, pointing to the mess on the kitchen floor. At that moment Rebecca walked into the kitchen.

"Oh, the leetle dog, is sick," she said with a frown.

Taz watched as the maid walked over to the counter and tore off paper towels. She bent and started cleaning up the dog barf.

"I'm taking Butch to the vet, Taz. Just to make sure, I want to have him looked at," Storm said.

"Should I have David get the limo ready?" Taz asked. Storm looked so sad, all he wanted to do was to reach out and take him into his arms to comfort him.

"Oh, would you, Taz?"

"No problem." He turned and walked away as Storm comforted his little dog. He left the kitchen and walked through the house to the front door, pulling out his phone and punching in a few numbers. When David picked up, he gave him instructions to get the car ready.

David lived in a small guest house at the rear of the property. Taz just hoped he'd discouraged the driver. Considering the fact Taz was involved with Storm, he didn't want David to come on to him again. He'd witnessed the way Storm had looked at them before and he knew Storm must have overheard his conversations with David in the limo. At the time it happened, Taz hadn't cared what Storm thought, except for the fact David had made it clear he wanted Taz. Although his relationship with Storm had changed dramatically, he didn't necessarily want the rest of the help to be in on their private life. It was bad enough that Rebecca had walked in on them with Storm's breakfast. He just hoped she was discreet enough to keep it "all in the family" as they say.

When he walked out of the front door, David was coming around the side of the house. He was dressed in his chauffeur uniform and was putting on his hat. When he saw Taz, his expression lit up with a smile.

"Good morning, sexy," he greeted.

"Hey, David," Taz said, walking up. He was going to put the kibosh on whatever David had in his mind right now. "Storm's little dog is sick. He needs to take him to the vet," he said.

David moved closer, reaching out to touch Taz cheek. "That's perfect, gorgeous. While he's inside, you want to…"

His words were cut off as Storm walked out of the house. David dropped his hand and they both turned to Storm. He was holding a very sick looking little dog and the look on the superstar's face wasn't much better. Taz knew Storm had seen David touching his cheek and he was pissed with himself for getting close enough to the driver to let it happen. Storm looked at both of them and his expression was as sad as it could possibly be.

Taz immediately stepped away from the chauffeur and walked over to Storm, standing right in front of him. The urge to touch him and comfort him came back tenfold but with David standing there looking on, he just stood still, watching his lover.

"The car is ready, Storm."

Storm's expression hardened as he transformed into the snobbish actor all over again. "Fine. I called Dr. Norman and he's expecting us," Storm said.

He turned and walked over to the door which David had opened for him to climb in. He sat down and then looked straight ahead, ignoring Taz completely. His expression and actions couldn't have been more different than the way he was just a few minutes before and Taz knew it was because of the driver. As David shut the door to the car, Taz walked around to the front passenger seat. He knew he'd have to talk to Storm later, but for now, there was nothing he could do about the way the star was feeling. The drive to Butch's vet was the longest Taz could remember in a long time.

****

"He's been poisoned!" Storm said as he walked out into the reception area at the veterinarian's office.

Taz had been sitting in the doctor's office for well over two hours and he'd been up to the reception desk two times to ask what was taking so long. The receptionist was a young woman who simply told him they were running tests to see what had happened to the little dog and that it would take some time.

"What do you mean?" Taz asked, rising from the chair he'd been occupying as a stricken Storm walked over to him.

"Well, Dr. Norman isn't one hundred percent certain he's been poisoned but he says the signs are there," Storm said. He reached out a hand and Taz instantly took it in his own, turning toward the chairs in the empty reception area. As they walked over and sat down, Taz could feel Storm grip his hand tightly. He looked absolutely ill himself.

"Sit down and tell me what the doctor said," Taz said, quietly. He knew he was frowning but he couldn't help but be concerned about Storm. He was obviously beside himself with worry.

"He said he has to keep Butch here and run more tests. He gave him some medicine to bring up whatever was left in his stomach, but Dr. Norman says Butch is behaving as if he got into some sort of a pesticide." Storm looked over at him and Taz was distressed to see tears fill the star's eyes. "He says the poison attacks the blood cells, destroying them. What if he dies, Taz? What will I do?"

Taz was already holding one hand and he reached out with the other hand taking both of Storm's in his. He was feeling wholly inadequate, not knowing what to say or do. If he had a magic wand, he knew he would have made Storm's distress vanish but as it was, all he could offer was a squeeze of his hand and a few comforting words.

"I'm sure the doctor knows what he's doing, Storm. All we can do is wait and see what he finds." He was a little surprised how invested he'd become in the little dog's well-being. As a kid, he'd never had a dog, due to his mother's allergies to most animals, but he'd always liked them well enough. As they sat there holding hands the door to the reception area opened and a man dressed in a white lab coat came out. He was tall, gray-haired, and very good-looking, but the expression on his face was serious. They both stood up immediately as he walked up. He nodded to Taz and then turned to Storm who was wiping tears from his face.

"He's stabilized, Storm. I've hooked him up to some IV fluids and I want to keep him overnight," the doctor said to Storm. "As best I can determine, he's been poisoned with some arsenic based toxin, similar to what you'd find in rat poison. It's very deadly on small animals but you got him here right away," he said.

Storm looked like he was going to faint as the doctor continued.

"The poison attacks the internal organs, primarily the liver and kidneys. I've given him some medicine to speed the progression of the poison through his system and he seems to be doing a little better. We'll run more blood tests later this afternoon, once he's had time to metabolize the medication," the doctor said. He reached out and put a hand on Storm's shoulder. "I don't want you to worry too much. You got him here shortly after he got into whatever it was that made him sick. If you had waited… well, Butch may have died."

Taz looked over at Storm when he choked back a sob, putting a fluttering hand to his lips. He looked absolutely devastated as more tears rolled down his face.

The doctor patted him on the shoulder again. "Come… come now, all we can do is wait. It's going to be several hours. My advice to you is to go home and get some rest, Storm." The doctor looked over to Taz, seeming to see him there for the first time. "Hello," he said, "I'm Doctor Norman, Butch's vet." He reached out a hand to shake.

"This is Balthazar, my bodyguard," Storm said shakily as Taz shook the man's hand. His voice was thick with emotion.

"Nice to meet you, Balthazar," Dr. Norman said.

"Please call me Taz."

"Taz, then. Please take Storm home and put him to bed. He looks worse off than little Butch," the handsome older man said with a smile that lit up his whole face. He dropped his hand.

"I'll do that," Taz promised the man.

"Are you sure, Dr. Norman?" Storm asked.

"Yes, Storm. You go home. Get some rest and I promise I'll call you as soon as I know anything," the doctor said, turning to Storm.

"Okay, doc."

Storm stayed to settle the bill with the vet's receptionist, and then Taz escorted him out to the limo where David had been waiting for them. The chauffeur jumped out of the driver's seat and opened the door for Storm to get in.

Storm turned to Taz. "Please sit with me," he said. He looked so sad that Taz nodded to him and climbed into the back.

David closed the door and Storm immediately scooted close to Taz, laying his head on his shoulder as he reached around him with one arm, holding on to his waist. Taz pulled Storm into his arms and held him close, feeling protective and just plain wonderful with him in his arms. Storm moved his head so it was resting on Taz's chest and he leaned his chin on top of the star's head. When he looked up toward the front of the car, David was staring at him in the rearview mirror. He had a very knowing smirk on his face and Taz ignored him, closing his eyes and leaning his head back on the seat as the driver started the car. The movement of the car as David drove them back to the mansion lulled Taz into a comfortable state of being. He loved having Storm in his arms and he felt as if that's where he belonged. He couldn't care less about what the driver thought. *Storm's exactly where he belongs… in my arms.*

CHAPTER TWELVE

When they got to the house in Malibu, the sun was setting and the weather had grown chilly. David opened the back door to the car and once again shot Taz a knowing smirk as Taz got out of the car with Storm's hand in his. Taz ignored him and walked Storm into the house with the single-minded thought of putting the emotionally exhausted man to bed to let him sleep until the doctor called to update him on Butch's condition. He honestly hoped the little dog would be okay because he'd grown to love the dog in the short time he'd spent at the mansion and above all else, he didn't want to see Storm experience any pain if something happened to the small pet which he clearly loved.

Storm clung to him as they walked through the front door. Rebecca was waiting for them in the foyer, wringing her hands with a look of worry on her sweet face. Gone was the teasing maid she'd been that morning and early afternoon. After assuring her Butch was being taken care of, she told them she'd prepared a hearty vegetable stew for dinner and left it on the stove. She picked up her handbag and left shortly afterward.

"I'm not hungry, Taz," Storm said, once the maid had gone. "Will you come to bed with me?" He looked like a little boy, so forlorn and lost, Taz didn't know what to say. The truth was, he desperately wanted Storm but the whole day he'd been kicking himself for drinking too much wine and letting it cloud his usually good judgment.

"I don't think that's such a good idea, Storm," he said. The look in Storm's eyes was sad and sexy as hell and he knew one more word of encouragement and his fragile resistance was going to shatter.

Storm moved closer to Taz, reaching out and taking his hands in his own as he looked up the few inches that separated them in stature. His expression was sweet, sexy, and pleading. "I really need you to make me forget how awful I feel for a little while," he said, focusing his stare on Taz's lips.

Taz smiled at him, feeling his shaky opposition to Storm's request melting away as he began to lose the battle within. "Okay, Storm," he said.

Storm smiled and turned, Taz's hand still in his as he pulled him up the stairs of the quiet house. As they got to the top, Storm's cell phone began to vibrate. Storm stopped at the top of the stairs, glanced at Taz, and pulled the phone out of his tight jeans.

"Anthony?" he said, "Yes, I know… I had a bit of an emergency here. What? Okay, I will see you in the morning then… Ten? Okay, I'll be here." Storm glanced back at Taz, replacing the phone in his jeans as he glanced at him. "That was my business manager. Apparently, whatever it is, it's important. He'll be here in the morning."

They walked into the bedroom and Taz noted the bed was made up as if they had never slept in it and the mess from the encounter with Rebecca had been cleaned from the carpet as well. The room was neat and clean and it looked put back in perfect order. Embarrassment washed through him as he noted candles had been lit in the room and the fireplace was glowing once again. He honestly hoped the maid did this for Storm every night and not just to set the mood for her hopeful encounter between them. Taz marveled that everyone in Storm's life seemed to be so encouraging of his playboy lifestyle and had he not known Jules and Rebecca better, he was certain everyone catered to the superstar because of his money. He was removing his jacket as his own phone rang. He pulled it out of his coat pocket and swiped the screen, putting it to his ear where he could talk while he removed his gun from his shoulder holster, setting it on the dresser.

"Mom?"

"Yes, baby," his mother said.

"Hi, Mom." Taz was genuinely happy to hear from her but as he watched Storm undressing on the other side of the room, his own thoughts were about him and not his mother's piss poor timing.

"Taz, we're havin' a barbecue tomorrow. I wanted to tell you to be here at three. Your daddy's lookin' forward to it," she said.

Taz knew those were code words for "I'm looking forward to seeing you" but he didn't say anything; he just smiled.

"Mama, I'm working tomorrow," he said.

"Aw, Taz, it's supposed to be your day off. Did that change?" she asked, sounding genuinely disappointed. He looked over at Storm as his phone rang again and he watched as the star dug the phone out of his jeans. He had stripped off his shirt and the nipple rings were glinting at Taz in the firelight. He looked absolutely edible as he put the phone to his own ear and began talking to Jules.

"I was supposed to have the day off," he said quietly, walking into the bathroom for a little privacy. The truth was, he wanted to stay with Storm and be with him when Butch came home.

"Then what's going on that I can't have my little boy at home with his family for a barbecue?" his mother asked.

Good question. "The man I work for, Mom… , I'm gonna be working; that's all."

"Bring him along, honey. We all want to meet Storm Ellison. The girls have been talkin' about it since you went to work for him… or are his britches too big to go to a barbecue with regular folks?" she pressed.

The door to the bathroom opened and Storm walked in. He wasn't holding his phone but he was naked and when he slipped his arms around Taz and hugged him from behind, kissing him between the shoulder blades, Taz melted.

"Fine, Mom, I'll ask him," he said.

"Ask me what?" Storm, said, brushing his lips on the side of Taz's neck and sending sexy shivers running through him. He turned his head to the side and met Storm's lips in a quick kiss.

"It's my mom. She wants to ask if you'd like to come for a barbecue tomorrow. I told her that you're busy and I have to work," he said, holding his hand over the phone.

Storm's pretty face lit up with a smile as he moved in front of Taz, circling his waist with his arms. "I'd love to go, provided Butch is home and he's okay," Storm said. "Tell her we'll go."

"Taz, is that your Mr. Ellison? Tell him he's welcome to come," Taz's mom said into his ear.

222

"He's not my Mr. Ellison, Mom," Taz said, gazing into Storm's eyes.

Storm grinned at him and nodded vigorously. *Oh yes I am*, Storm mouthed and then quick as a rabbit, he leaned forward and stole another fast kiss. Taz laughed.

"Okay. Okay, Mom. Fine, we'll be there," he said, feeling like a million dollars when he thought of belonging to Storm.

"Wonderful, honey, we'll see you then," his mom said and hung up.

Taz lowered the phone and Storm swooped in, taking his lips in a blistering kiss as Taz reached out and wrapped him in his arms, reaching blindly behind Storm to the countertop, where he set down his phone. They kissed desperately, as if they couldn't get enough of each other and any misgivings Taz had about making love with Storm again flew right out of his head. He had the sexiest man on two legs in his arms and he knew he'd be an absolute idiot not to take the opportunity to make love to him again.

Storm backed up against the counter, taking Taz with him. When he pulled his mouth away and looked at him, his eyes were filled with lust and longing. "I want you to fuck me," he said.

Taz was slightly stunned. When they'd made a half-assed attempt at it the night before as he'd responded to the same request, it hadn't gone so well. Taz had lubed him up pretty well when he realized the condom Storm had given him had been wholly inadequate for a man of Taz's size. He'd gone off to his room to retrieve one at Storm's urging, only to find, after attempting the act for about fifteen minutes, it just wasn't going to happen quickly and that had become too much for both of them. After all, they were still so new to each other; holding back at all was frustrating as hell. In the end, they'd opted for the easy route, and Taz had flipped onto all fours and received the king of all rim jobs and an ass fucking that, if he could, Taz would have handed Storm another award for. Storm was proficient as a top and somehow, he'd managed to hit Taz's prostate so perfectly that he'd left a sticky mess for both of them to sleep in.

"You sure you wanna try again, Storm?" Taz asked.

"You know I do," Storm said. "If we weren't so impatient last night, things would have gone a lot smoother."

"Fine," Taz said, kissing Storm quickly. "Let's take this to the bedroom."

"Tell you what, let's not," Storm said. "I want to see you from all angles, Taz."

Taz looked past Storm to the long mirror above the granite countertop. It began at the counter and went all the way to the ceiling, covering the entire wall. He imagined how sexy Storm would look, naked in his arms, riding his cock with his ankles wrapped around his back. Taz's cock was pounding behind his zipper just thinking about it. He nodded.

"Okay, Storm," he heard himself saying.

No wonder the superstar got whatever he asked for. He watched as Storm's face lit up and he began stripping out of the suit while Storm raced out of the bathroom and then returned a minute later, holding one of the condoms Taz had left in the bedroom the night before in one hand and the bottle of lube in the other. Storm was hard as his own impressive length bobbed in front of him.

"I'm ready, Taz," Storm announced.

"We'll see about that. Turn around and let me get you lubed up," Taz said, taking the condom from him.

Storm shook his head and reached out, running a hand down Taz's naked pectoral muscles and over his abs down to his cock where he circled it with both hands. "I want to watch your eyes when you fuck me." He gave Taz's cock a few pumps with his hands, then let go, backing up and reaching behind him as he grabbed the countertop. As Taz watched, Storm boosted himself up, lifting both legs and putting both feet on the counter, before scooting forward and leaning back, widening his knees so his pucker was exposed.

"How's this?" he asked.

"You seriously need to ask?" Taz asked with a grin.

He pinned him with his sexiest look and then reached out, taking both legs behind the knees and exposing him even further until Storm was nearly folded in half when Taz kneeled in front of him. Storm's manscaped balls hung between his legs like a pretty smooth feast and his long, thick cock lay up against his belly. A string of precome had already begun to hang down from Storm's slit almost to his stomach. *I need to taste him.* Taz leaned forward between Storm's legs and nuzzled into his ball sac with his face. He inhaled, savoring the musky scent of the man and couldn't help but open his mouth to suck in one of his balls. Storm groaned as Taz rolled it gently, tickling it with his tongue, eventually moving to the other side and repeating the gesture. Storm wrapped his fist around the shaft of his cock and began pumping it as he looked down the length of his body and watched Taz paying homage to his private parts with his lips and tongue.

"God! Taz… oh…" was all Storm could say.

The words were not coming easy to him and that's just what Taz wanted. He moved lower, licking under his balls at the smooth, fresh smelling skin, working his way toward the pink puckered opening which awaited his attention. When he firmed his tongue and stabbed through it, Storm nearly levitated off the countertop. One of his hands grabbed the back of Taz's head, holding it in place.

"Ahh…ah, that feels so good, Taz! Oh my God!"

Taz continued his assault, fucking Storm's hot hole with his tongue. Storm was wiggling and Taz licked and sucked him, loving the way he could make him moan.

"Fuck me! Fuck me! Fuck me, Taz!" Storm began to chant. His voice was gravely and thick with sex.

Taz took one last lick from his hole, sliding the point of his tongue all the way up the shaft of his cock and over the head where he lapped up a dribble of precome. Storm tasted amazing. Taz stood up and leaned forward, pinning Storm with his gaze. Storm's expression was intense and when he looked down toward Taz's groin, he felt himself grow even harder than before. Something in the way Storm looked at him with such devotion made Taz feel very special and very wanted, and that feeling was amazing.

Taz stepped back, grabbing the condom as Storm reached for his cock to give it a few pumps. It was rare that Taz was able to take a man the way he wanted to take Storm. He wanted to feel himself buried in Storm's body, making love to him with his whole heart and soul and he did know that feeling was foreign to him. Because of his size, the moment men saw him, they began drooling over him, lusting for him. Taz mostly hated it. People looked at him as a conquest and when they weren't able to take him, they often tried to shame him as if it were his fault. The one woman he'd tried to have sex with when he was in the military overseas hadn't been able to take him and it had been a thoroughly humiliating experience, so he'd given up the idea of topping most men. When he did, it generally ended the way it had with Storm the other night but he was determined to redouble his efforts with his sexy lover. If they were to be together, he wanted it to be without anything between them; that's just the way Taz did things, all or nothing. He rolled on the condom as Storm watched and grabbed the lube.

Storm reached out and took the lube from him. "Give that to me. I want to get you ready," he said, sexily.

Taz handed it over and stepped up, watching as Storm poured a healthy amount into one palm, then rubbed his hands together before taking his cock in both hands and sliding the slippery concoction up and down the shaft. After he'd lubed him up pretty well, Storm leaned back again, and bracing himself with one hand on the countertop, he began slicking his own

227

hole, digging in first one and then another finger until he'd worked it well. Taz watched with utter fascination as he began panting with arousal. After Storm had been able to take three fingers, he pulled them out and Taz handed him a towel.

"I'm ready," Storm growled, "We'll go slow."

Taz nodded, stepping into the vee of Storm's legs as Storm threw the towel aside and grabbed the edge of the countertop. Mirrors on three sides of them gave Storm the perfect view he wanted, and as Taz put the head of his cock up to Storm's slick hole, he felt Storm blow out a breath and felt him relax his body. Taz grabbed Storm's knees, widening them farther as he pushed slowly. He watched Storm's face for his reaction and it was only of encouragement.

"Come on, baby," Storm whispered. "That's right," he said as the head of Taz's cock breached him fully.

Taz halted, waiting for Storm's tight body to adjust, knowing the worst was yet to come. Storm's face was serious, his jaw set, but the expression on his face was so sweet and welcoming and when he nodded, Taz pushed farther, making a slow advance. It was difficult holding back; Storm was tight but then because of his size, Taz had never known a lover who wasn't, so he made slow progress as he pushed in. He looked down at their connection; it was so unbelievably sexy and Taz had to hold back from pushing harder and faster. When he was halfway there, he gave his own little encouragement.

"That's it," he ground out, "God, baby, you're so tight; you're taking all of me. Just look at us."

Storm turned his head to glance into a mirror on the wall on the side of the countertop and Taz met his gaze. They watched each other as Taz made his slow advance and Storm lowered his gaze to where they were connected, blowing out another breath as Taz approached full penetration.

"You okay, Storm?"

Storm was concentrating on his breathing, his abs and chest rising and falling rhythmically as he relaxed his sphincter around Taz, letting him in. He glanced up at Taz, nodding. "Keep going. I've got you, Taz."

The words encouraged Taz like never before. He wanted this so badly but more so, he wanted to give Storm the ride he'd been asking for from the beginning. "Two more inches," he growled through gritted teeth. His cock was throbbing and he hoped he could make it all the way before he came but the fact Storm's body was hugging him like a tight glove as it stretched around him and the look on his beautiful face as he accepted all of what Taz offered were encouraging.

"Now, Taz," Storm said.

Taz felt him relax and he pushed, feeling Storm push back, watching as Storm's body accepted the last two inches.

"Oh, God!" Storm suddenly shouted.

Taz watched as come shot out of Storm's erect cock, painting his chest with thick white spunk. *He's not even touching himself. How fuckin' hot is that?*

Storm screamed, squeezing his eyes tightly shut as Taz pulled out two inches and repeated the thrust. When Storm screamed again, Taz knew he was hitting his gland. Storm's cock bobbed and Taz's gaze was riveted on the head as two more thick streamers shot out, hitting as high as Storm's clavicles. His nipples with their silver rings were glinting in the glow of the strong lights above them on the bathroom ceiling but most sexy of all was the come that pooled on Storm's cut six-pack abs.

Taz pushed back in and the going was a little easier.

"Fuck me, fuck me, fuck me through it!" Storm said and if he could have said anything sexier, Taz wasn't sure how.

"God, that's so fucking sexy, Storm. You have no idea what you look like right now." Taz could hear the deep throaty words in his own growling voice, and he let go of Storm's legs, reaching around and gripping his ass cheeks in both hands and lifting him clear off the counter.

Storm instantly wrapped his long legs around Taz, hooking them behind his back as he straightened, while sliding his arms around Taz's neck. Storm held on for dear life and Taz leaned forward to find his lover's mouth with his own. They kissed long and frantic as Taz used his hands to lift Storm up and down, impaling his ass on his own thick cock, as he approached his own climax. Storm moaned into his mouth as Taz sucked on his tongue, all the while thrusting his hips and fucking him deeper than he'd ever taken another man. His inner beast roared from deep inside him and he growled into Storm's mouth. He tore his lips away and rested his forehead against Storm's, staring into his eyes.

"Come on, baby," Storm whispered. "Come deep inside me. Give me all you have."

Storm's words of encouragement, the way he was tightly milking the shaft of his cock from his orgasm, and the throbbing in his own full balls sent him over the edge. Storm seemed to know when it was going to happen because he lowered his teeth to Taz's shoulder and bit down on the thick muscle. Taz's orgasm roared through him and he shouted, feeling his cock throb as he emptied himself into the condom buried deeply in Storm.

"Jesus!" he cried into Storm's neck. His taste was salty and slick with sweat as he licked at the corded muscle, feeling the burn from his lover's teeth for the first time. His cock pulsated again inside the confines of Storm's tight hole for what felt like a full minute and only then was he reminded that he carried Storm, supporting his weight completely. His heart pounded wildly in his chest and his muscles began to sag as he relaxed his arms, and Storm instantly reacted by unhooking his legs and straightening. Taz's cock slid out and hung down as Storm regained his footing; Taz steadied him in his arms until he could stand on his own.

Storm leaned forward and kissed him, sliding his arms around Taz as his condom covered cock hung between them. Taz wrapped him in his arms, pulling Storm against his chest, loving the way the smaller man felt in his embrace and feeling him shudder slightly. They were both covered with sweat, Taz from the exertion of fucking Storm while supporting his considerable weight, and Storm probably from working at taking a man his size.

"That was…," Storm blinked his incredible blue eyes up at Taz as he spoke against his lips.

Taz felt himself smile. "Yeah…, it was."

Storm kissed him again. "You're a hell of a man, Balthazar Grant," he said, hugging Taz tight.

"No one ever took me that deep, Storm," Taz heard himself saying against Storm's hair as he hugged him tightly. As nasty and slippery as they both were, there was no way Taz wanted to let go.

Storm pulled away so he was looking in Taz's eyes again. "I can't believe that," he said. "Sure, you're a lot of man but I feel so honored. You must have had some seriously selfish lovers, Taz."

"The truth is, I haven't had many lovers at all, Storm," he said.

Storm looked at him like he had two heads.

"The fact is, when they see me, either they want to run away or to brag they've had me. I've had men walk right out of my apartment and brag they've had me later," he admitted truthfully. Opening up was very hard for Taz. He'd always been self-conscious about his size. There was something about the way Storm looked at him like he cherished him that made Taz warm inside. Somehow, he knew Storm was genuine and wouldn't ever mock him the way others had.

Storm kissed him again. "That's seriously fucked up," he said.

Taz let go of Storm's waist, agreeing with him. "Look, you'd better go call the doc. I'm gonna get into the shower," he said.

Storm smiled, sweetly. "You read my mind, lover." He eyeballed Taz, perhaps looking to see his reaction to that word but Taz carefully schooled his features. The word still gave him pause though he'd become more comfortable with it over the last twenty-four hours. "I'm gonna call Doc Norman right now."

Taz watched as Storm turned and walked into the bedroom and he reached down, taking some toilet tissue and dealing with the sagging condom before leaning into the shower stall and turning on the spray. Storm's bathroom was white marble and it was beautiful. He was amazed that Rebecca was able to keep the large mansion so clean by herself, as well as having time to prepare Storm's meals and wait on him.

He stepped inside the shower and let the warm water sluice over his head and shoulders for a few moments before reaching for the shampoo in a recess in the wall. Taz's hair was shaved very close to his head but he wasn't completely bald. He had very little body hair, a fine line between his pectorals and a short bush which he kept closely-trimmed at his groin, as well as very short armpit hair which was also trimmed close. He liked being well groomed and smelling clean and he liked his men that way as well, though Storm was always neat and clean and smelled amazing. He felt truly fortunate to have a man like Storm as a lover but when the shower door opened and Storm stepped in, slipping his arms around his middle and hugging him from behind, he felt as though he'd truly come home.

"Butch is going to stay the night at Dr. Norman's. He wants to observe him another twelve hours. We've got a busy day tomorrow. Anthony's coming at ten."

Taz loved the way Storm's hands spread scented body wash over his stomach and pecs. He turned in his arms so he could lean down and kiss Storm. Storm turned up his face, meeting his lips where they kissed leisurely. When he finally pulled away, Storm was looking up at him, blinking to keep the water droplets out of his eyes.

"Let's finish up here. I wanna take you to bed and hold you all night long," Taz said.

Storm grinned, lowering his gaze to Taz's lips as he spoke. "I thought you were concerned about what was happening between us," he said.

Taz signed. "I am but only because I need to remain objective. I've decided that if this is going to continue, I need to step aside as your bodyguard."

"You can't do that, Taz." Storm looked stricken and Taz closed his eyes, deliberately turning his back and reaching for the faucet, shutting off the water before turning around. He opened the shower door as Storm continued his protest. "I feel safe with you. I need you at my back," he said. His lips looked so adorably pouty, Taz couldn't help but kiss him again.

"I want someone to give their complete attention to you," he said, reaching for a towel, reaching out and drying Storm and then himself.

"But I want you paying attention to me, not some stranger who doesn't care about me. You care about me, don't you?" Tears appeared in Storm's eyes and Taz's stomach did a little flip-flop. The last thing he wanted was to cause Storm any emotional pain.

"I care more about you than I've ever cared about anyone, Storm. This thing we have between us is…"

"Amazing," Storm finished, looking more sincere than Taz had ever seen him.

Taz smiled. "Totally amazing."

"Please don't stop guarding me. I don't want anyone else. I promise I won't do anything you don't want me to. No more guys like Petros. I promise, Taz."

Storm was getting himself really worked up. He'd had enough upset for the day so Taz relented. He reached out, taking the superstar in his arms and pulling him into a tight embrace where he kissed him slowly, savoring every last thing about the man he was falling hard for before slowly pulling back. Storm's face was sweet and his lips were swollen from Taz's kisses. He looked sexier than hell.

"Okay. But you have to promise to behave," he said, finding himself smirking as he watched Storm's face light up.

"Cross my heart and hope to die," Storm said with a grin. He made the little X over his chest as Taz looked on.

"It won't come to that if you behave," he said. *If you listen and behave.*

****

The next morning was a flurry of activity at Storm's house. They woke in each other's arms with no time to make love which Storm desperately wanted. Instead, they had to settle for mutual blowjobs before getting out of bed and piling into the limousine and driving out to the veterinarian's office where they picked up Butch. Thankfully, there were no paparazzi waiting on Storm's street when they drove through the gates. He would have lost his shit if he'd had to fight with anyone today. The little dog jumped up when he saw Storm and Storm got tears in his eyes when he picked up the little guy only to have him cover his face with licking kisses. Taz laughed and Storm once again marveled how lucky he was to have such a gorgeous man for a lover. David drove them back home with Taz sitting in the back holding his hand and when they got out of the car back at the house, Storm was relieved he didn't have to say anything to David. He'd been ready to have to fire the chauffeur if he'd dared to come on to Taz again. The fact was, Storm was very territorial, more so now that he had a firm commitment from Taz that they were going to try to make things work between them, and if he'd so much as seen David attempt to poach Taz from him, he wouldn't have been forgiving.

Anthony was waiting for them at the house when they drove through the gates to the mansion. David parked the car and rushed around to the side where he opened the door, letting Taz out before he followed. Anthony greeted them when he went inside and he put Butch down in the foyer, turning to instruct Rebecca to discard the food which had been in his bowl and what remained in his bag. Something had gotten the little guy sick and though they didn't know what, he wasn't going to take any chances. Rebecca was very distressed about little Butch so she offered to make him something special. Butch followed her into the kitchen and Storm turned to Taz.

"We're going to go over some business in the library," he said.

Anthony, a small, slight man, blinked up at Taz and Storm turned to look at him when Taz gave him his scariest look. The man looked as though he was about to pee his pants right there in the foyer.

"Come on, Anthony. He's harmless," Storm said, taking the twink's hand and pulling him into the library while Taz followed.

The smirk playing around the corners of his lover's mouth was delicious, and he remembered the way his gorgeous, full lips looked wrapped around his paler cock. Forcing himself not to grow hard, he went into the room and over to the desk where Anthony laid out the ledger he'd brought with him.

"So, what's so important, Anthony?" he asked, noting Taz take up a position next to the door of the study where he could observe them from behind the infernal reflective lenses.

"That's just the thing, sir," Anthony began. "I've never questioned your investments before, sir, but this was so glaring, I knew I needed to bring it to your attention immediately. This is very important."

Storm could see the accountant getting worked up like crazy. He looked at the column of numbers and spreadsheets he'd laid out in front of him.

"What are you showing me, Anthony?" Storm asked, not being able to make heads or tails of the columns of numbers Anthony was so focused on.

Anthony puffed up and began to explain that Brian, Storm's previous business manager, had been handing out large sums of money to the contractors since the beginning of Guru Shamsa's temple building project. He explained it was customary for contractors to receive no more than ten percent of the cost of a construction project at the outset of the building but the temple's contractor had been given a full twenty-five percent of the funds necessary to complete the project at the very beginning. In addition, it was customary to get several bids on a construction project and those competing bids, if they had ever been sought, were nowhere to be found. After the outlay of the initial twenty-five percent, several other large payments had been made up to the point when Brian had passed away from kidney failure and the sum of those payments was equal to well over seventy-five percent of the project total.

"But the temple isn't even half built," Storm observed.

"That's why I felt it important to bring this to your attention right away, Mr. Ellison," the mousy man said. "It's all very unusual."

Storm looked over at Taz who just shrugged. "Do you think something is amiss here, Anthony? Please be honest."

The man puffed up again, looking very smug and satisfied that he'd finally gotten the point across. "Well, sir, I can't really say…" He cut a glance at Taz to make sure Storm's huge bodyguard was still across the room where he was little threat.

Storm smiled, knowing full well that Taz could snap Anthony like a twig in a heartbeat if necessary. He'd seen what was left of Petros's guards after the two of them had dared take Taz on alone and in addition to that, he knew Taz was packin' a huge weapon under that suit… and not the one he'd had so much fun with in the shower. He began to grin and then looked back at Taz with a question in his eyes.

"Why don't you let me look into the irregularities Anthony has found, Storm? That may set your doubts to rest," Taz said.

Anthony looked exceptionally pleased. "If you have those resources, I'd say it would do to use them and as soon as possible," the small man said.

"Meanwhile," Storm said, "don't issue any further payments to this contractor."

"Yes, sir," Anthony said. It was obvious he was very pleased with the outcome of the visit. "Well then, if that's all, I'll be taking my leave," the accountant said. He slammed the books closed. Clearly, he wanted to get out of Taz's way as soon as possible.

"Thank you for your observations, Anthony," Storm added, shaking the man's hand.

Storm escorted the business manager out of the library with Taz following. Something sure stank to high Heaven. Anger bubbled up inside of him and he felt stupid as though he'd somehow trusted the wrong man. Whatever it was though, he was confident Taz would root out the problem and for the time being he decided to put it aside; after all, they had a barbecue date at Taz's house.

CHAPTER THIRTEEN

As soon as Anthony had gone, Taz reminded Storm that his parents were expecting them for the barbecue. He was slightly intimidated about bringing a star like Storm Ellison to his folks' house. They knew Taz was gay so that wasn't an issue; his parents accepted him for who he was and he appreciated that more than they knew. When Jules showed up at the house for a pre-arranged shopping trip Storm had forgotten, Storm begged her to come with them; as far as Taz knew, Storm hadn't told her about the two of them. He wasn't even sure he wanted Storm to. They were new and though Taz's feelings were becoming more and more wrapped up in his beautiful young lover, he wasn't sure what they were yet. Would Storm expect him to introduce Storm as his boyfriend to his parents? They knew he worked for Storm so that was most likely how he was going to leave it. He decided he'd let the cards fall where they would.

Taz's parents' house was on the south side of Los Angeles, in an old neighborhood called Inglewood. The population was heavily African-American and as Taz drove them there in Storm's Land Rover, he explained that his great grandfather had built the house over sixty years before, telling him that four generations of Grants had grown up in the house. Jules sat in the back of the car dominating the conversation. She'd just finished telling them about a reception at the Brazilian embassy which her mother had made her attend the night before. Taz was enthralled by her lively, upbeat personality, and her description of some of the men her mother introduced her to had Taz laughing so hard, tears were falling from his eyes as he drove. She lit up the room when she walked in and he could easily see why Storm was best friends with her. She was just darling.

"So that about covers my wildly exciting love life," she said, leaning forward between the two front bucket seats. "Now, tell me about how it feels to be together."

Taz glanced in the rearview mirror, to see Jules's eyes sparkling with glee and undisguised mirth as she grinned ear to ear. When he shot a frown at Storm, he looked as surprised as Taz felt.

He shrugged his shoulders. "Don't look at me. I didn't say anything," Storm said. If he hadn't looked so damned serious, Taz wouldn't have believed it. Jules reached out from the back and slapped Taz on the shoulder, earning her a frown into the rearview mirror.

"You've got to be kidding me, Taz. Storm didn't tell me anything but you just confirmed it with that look," she said with a smug smile. "So… details… I want all the horny details."

Storm snorted and Taz glared at him. He was covering his mouth and cracking up into his hand.

"There's nothing to tell," Taz said, shooting her another glance into the rearview mirror.

"Oh puhleeze!" she said.

"You may as well tell her, Taz. She's not going to leave you alone until you tell her," Storm said.

"Yeah, I'm not going to leave you alone until you tell me, Taz. Do your parents know? Are you even out to them? How come I'm the last to know about you and Storm? Who seduced who? How long has this been going on?" The questions came in rapid-fire succession.

"Seriously, do you have an off switch?" Taz asked, completely at a loss as to what to say.

"So is he hung, Storm?" Jules asked, leaning forward to whisper not so conspiratorially to Storm.

"Hello! I'm sitting right here," Taz said, disgusted.

"Come on. I have to live vicariously through Storm, Taz. It's not like you bat for both teams... or do you? Is there any chance for me?"

Taz glanced over at Storm who was doubled over in the front seat of the car, laughing so hard he was turning red in the face.

"Seriously?" Taz asked, meeting Jules's sparkling eyes in the rearview mirror.

"Okay, okay," Storm gasped. "We've been together only a couple days. This is our actual first date."

"This is a date?" Taz asked, glancing over at Storm.

He grinned back. "Isn't it? Or, was taking Butch to the doctor our first date?" he asked innocently.

"Oh fer..." Taz began.

"Aw, see? That wasn't hard," Jules said. Now, tell me more... tell me more. How's Storm in bed?" I've heard..."

"Please! We're not sharing any details, thank you," Taz added, warming to Jules prying. Storm was having such a genuine laugh about things, it was hard to get angry with her. Besides, she was as cute as could be and if he had been as open as he wanted to be, he probably would tell her everything she wanted to know… that is, everything but the intimate details about their romps in bed. That was no one's business but his and Storm's and he loved the fact the two of them had that very special part of their lives which belonged to no one else and only to them.

"Oh, poo!" she said, flopping back onto the seat where she folded her arms and stuck out her bottom lip. "So, can you at least tell me if you're out?" she asked Taz when he looked at her in the rearview mirror. "Oh, please be out! I want to take you to WeHo and show you off to the pretty boys. Won't they be jealous? Storm remember that time when…"

"Jesus!" Taz said. "You don't have an off switch, do you?"

"Well… um… do I, Storm?" she asked innocently.

"You should," Storm said, leaning between them to look into the backseat. "And yes, Taz is out to his family and they are very accepting of it. And, no, they don't know we are a couple. And, no, I am not telling you whether Taz is hung or not."

Taz glanced over just in time to see Storm waggling his eyebrows and winking at Jules.

"Really?" he asked, throwing him his best glower though he was smiling inside; he was not about to let on that he was happy about his relationship with Storm. In fact, he was utterly giddy. He was crazy about Storm, to the point where he'd almost told Storm that despite his objections, he was going to find a replacement for himself regardless of whether Storm wanted it or not. Not because he was afraid he couldn't do his job, but because he was concerned that he'd die inside if something happened to Storm on his watch.

"I'm a terrible liar, lover," Storm said to him, blinking innocently.

Taz looked at him and the sweet expression on his completely gorgeous face was impossible to resist and the funny thing was, he didn't want to resist Storm in any way. He wanted to be completely owned by him. *I'm so over the moon for this guy it's crazy.*

Storm reached out and put his hand on Taz's bicep. He was wearing a black muscle T-shirt and camouflage cargo shorts and he loved the way Storm touched him.

"Look, you can say anything you want about me to my family, Jules, but can we not talk about our sex life? My parents are slightly old-fashioned," Taz said.

"Of course, Taz. I only hope you know I was teasing. I love seeing Storm happy and if that's because of you, I wholeheartedly approve," Jules said, patting his arm.

"Okay, thanks, Jules."

They drove a few minutes in silence until entering an old neighborhood with majestic homes on large lots.

"Oh, Storm, that's my house," Taz said, turning onto their wide street. Fall leaves were all over the street, on cars, and filling the gutter. As the wind kicked up, lifting them into the air, Taz suddenly got very homesick. He'd grown up here, riding his bike and swinging in the huge tire swing that hung from a massive oak tree in the front yard. His grandfather had hung that swing over thirty years before and his father had swung in it along with his siblings as children. As they drove up to the old Craftsman style bungalow with its wide single-story design and wrap-around porch, Taz found a spot in the street to park. The single car wide driveway leading to the detached garage in the back was filled with four cars, those of his parents and his siblings, one behind the other in a straight line to the curb. The sidewalk was cracked and raised by thick roots from eighty-year-old trees which had been planted when the neighborhood was new.

"Uncle Taz!" A little boy of no more than five came running from the porch and leaped right into Taz's arms as soon as he got out of the car.

Taz scooped up his nephew, Tyson, spinning him around in circles right there on the sidewalk. "How you doin' kiddo?" he asked, setting down the giggling child.

"Good, Uncle Taz! Mama says you brought a star with you." Tyson looked directly at Storm and then at Jules, a look of puzzlement on his face. "I don't see no star, Uncle Taz."

Taz laughed. "This is my friend, Storm Ellison, and his friend Jules, Tyson. Storm's a TV star."

The little boy stared at Storm for a second and then tugged on Taz's shorts. "Is he an action star, Uncle Taz? I love 'The Avengers', Uncle Taz. Is he in 'The Avengers'?"

Taz couldn't help but laugh some more. "No, little guy, Storm isn't in 'The Avengers'. That's a movie. He's on 'Trapped on an Island'."

The little boy pinned Storm with another curious look. "Oh, my mama watches that show. Daddy says it's shit."

Taz looked over at Storm who burst into laughter. The happiness on his lover's face was priceless and he couldn't help but laugh.

"Tyson, where's your manners? Don't let your nana hear you talk like that or she'll take a wooden spoon to your behind."

Rodney, Taz's brother-in-law, came walking down the steps in front of the house. His son looked over at his father a little sheepishly as the man stuck out his hand and shook Taz's. "Nice to see you, Taz," he said with a smile.

"Nice to see you, Rod," Taz said back. Rodney was married to his oldest sister Janelle, the teacher, and he genuinely liked the man. "I'd like you to meet Storm Ellison and his friend Juliana Ortiz," Taz said. They took turns shaking Rodney's hand.

"It's nice to meet you. Come on in then. The family is super excited to meet the TV star," Rodney said with a smile.

Taz shot a glance at Storm and noted he seemed to be taking everything in with interest. He wondered about Storm's family and reminded himself he needed to ask about his family and his upbringing.

"You ready for this?" he asked quietly.

Storm nodded and for some damned reason, he had a huge smile on his face.

"Are you kidding? I love family gatherings. We never had too many," he said. His blue eyes were sparkling and he actually looked very excited as he stepped right past Taz with Jules' hand in his, following Rodney and Tyson up the three steps to the house.

Taz marched right behind them, happy that Storm looked so happy and wondering whether he liked family gatherings because he had no siblings. Regardless, he was glad he'd decided to ask Storm and Jules to come along. When he walked into the house, his two brothers, Phillip and Thomas, and his sisters, Janelle and Erica, had joined his father in the front room. Jules and Storm were shaking hands and the room was buzzing with noise as they all introduced themselves at once. Taz was proud of the fact his family had closed ranks around Storm and made him feel welcome the minute he walked inside.

"Well, who do we have here?" his mother asked, coming out of the kitchen with a dish towel in her hands.

Taz walked over and kissed her cheek before turning to Storm. "Hi, Mama. This is Storm and his friend, Jules."

His mother turned her intelligent eyes up to him and grinned. "Hello, baby." She looked over at Storm and held out her hand. "Thank you for coming today, Storm. I know you must be very busy but we're tickled to have you. You too, Jules," she said, shaking Jules' hand as well.

"Thank you, ma'am," Storm said. "It's an honor to meet Taz's parents."

"You just come on out to the kitchen, Taz. Let the family get acquainted with Storm and his friend. I have a potato salad to finish up."

"Yes, Mama," Taz said. He knew better than to argue with his mother and he listened briefly to the cacophony of noise in the house while he followed her into the large kitchen. The room had been appointed with state of the art new appliances even though the house was very old and it smelled delicious as they walked through the swinging saloon doors to the back.

"Put this on, dear," his mother said, handing him an apron, "and peel those potatoes. Now be careful, they're hot."

"Yes, Mama," Taz said, picking up a steaming potato and a butter knife. He spun around to the sink, turned on the cold water, and began peeling it under the stream. Taz worked in silence for several minutes, knowing that his mother would broach the subject of Storm and his relationship with the star when she was ready.

"So, you and this Storm Ellison… you're serious?" she finally said, breaking the silence in the room.

Taz turned to look at her. He hadn't said anything about their relationship to either of his parents but then again, he didn't need to. They were both extremely bright individuals and he never brought men home when he came to visit, even though they always made him feel comfortable about doing so if he wanted to. "I think so, yes, Mama." He looked over at his mother who was slicing radishes for the potato salad.

She smiled. Beverly Grant was about fifty and had just begun to gray with white appearing here and there in her short hair. Taz had always thought both his parents were good-looking but she was exceptionally beautiful. She had kind silver eyes, the ones Taz had inherited, and he'd always felt fortunate about that. He could just as easily have gotten the brown eyes his siblings and his father had. Growing up, he'd always been the closest of all the kids to his mother and as a child, he'd attributed that to the fact they shared the recessive gene which gave them both their light eyes.

"That's good then. I know he must be a good man if you picked him. Your daddy and I have been waiting a long time for you to find a man good enough for you."

"He is a good man, Mama, despite what the tabloids say about him," Taz said. He watched the emotions play over her features.

"Well, that's good. I knew that of course. Those papers never get the whole story. We just want you to be happy, Taz," she said, seriously. "I know you know what you're getting yourself into here... but then, gay marriage is legal in California now."

"Mama, we've only known each other a short time. We haven't even talked about marriage. I don't even know if Storm wants marriage."

"Is the sex good?" she asked.

Taz stared at her with what could only be shock.

"Oh, come now, I know men, son. You are very physical creatures. If anyone understands how sex makes a bond between two people strong, it's me," she said with a smile.

"Mama, please..."

"Mama, please, nothin', Taz. Your father and I knew we were soul mates from the moment we first went to bed together. There's nothing like a good romp in the sack to put everything in perspective."

"Mama, please... the last thing I want to do is to hear about you and Pops in bed together," Taz said, finding his voice after swallowing his tongue moments before.

His mother put down her knife and walked over to where he was standing; she put a hand on his sleeve. Her eyes were sparking and a smile hinted at the corner of her lips. "Darlin' it's okay. Someday, I'd like to see you walk down the aisle with your daddy."

Taz nearly choked on his laughter. "I'm not a daughter, in case you haven't noticed," he said.

"Yeah, that part can be worked out later. The important thing is, we just want to see you happy like we are," she added.

"Okay, Mama," Taz said, putting down his own knife and hugging her petite form to himself.

"Okay, son. Now, let's get this salad thrown together and get out there and rescue Storm," she said with a laugh.

The thought of Storm needing rescuing from his family tickled Taz to no end and he had no idea why but the fact was, he was inexplicably happy for the first time in a long time.

****

The day turned into evening so quickly, Storm didn't want it to be over. Taz's family was wonderful. Storm felt so at home in his bodyguard's house, he didn't want to leave. He spent most of the afternoon in the backyard laughing his ass off as Taz, Phillip, Thomas, and Taz's father, Ben, poked fun at everything they possibly could. The family loved to laugh and they were very down to earth, something Storm hadn't known for what seemed like a long time. His world of late had revolved around Gucci, Manolo Blahnik, and Dolce & Gabbana. His world of fame and fortune wasn't the real world… this was, and they made him feel like he was a part of all of it. Spending time with Taz's family really made him think about where he came from. In addition, the urge to cut himself had been gone since Storm had begun seeing his gorgeous bodyguard and for the first time in a long time, he remembered who he really was and that he'd come from roots very similar to these. Storm's adoptive parents had been very much middle-class and he'd lived in a small tract house growing up. He only wished he'd known his birth mother and why she'd given him up.

On the way home, Storm turned on his cell phone and listened to the messages. He'd purposely kept it off and there were three from Alan Steinberg, one more frantic than the next. Apparently, Alan had set up a meeting to sign the final contracts for "Silver Bullets" in the morning and when Alan couldn't reach Storm, in the final message, Alan had nearly been in a panic. Storm quickly called Alan's phone and it rang and rang. He glanced across the car to Taz who was driving them home, thinking how unusual it was that Alan wasn't picking up after trying to reach him so many times. He made a mental note to call his house phone in the morning if he still hadn't heard from him. As it was, Alan had said they had an appointment at his office at noon with the executive producer and director of "Silver Bullets", GA Hauser, and Storm's lawyer. If Alan didn't turn up for that, Storm decided he'd begin to worry. He was excited to hear that the producer and director of the movie would be GA Hauser. She'd directed two other gay films, "Capital Games" and "Naked Dragon", both box office hits.

"What is it? You look worried," Taz said, glancing over at Storm from the driver's seat.

Storm reached across the console and took Taz's hand. "Nothing. Alan left me a few messages and now he's not picking up."

"Well, try him again in the morning," Taz said. "I have plans for you tonight." He waggled his eyebrows and Storm could see the unspoken promise in his pretty eyes. He turned to look in the back and noted Jules was fast asleep in the backseat. He glanced back at Taz and grinned.

"Yeah, promise?" he asked.

Taz reached down to his crotch and adjusted the large bulge there. "You better believe it. Good food always puts me in a sexy mood."

"I'll remember that, big boy," Storm said, squeezing his hand. If the truth be told, all he wanted to do was get his big gorgeous bodyguard home, get him naked, and climb him like a tree. He smiled when he thought about it.

"Uh-oh. Someone definitely has big plans," Taz said with a smile.

"Yeah, get us home, Taz."
****

When they got to Jules's apartment, Taz escorted her to the door while Storm waited in the car. He made sure she made it inside of the apartment's lobby, keeping an eye on Storm the whole time. He was honestly surprised they had dodged the paparazzi since the incident at Devon and Clive's house but he knew there was always the possibility they'd swoop in at any moment, so he remained vigilant. When he returned to the car, Storm was hanging up the phone.

"Who was that?" he asked, climbing into the driver's seat of the Land Rover.

"That was Devon, letting me know that Clive is responding to the medication they gave him. He was in almost total kidney failure when they got him to the hospital. The doctors thought he may be simply off his bi-polar meds but when they did blood tests to check his body chemistry, his kidneys were failing. They can't understand it but they are attributing it to the herbal meds he got from the Chinese store," Storm said, frowning. "They told him to throw away whatever he got from the store and never take it again. I'm just glad they figured out what it was and put an end to it. He'll be released in a couple of days. Devon says she's going to stay with him until he's stabilized. If things work out, she may even let him move back in but he would have to promise to stay on the medication he was on before he started taking the herbal stuff. Would it be okay if we went to visit, once they get home?" Storm's face was so innocent and open and there was no way Taz wanted to tell him no.

He realized, Storm's happiness was very important to him. He was becoming more and more attached to the superstar and for the moment, he decided he wasn't going to second guess anything. He was just going to let things play out and see how it went. "Of course, Storm. I really hope he stays on his meds. Those herbal medications seemed to have a really adverse affect on him." He was instantly suspicious but then he had never really liked Storm's guru to begin with. If the guy had been referring him to a store that sold tainted medication, Lord knew what else the man had his hands in. He made a mental note to check into him.

"Yeah, I don't understand it really," Storm added. "Guru says they'd be better for him."

"You put a lot of stock in what this guru guy says, don't you?" Taz asked. It bugged him that Storm was so trusting of the guy. He looked harmless enough but after they'd talked to Storm's business manager, Taz wondered how much of Guru Shamsa was honestly trustworthy. He glanced at the clock, noting the time. It would be 10:00 p.m. in Texas, but he decided before turning in with Storm that night, he'd make a phone call.

"I do trust Guru Shamsa. I had to trust someone. I think building his temple will give a lot of people a place to go for reflection and it will offer peace in a tranquil environment. The tranquility alone can be lifesaving. In addition, there are various outdoor areas for meditation and he surrounding hills are beautiful," Storm said, seriously. He looked a little put out by Taz's question. "I'm sure if there were issues with the contractor he hired, he didn't know anything about it."

"I'm not saying he knew anything about it. I just feel like… ah hell, I have no right to give you any advice, Storm," Taz said. He was suddenly feeling just slightly miserable about all of it. The truth was, he was a bodyguard to Storm, and no matter how else he'd been feeling about the star, he didn't want to make too much of it. Storm was his boss, they'd not confessed their deep love for each other, and he really had to stop thinking it could eventually be more. The truth was, Taz had been hopeful their relationship would grow

254

into something deeper but they'd only taken it to the level of fucking a short few days before and Taz was a cautious guy. He certainly didn't want to jump the gun and start thinking Storm should give his advice any credence… not after only a couple of sexual encounters. It was pretty easy to get along under the sheets; though Taz had had his share of sex, he hadn't had what some would call a deep and abiding relationship with a man, at least as an adult. In his mind, high school fumbling with an adolescent boyfriend didn't count as a relationship, and that had been his only real experience with a guy other than a one-night stand here and there.

"But, Taz, I want you to give me advice," Storm said emphatically. Taz could hear the sincerity in his voice and he knew Storm meant what he said. "I don't have too many people I can trust, Taz. I knew I could trust you from the minute I met you. Your advice and wisdom are very important to me. I appreciate it more than you know."

Taz glanced over to Storm, sitting in the passenger seat. He was so open, Taz knew he must honestly mean what he was saying. It was very hard to live up to other's expectations and he wanted to be able to do it. "I hope I can live up to that, Storm," he said.

Storm laced his fingers with his own as he looked over to him with a loving expression. It made his pretty blue eyes sparkle in the car. "I feel safe with you, Taz," he said, quietly. "The truth is, I've only had Jules to this point. With my parents gone… well… let's just say, I am trusting you with more than my safety."

Taz understood what he was saying. He was trusting Taz with his heart as well and that made him feel ten feet tall.

****

Storm excused himself to go upstairs and shower when they got back to the house while Taz went to make his call. He sat down at Storm's desk in the library and dialed Rome's number, knowing his friend would be able to find out the things he had to know.

"Taz?" Rome answered.

Taz glanced at the clock which read ten thirty. "Hey man, I hope I didn't wake you."

"No, I'm awake; what's up, buddy?"

"I need you to write down a couple of names. You have a pen?" Taz asked.

"Shoot."

"Okay, I need you to look into Guru Shamsa. He's Storm's yoga instructor but Storm has also invested a shitload of money in a construction project he's got going on here in Los Angeles. It looks like the contractor he hired may be shady and I want to find out if Storm's investing in a project that isn't completely aboveboard. The contractor took a larger than average up-front deposit and Storm's previous business manager may have been in cahoots with the builder. I want it checked out," Taz said.

"Storm, huh? Not Mr. Ellison? Let me guess. You made the one mistake a bodyguard should never make… you got involved with the guy," Rome said. He didn't sound angry. In fact, he sounded as though he'd known it was gonna happen. "You know how dangerous that can be. Have I taught you nothing?"

"Yeah, I got involved with him," Taz admitted. "Truth is, I'm not even gonna try and make excuses for it. I just let it happen. Oh, and thanks for the wine, by the way."

"Ha ha. Perfect." Rome chuckled. "Couldn't keep your hands off him after a couple glasses, huh?"

"Laugh your pretty ass off, Rome. That stuff's lethal."

Rome chucked some more. "Okay, so I'll check out this Guru guy. Anyone else? You said there were a couple names."

"Actually, two more. Alan Steinberg is Storm's agent. He's been pushing him like hell to hurry up and sign a movie deal and Storm's excited about it, but I overheard a conversation between him and a bookie. That, combined with the irregularities in the books which his new business manager found, make me wonder if Storm isn't getting ripped off big time."

"Okay, got it. And the third?" Rome asked.

"Brian McGee was Storm's business manager before he died of kidney failure. Storm told me he was a young man and he didn't realize he was sick. You know the rule when it comes to otherwise healthy young people dying," Taz said.

"Yeah, I do. Anytime someone buys it before their time, the cause should be checked out."

"Right," Taz said. "I was hoping you could get a hold of the coroner's report."

"I can do that, through Herman's office or a friend of mine in the LAPD," Rome said. "They've got connections in Los Angeles. Is that it?"

"For now. Thanks, Rome."

"You got it buddy. So, this Storm Ellison isn't what they say in the tabloids, huh? Not that there's any surprise there," Rome added.

"Yeah, he's surprisingly down to earth. In the beginning, he was a little…"

"Difficult?" Rome asked.

"They're always difficult, Rome, but now that I've gotten to know him, I think he's a genuine guy. The spotlight has his head screwed up in some ways… you know, the money comes easy and shit," Taz said.

"But aside from that, he's the real deal?"

Taz smiled to himself. "That's exactly right. Storm's the real deal."

"Well, I'm happy for you both. I hope he knows what a special guy he's getting," Rome said.

"Aw, stop crushing on me, Rome," Taz said with a grin.

"Hell no. I have two people to answer to if my eyes begin to wander, an FBI agent and a Marine," Rome laughed.

"Yeah, if you want to keep your twig and berries, I'd watch that," Taz joked. "Thanks again, Rome."

"You're welcome, man. I'm guessing time is of the essence?"

"Yes, thanks again." Taz swiped the phone, disconnecting the call. He had a man waiting on him and just anticipation of the night to come was making him hard. He stood up and headed out of the library toward the stairs. *Time to claim my man.*

CHAPTER FOURTEEN

Taz had barely walked into the bedroom when he noticed it was lit only with candles. It took a few seconds for his eyes to adjust before he realized Storm was lying naked on the bed. He had his erect cock in one hand and he was slowly stroking it. To say Storm looked utterly edible stretched out on the purple satin sheets was an understatement. He noted the bed had been freshly made up; there certainly hadn't been purple satin sheets on it when they'd woken up that morning and he wondered how much of it had to do with Rebecca walking into the bedroom and finding out Storm was no longer alone there. Taz feared the subsequent losing of the towel had given the maid the shock of her life but even at her sixty-some-odd years, the woman had been drooling when she'd walked out of the bedroom after the pancake incident. Storm smiled that killer Hollywood smile at Taz and he rolled to his side, patting the empty place on the bed beside him as he walked up. *God you're so damned beautiful. I bet you could have any man in the world in bed beside you, and you want me. I'm a fuckin' lucky ass dog!*

"Look at you, Storm," Taz said, ripping the shirt over his head as he walked up, tossing it onto the floor. *I have a habit of doing that when Storm's around.*

Storm crooked one finger and said, "I want you, my bad boy. Come here and show me how much you want me." He patted the bed, throwing Taz his most sultry look. Taz had seen that look before. The producers of Storm's television show had written in a character who was meant to be a gay love interest for Storm, and the two had carried on an onscreen affair in

259

the first two seasons of the show. They had terrific onscreen chemistry and many of Storm's rabid fans speculated it was a real life relationship. When the producers had written the character out of the show when contract negotiations with Storm's co-star broke down, the two onscreen stars had a tearful split in the last episode of the second season. That had been a year before, and when no new love interest had been written into the show for the entire third season, the producers had gotten more mail from viewers for Storm's character than for any of the other cast members for all the three seasons combined. *That however, is something for a later time. For now, the star is mine... and for this night, and as long as I can make this last, Storm will be mine.*

Taz walked to the side of the bed, watching Storm's face as he slowly undressed. As aroused as he felt, he wanted to savor every moment with the man he was falling so hard for. In his heart of hearts, he knew being with Storm in the long run just wasn't going to be possible. Too many people wanted and deserved a piece of the fabulously beautiful young star. Storm had talent as an actor and decency as a human being. He deserved so much more than what Taz could provide for him and the simple fact was, Taz had been considering the idea of them becoming involved on a deeper level, obstacles and all. He'd considered it for about thirty seconds; there was no way, he'd step in the path of Storm's success and no matter how one sliced it, he'd eventually get in the way. Right now, Storm's popularity was because he was a single, searching, ever bawdy playboy, who partied hard and fucked everything he could.

If his public learned… hell, if his fans learned, that he was involved with a mere bodyguard, they'd leave him high and dry. His public image, so carefully crafted by Alan Steinberg, was one of hedonism and loose morals. It made for better contracts, more money, and hell, even for the starring role in a feature length motion picture. So what if it was a gay film… so was Brokeback Mountain and the difference was, "Silver Bullets" had a happy ending. As soon as Taz had learned about the book, he'd bought it and devoured it in one sitting. Storm's role of Michael Francis was as though it had been written for him. Taz realized this movie character was perfect for Storm. He and the character Michael Francis both started out as selfish bastards and eventually came around, grew a soul, and became great men. Of course, it veered off from that scenario in one respect. Storm had always had a soul and had never been selfish. The people judging him had been soulless and blind to the beauty inside Storm.

I'm falling in love with him.

Taz shook the thoughts out of his head and climbed onto the bed naked. He was hard and ready for Storm. He'd loved fucking his young lover like he'd never been able to fuck a man before and he was anxious to bury himself deeply inside Storm's tight body. This night, they were going to do it his way. He grinned as he crawled up to Storm on his hands and knees. Storm smiled back and when Taz pushed at his shoulder, he lay flat, widening his legs for his lover to climb between. Taz was over him in a second, his gaze locked with Storm's licking his lips as he prepared to devour his gorgeous lover.

"I love your body," he said, running his hand down Storm's rib cage, stopping at his waist where he stroked onto his belly. Storm's muscles rippled and Taz smiled as he giggled.

"You're tickling me, Taz."

"I could touch you day and night. I love your skin," he growled, leaning down and kissing Storm's belly. His scent rose up from his pale skin and Taz once again marveled at the contrast between their skin color. *Cream for my coffee.* As he scooted down the bed, Storm's cock bobbed at the level of his face and once again his scent rose to tempt his senses. The head of Storm's cut cock wept with a droplet at the slit and Taz snaked out his tongue, capturing it, letting the flavor of his lover explode in his mouth. He reached up and grasped the thick length, drew it to his lips, and went down for the feast. Taz sucked the spongy head inside his mouth, lapping at the slit while he sucked it deeper into his mouth and Storm's answering groan was all he needed to encourage him further.

"Oh, yesssss," Storm hissed, grabbing the back of Taz's head with one hand and as Taz glanced up, he could see Storm's gaze focused on their connection. Storm bucked his hips off the bed and Taz firmed his hand on Storm's hip holding him down against the slippery sheets.

He pulled his mouth off of Storm's cock with a pop. "You like that, baby?"

"God, Taz, your mouth is magic. I never ever want to leave this bed. Can we just stay and die here in each other's arms?"

The question was unexpectedly sweet and a feeling of possession once again rolled through Taz and warmth bloomed in his belly like nothing he'd felt for a very long time. "You want me that bad, Storm?" he asked.

Storm's expression turned serious. "Do you believe in Karma, Taz?"

"I hadn't given it much thought, Storm," he said, letting go of Storm's cock and crawling up to him where he could pull him into his arms.

Storm snuggled into his embrace, laying his head on Taz's broader chest as he looked up at his face. His eyes were bright blue and he was the most beautiful person Taz had ever seen. "I believe in Karma, Taz," he said. "I believe when two people are meant to find each other, they will and I believe with all my heart, we were meant to be together. Do you believe that?"

Storm was laying his heart at Taz's feet and no man, even the boy he thought he'd loved in high school, even his last lover, Gregor, had ever done that before. The truth was, Taz had felt the connection between them since the first time he'd kissed Storm and then when he'd carried him up the stairs and spent the night with him, he'd only hoped what he was feeling was real. *This is real.*

"My mother told me that she knew my father was meant to be her love from the very first time she met him, Storm. If you'd have asked me a month or even a week ago, if I thought I could feel about anyone the way I feel about you, I would have said you are crazy. Now… I think I'm falling in love with you." He paused, gazing into Storm's beautiful eyes. The emotion was clear.

"I'm in love with you, Taz, and I never want this feeling to end," Storm said.

Taz looked at him for a second, the feeling of pure joy rushing through his veins as he felt a weight lift from his shoulders. He realized it must have been there for days, at least since he'd seen the love and caring Storm gave to everyone he held dear from Jules, to Rebecca, to Devon, to Clive and even to his precious little Butch. He knew for a certainty the man he loved was capable of loving others deeply and the knowledge that he was counted among those Storm loved was the most amazing feeling Taz had ever had in his entire life.

"I'm not a man of eloquent speech, Storm, but I want to show you how I feel as I make love to you," he whispered.

Storm's face lit with an expression of such devotion, it knocked him flat. "Make love to me, Taz," he said and then just as suddenly, he was kissing Taz and for a few precious minutes, Taz was lost in his beautiful lover, tasting the man he hoped he'd spend the rest of his life with. They kissed slowly, leisurely, safe in Storm's bed... reveling in what they'd found in each other's arms. When Storm finally pulled away from Taz's mouth, he said, "Can I ride you?"

Taz was a man of few words and if he'd been asked to speak, he couldn't have at that moment. Instead, he rolled off Storm and lay flat on his back as Storm leaned toward the bed table, pulling open the drawer where they'd stashed Taz's condoms the last time they'd been together. When Storm returned, he threw a leg over Taz, pulled a condom out of the package and ripped it open, reaching for Taz's hard cock, and rolling it on to the length of it.

Taz watched as Storm popped the lube open with a snick and drizzled a large amount over the condom, smearing it on with his hand before reaching behind his back where Taz knew from his expression he was preparing himself for their lovemaking. Storm groaned as Taz watched his mouth fall open when he began to pant. When several moments had passed, Storm looked down at Taz and locked his gaze with him. His light blue eyes had darkened with desire and Taz felt a wave of lust crash through his body. He wanted to get inside Storm and he wanted it now.

****

Storm had prepared himself as much as he could for Taz's cock. He'd never had a man of Taz's size before and until the night they'd made love, he hadn't any hope of them connecting in that manner. When he'd bottomed for Taz, the giant had been as gentle as a lamb, so sweet and careful so he wouldn't hurt Storm or damage his delicate tissues with his size. Taz was a man unlike any Storm had ever hoped to have and in truth, until he'd met Taz, a man's endowments meant little to him. A deep connection between him and his lovers was something Storm had always wanted but until his huge, beautiful bodyguard had come into his life, he'd never expected to ever find such a man to share his bed with. He'd certainly never dreamed of finding a man like Taz when Alan had insisted on hiring the massive, intimidating bodyguard.

"I'm ready, baby," he said, reaching behind himself and grasping Taz's dick, positioning the head at the entrance of his body.

"We'll go slow," Taz growled and Storm nodded, completely relaxed as he lowered himself onto the head of Taz's cock. The crown was wide and for just a second, Storm tensed as it stretched him, almost more than he thought he could bear. And then, slowly but surely, as Taz stilled beneath him, Storm was able to slide over the slick head until it was completely buried in his body. The burn was almost too much and he forced himself to concentrate and relax again, blowing out a long breath as he waited for the initial sting to abate.

"Take your time," Taz grunted.

Storm knew he was holding back. He loved him all the more for the gentleness he showed Storm as he eased himself farther down, down, until he was nearly sitting on Taz's thick thighs. He put both hands on Taz's thighs and pushed back up as Taz's large cock retreated from his body, only to hold himself steady at the head and then slide back down.

"That's it, babe. You can take me. You're so beautiful," Taz encouraged in his totally deep, completely male voice.

"You're so big, Taz," Storm gasped. The look in his lover's eyes encouraged him and he concentrated on his breathing, watching Taz's chest rise and fall, his pecs tight with the strain as he tried his best not to push Storm too hard. Taz grasped him by the waist and lifted him and again he slid nearly out, letting the thick head stay buried in his body before sliding back down all the way. A whimper escaped his lips and Taz leaned up as he buried himself, taking Storm's lips in a desperate kiss. *My God, I dearly love this man.*

"You're so tight, my love," Taz breathed as their kiss ended. Storm felt his body ripple around Taz's cock and the pressure of being filled as he never had before, nearly undid him then and there. "I want you to come all over my cock, Storm," Taz encouraged. "That's it… ahh…" he sighed. His hands lifted Storm up and nearly off again and Storm felt beautiful in his arms. He sank back down, moving more quickly as his body accommodated Taz. They rocked together and Storm felt his orgasm begin. When Taz scraped past his prostate, it was all Storm could stand. He cried out as his climax hit and Taz reached for his cock closing his fist around it as it began to spurt. Come shot out of the slit and over Taz's chest and abs, coating them with spunk as he stroked.

"Ah… ah… ah!" Storm cried out as he felt a throbbing deep inside and as his climax continued, Taz gasped out his own.

"Storm!" he cried, and Storm felt Taz's fingers tighten on his hips almost painfully. He held Storm tight against his body and as Storm calmed, Taz blew out a breath, throbbing once again buried deep up inside his body. "My God, Storm," he groaned, pulling him down.

Their lips touched again and Storm sighed into his mouth as Taz's tongue stroked languidly across his own in a sweet, soft kiss. His lips were Heaven sent and soft as a feather. They kissed that way for several minutes until Taz's cock slipped from Storm's body. Storm sighed, kissed his lover once more for good measure, and rolled off to the side, immediately reaching for tissues and handing them to Taz so he could deal with the condom. Taz looked up and he smiled at Storm, holding out his arms. Storm scrambled back to him and laid his head against his chest feeling as perfectly at home as any place he'd ever been in his life.

"I still love you," Taz said. His low, soft voice was like a warm welcome purr in Storm's ears.

Storm chuckled. "Good to know you didn't stop loving me after you came." He glanced up, searching for Taz's silver eyes in the darkened room.

"You know, I carry a gun," Taz said, grinning.

Storm laughed, running his hand over Taz's beautiful muscled chest. Tiny whirls of curly dark hair nestled in the crease between them. "No, actually you carry two," he said, running his hand down the washboard abs to the flaccid beauty between his legs. Taz's low chuckle filled the room as Storm's head rose and fell on his chest. "I'll never tire of this… of you," Storm said, quietly.

Taz leaned over and kissed the top of his head and then Storm lifted his face to Taz's and he was kissed again and again while Taz rubbed his back. After several sweet minutes, Taz pulled away, laying his head back on the pillow and pulling Storm close with both arms around him. As Storm drifted off to the soft huffs of Taz breathing, he thanked his lucky stars for bringing the gentle giant into his life, knowing he'd found happiness beyond measure.

****

Taz and Storm woke up in each other's arms. After Taz kissed his beautiful lover on the top of his head, he rolled over in the bed, sat up, and swung his long legs over the side. Taz felt Storm's hand on his back as it stroked down to his hip and he turned around, looking at him. His spiky blond hair was sticking up all over the place and he looked soft, warm, and well fucked lying in the bed. Taz smiled as the thought struck him.

"What are you going to do, today?" Storm asked, sitting up and stretching. He looked edible and Taz had to reach down and tame his cock as he started to get hard. He had no time to waste. He knew Storm had an appointment with Alan and the producer of the movie today and he really wanted to talk to Rome beforehand. If Alan Steinberg had anything to do with the irregularities the accountant Anthony had found, Taz wanted to know about them. Now that he was invested in Storm's future, he wanted to make certain his lover wasn't railroaded into a contract that wasn't beneficial to him and if Alan had a gambling problem, he wanted to let the man know Storm was aware of it and he'd be scrutinizing the contract.

"I have a call to make. Last night, I asked my friend Rome to look into your guru's contractor," he said without apology. "If Guru Shamsa knew about the contractor, assuming he's crooked, well…"

"You just want to protect me," Storm said.

He looked very vulnerable and sweet and Taz wanted to rip the heart out of anyone who'd hurt him. He'd felt the same way when he'd seen the families who were devastated by the war during his time in the Middle East while in the Marines. No way did he want Storm taken advantage of… at least not any more than he already had been. "That's right. You're mine now and I take care of what's mine."

Storm whipped off the sheet and crawled over to Taz, taking him around the neck as he blanketed his back. He kissed his lips and then touched his forehead with his own. "That's only one thing I love about you, Taz. You take care of me, body and soul."

Taz's heart soared and he smiled before kissing Storm on the lips, lingering just a little longer than he'd planned but every second he spent with Storm got better and better. "I love you too, babe." He pulled away and stood up as he felt Storm's eyes follow him into the bathroom. He hadn't showered the night before and he was feeling especially grimy after their sweaty lovemaking.

As he closed the door, he heard Storm's phone ring. A few minutes later, he walked out of the bathroom only to find Storm sitting on the side of the bed with tears running down his face. When he looked up at Taz, he rushed over and sat beside him, pulling him into an embrace. "What happened? Who was on the phone, Storm?"

"It was Marjorie Steinberg, Alan's wife," Storm sobbed. "Alan died yesterday. She said he collapsed while they were at a friend's house playing cards and by the time the paramedics got there, he was gone. They tried to revive him all the way to the hospital but the doctors told Marjorie that he suffered a massive myocardial infarction," he said against his chest.

"A heart attack?" Taz asked.

"Is that what that means?" Storm asked, pulling away and blinking his red-rimmed eyes up at Taz. He was clinging to Taz's hands and staring into his face, looking devastated.

"Yes, honey," Taz said, pulling him back into his arms again and rocking him as he sobbed against his chest.

"He was only fifty," Storm said. "He was healthy, Marjorie said. He always ate salads when we went out to eat, well... salads and a burger."

Taz realized that meant a lot to Storm. He knew Storm was not a meat eater, and rarely ate anything but salads. His lover was very tenderhearted and Taz's heart went out to him.

"I know, sweetie. For now though, you need to pull yourself together. Do you still have to get up? I mean, I would suggest you rest, unless..."

"My meeting is cancelled, obviously. Marjorie was crying so hard that I could barely get anything out of her but she said she had Alan's secretary cancel all his appointments," Storm said, sniffling. "I guess that means the contract for the new movie won't be finalized. Hell, without Alan, I wouldn't even have that contract. They may just back out completely at this point."

Taz petted Storm's spiky hair, looking into his eyes. His heart went out to him. Not only did he just lose a man he called friend, but if it turned out that Alan had been embezzling somehow to feed his gambling addiction, it would kill Storm. In addition, the movie roll he'd really been excited about might be a thing of the past as well. He leaned in and kissed Storm softly. "Why don't you lie down, Storm. I'll have Rebecca bring you some breakfast."

"I can't eat anything, Taz. My stomach is just sick," Storm said miserably.

"Some tea? I'll have her make some chamomile tea. That should help you go back to sleep," Taz offered.

Storm looked at him again, blinking his lashes over the red-rimmed eyes. He looked exhausted even though they'd only just started their day. "Okay, tea," he sighed, lying back down and snuggling into the pillow, closing his eyes.

Taz got up from the bed, took the wet towel he'd dropped when he'd seen Storm crying, and hurriedly dressed. He wanted to get a hold of Rome now even more than ever. Storm was sleeping when he walked back into the bedroom after shaving. He adjusted the cuffs on his white sleeves, buttoning them, though he knew they probably wouldn't be going anywhere today. He walked over to the bed and looked down at Storm who was lying on his side with the pillow scrunched up under his head, another in his arms. He looked angelic and Taz could understand why all of America wanted him. His fan club had been growing with every season of the show's three seasons and now that he had a movie deal in his immediate future, Taz knew even more demands would be made on the man he loved.

He marveled at how quickly he'd grown to love Storm. Though he'd thought him a spoiled slutty brat when he'd first met him, now Taz believed all that behavior was a result of his insecurities. He wondered again at Storm's ancestry. He knew that his mother had given him up for adoption but that's all Storm really knew about her. He wondered if he could ask Rome for one more favor. He reached down and picked up the smartphone on the bed table, turning and walking away from Storm and quickly out the door. Taz walked to the edge of the staircase, holding the phone. He wanted to be far enough away from the bedroom that he wouldn't wake Storm up when he called Rome. Besides, he had no pen to write things down. He headed down the curving stairs and as he got to the bottom, he caught sight of Rebecca. She was standing in the living room having an animated conversation in broken English with whomever was on the end of the line. When he heard his name, he stopped and stared at her.

"I mean, Loueeesa, Meester Taz… he was a beeg… he was a beeg beeg man." The maid had the telephone receiver between her cheek and her shoulder and the palms of both hands were held about twelve inches apart while she animatedly described what could only be his own anatomy. Embarrassment flooded his veins and then when she looked up, her mouth flew open and the phone fell from her head and clanged onto the marble floor.

"Hello? Hello?" Whoever was on the other end of the line had been left hanging… literally. Rebecca stared at him as he stood with his hands on his hips and then she began smiling from ear to ear.

"Oh good morning, Meester Taz!"

"Yeah, yeah, howdy," Taz said, without humor. "When you have the time, please bring Storm some chamomile tea, Rebecca." He turned without another word and walked toward the library, shaking his head and wondering if he'd ever live his reputation down now. Pretty soon, all of the female maid community would know Storm's lover was well endowed… no, scratch that… by the time Rebecca got finished with the telling, Taz's dick would be touching the ground while he stood. He started dialing Rome's number as he entered the library and as it rang, he sat behind the desk. Rome picked up after two rings.

"Hey, I was just going to call you, Taz," his friend said.

"Yeah, well, good morning to you, Rome. You found out some things?" Taz could feel his breathing speed up when he heard the tone of Rome's voice.

"I did. First off, I checked on Storm's manager, Alan Steinberg. You were right. He's a regular at Los Alamitos Race Track, Hollywood Park, and the Bicycle Club Casino in Commerce. Herman's source at the casino say he's a heavy better but he does win half the time. My friend Rowley, an old SEAL buddy, has a brother who's a bookie in town and it seems Steinberg has been playing the ponies for years."

"And, does he win?" Taz asked.

"Most of the time, though lately, his bets have been getting heavier and heavier and he's currently down about thirty large. The bookie says people round town are getting nervous about extending him more credit. They aren't into leg breaking but…"

"Yeah, I know he's your friend, Rome, but we both know they're all into leg breaking when the times call for it," Taz finished for him. "But, as an aside to that, Storm got a call from Steinberg's widow this morning. It seems Alan Steinberg died of a massive heart attack yesterday," Taz said. "He just keeled over in the middle of a card game at a friend's home and he was dead before they even made it to the hospital.

"Oh, wow… well, there goes that problem, Taz," Rome said.

"Yeah, I guess."

"Okay, next, there's Brian McGee, Storm's ex-manager. Thanks to my friend Cassidy Ryan, who's a detective with the LAPD and is close friends with the coroner Linda Hastings, I was able to get a verbal on his cause of death from her autopsy," Rome said.

"And?" Taz asked.

"And it seems Mr. McGee did die of kidney failure but the coroner found lethal doses of an herbal supplement in his system. She's ruled his death 'suspicious in nature'. My guess is that means that she'll be doing further tests but at this point, he took something that fucked his chemistry up and caused his kidneys to fail."

"Wow, that's telling," Taz said, thinking instantly of Clive, Storm's friend.

"How so?"

"Storm's guru, this Shamsa character, recommended a Chinese herbalist to Storm's friend Clive, who's a psychiatric patient. He was rushed to the hospital in total kidney failure after taking the herbs. Storm says he nearly died. At first, his wife thought he'd gone off his prescribed meds and become depressed when the herbs didn't do what they were supposed to do. After hearing this, it sounds like he was poisoned," Taz said.

"That's too bad, Taz," Rome said. "And that brings me to the last thing."

Taz knew there was more bad news coming. "Let's have it."

"From what I can determine, this Guru Shamsa is a fraud from the top of his head to the tip of his toes. His real name is Leonard Melkowitz and he's got at least twenty aliases that I could find. His current gig, as Guru Shamsa, has been going on about two years as far as I can tell. He's got a foot long list of people suing him. I mean, there must be fifteen names on this thing... everything from individuals to corporations, it's a clusterfuck. In addition, he has a financial interest in guess what? A Chinese Herbal pharmacy. It seems the pharmacy has come under some scrutiny because some of the patients have been making complaints against them after becoming sick from medicines purchased there. Please tell me Storm hasn't invested his life savings with this character."

"Honestly, I have no idea," Taz added, feeling a stone in the pit of his stomach.

"At this point," Rome continued. "It looks like his contractor, A&M Contracting, is being investigated as well. I have some friends down here that own a contracting company and they say A&M is really bad news. No one's given them business in almost a year which may explain why they took such a big payment from Storm's business manager. That may also mean that Brian McGee was in on it or worse yet, judging by the way he suddenly died from kidney failure, maybe he found out about A&M's practices, made a stink with them, and then became expendable. No matter how you slice it, it all points back to Guru Shamsa, his contractor buddies, tainted herbal medications, and a dead body. That's not good," Rome said.

Taz knew exactly what Rome was saying. If Brian died of kidney failure when he was a relatively young and healthy man, it was too much of a coincidence that it had happened right around the time he would have given out large deposits to A&M.

Perhaps he'd gotten greedy and demanded more than he'd been promised by the desperate contractor. Brian dying might have allowed A&M to siphon off more money for the building project without Storm becoming aware of it. Add to it Clive's mysterious illness because of the Chinese herbal medicines which came from a shop Guru Shamsa aka Leonard Melkowitz, recommended, and there was no doubt in Taz's mind that the guru was a lying sack of shit who was ripping Storm off. Taz wasn't going to let it go any further.

"Rome, thanks man. I think you've saved my life and I definitely know you saved Storm's. I don't know how to thank you enough," Taz said.

"You really care about him, don't you, Taz?"

"I love him, Rome, plain and simple. I'd die for him," Taz said with conviction.

"You take the information I gave you, and don't do any dyin' for anyone, you hear me?" Rome's voice sounded as serious as Taz could remember. He was so relieved he'd made the call.

"Yeah, buddy, thank you. I owe you one." Taz swiped the phone and sat back in the chair, rage welling up in his gut as he thought of all the people the guru had hurt and perhaps even killed.

As soon as he finished telling Storm—*he's gonna be devastated*—Taz was going to rip Leonard Melkowitz's fucking head off. *No one hurts my man and gets away with it.* He stood up from the desk chair, knowing he needed to wake up Storm and tell him everything he'd learned. In addition, he was going to have to beef up security around the mansion big-time. He decided he would give Ranger Corrigan a call as soon as he was done talking with Storm. If nothing else, the addition of another solid bodyguard, and a man he could trust, would be a good start.

CHAPTER FIFTEEN

Taz walked out of the library, both anxious and worried about sharing his newfound knowledge of Leonard Melkowitz with Storm. He knew his lover wasn't going to like the news that his trusted Guru Shamsa was a total fraud, and a dangerous one at that. When he heard Storm's raised voice and Butch's barking coming from the kitchen, he immediately went in that direction. He walked into the kitchen to find a very stricken looking Rebecca standing with Storm over Butch's food bowl. They both turned to look at him as he walked into the kitchen.

"What's up?" Taz asked.

"Meester Storm… he mad because I give Butchy-Boy bad food. I no know it bad food. Meester Goo say it good food," the maid said. Her eyes were filled with tears as she stood holding a bag of dog food. Taz had seen it in the refrigerator marked with Butch's name.

"I'm not mad, Rebecca. I just don't want Butch eating that old food. I don't care who gave it to you. That could have been what made him sick," Storm explained to the frantic woman.

Taz walked over and took the food from Rebecca's hand. "You said Guru Shamsa gave you this food for the dog, Rebecca?"

"Si… si, Meester Taz. Meester Goo, he give eet to me for the leetle doggie."

"Don't you think it's a good idea if we don't give Butch any food that he had before?" Storm asked Taz.

Taz reached out and patted Storm on the shoulder. "Definitely not. As a matter of fact, I have to talk to you about the guru," he said. Taz turned to Rebecca. "I don't think you meant to hurt Butch, Rebecca. Why don't you make him some chicken or something?"

"Si… si, I make cheeken for the leetle doggie," she added quickly.

Storm looked up at Taz. "What's going on?" he asked, looking seriously confused. His poor eyes were still red-rimmed from crying earlier.

"Grab your tea and let's go sit down in the living room, Storm. I just got off the phone with my friend Rome."

Storm picked up the steaming cup of tea from the counter and followed Taz out of the kitchen and into the large two-story high living room. They sat down on the comfortable couches and Storm sipped his tea while Taz told him about the conversation he'd had with Rome. When he was done, Storm was crying again and sitting in total shock, staring at him with such a pathetic look, he wanted to hurt someone really bad… preferably Leonard Melkowitz.

"I can't believe it, Taz. Leonard Melkowitz? That's Guru Shamsa's real name?"

"Yes, and he's a really bad cookie," Taz said, frowning.

Storm seemed to gather himself up, squelching down his emotions as he put on a determined expression. "I'm going to call him right now, Taz. I'm going to tell that son of a bitch that I am pulling out of the project right now, having my lawyer to draw up paperwork to sue his ass and that of A&M

Construction, and if I find out he's responsible for killing Brian McGee and hurting Clive and my little Butch, I'm going to spend every penny I have to see him brought to justice."

"Honey, you won't have to spend any money to do that. If the man is guilty of poisoning your business manager and your friend and your dog, he'll go to jail for murder among other things," Taz said.

"I certainly hope so, Taz," Storm added, standing up. "Come here." Storm walked into Taz's outstretched arms, hugging him tightly before pulling away and removing the phone from his pajama bottom's pocket. Storm wore only his drawstring PJs and a wifebeater T-shirt. The silver nipple rings were visible beneath the soft, thin fabric and once again Taz was stunned by how gorgeous his lover was.

Storm began punching numbers as he walked away while Taz pulled his own phone out of his pants. He called Ranger and explained that he wanted him for additional security. When Ranger told him his car was in the shop, Taz offered to send David with the limo to pick him up.

"No thanks, man. I'll take a cab. My neighborhood ain't limo country," Ranger growled. Taz had always liked the gruff man whom he'd worked security with.

"You know what? Just text me your address, and I'll be by to pick you up in fifteen minutes," Taz said.

"Make it thirty, and you've got a deal," Ranger barked.

Taz chuckled. "You got it."

He hung up the phone and walked back into the living room from the backyard where he'd wandered while on the phone. Storm was blue in the face and fuming. He wasn't on the phone but Taz could guess that he'd just hung up. He couldn't remember ever seeing Storm so livid.

"What's wrong, Storm?" he said, walking up.

"Do you believe, that son of a bitch denied the whole thing? He denied cheating me out of money for the temple. He actually wanted me to come down to the temple building site and meet with his contractor so we could all talk together," Storm spit.

Okay, yeah, he's pissed. "Storm, look, honey. I have to go pick up my friend Ranger. He lives only fifteen minutes away. I'll be back in thirty minutes. I'm going to lock up the house. I don't want you to let anyone inside while I'm gone. No one. That goes for the contractor, or Anthony, or the paperboy, or for God's sakes, that Melkowitz character. Do you understand? I will be right back," Taz said.

Storm batted his pretty eyelashes as he looked up at him with bright blue eyes. "I promise. I'll be careful. I won't let anyone in, Taz," Storm said.

Taz reached out and pulled him in for a hard kiss, hugging him so tightly he squeaked. He let go and went to the front door. He looked back at Storm who looked worried yet determined as he closed the door behind him. Once he did, Taz listened as Storm armed the security alarm from the inside. Convinced Storm was safe and that he would heed his warnings, Taz got into the Land Rover and checked the dashboard clock. Taz told himself he had thirty minutes to make it to Ranger's house and back and he knew he'd sweat the entire time he was away from Storm, but rather than wait for Ranger to get a cab, he decided to pick him up himself. The faster he had increased security, the better he'd feel. He wasn't taking any chances with Storm's life.

****

Storm was angrily pacing in the front room fifteen minutes later. The more he thought about all the horrible things Guru Shamsa... correction... Leonard Melkowitz had done, the angrier he got. He couldn't stop beating himself up for how stupid and naive he'd been in believing in the fraud to begin with. As he thought of poor Clive lying on that gurney and being wheeled into the ambulance after he'd taken the herbal medicine Guru Shamsa had recommended he take, Storm wanted to start crying all over again. When he thought of poor Brian McGee, dead of kidney failure, or his poor dear, sweet, innocent little Butch, the victim of the same fiend, he wanted to pick up the priceless crystal vase in the foyer and hurl it across the room, smashing it into a billion tiny shards.

About fifteen minutes after Taz left, Storm heard the key in the front door and thinking Taz had made it in record time, he looked up, unconcerned. When he saw Jules come through the front door, he relaxed and smiled at her. He'd completely forgotten she had a key to his house. She came breezing into the house, bubbly as ever with a huge grin on her face. As she turned and began disarming the security alarm's keypad, his heart sank. Right behind her, dressed in long flowing saffron colored robes was none other than the bastard himself.

"Look who I found on the driveway," Jules said, unaware of anything that had transpired in the numerous phone calls that morning.

"Hello, Storm," Leonard said. The look on his face stopped Storm's pacing and a cold chill shivered up his spine.

"Jules get away from him," he cried out as his former guru slammed the door behind him. Storm took two steps toward them as Jules stopped and stared at him in surprise. Of course she couldn't have known of the danger she'd unwittingly just exposed them to.

"What's going on?" she said, looking terrified as she glanced behind her and off to the side where the man stood.

Storm rushed forward and grabbed her arm, pulling her toward him as the guru confronted them both.

"Step back, bitch. This is between me and the superstar," Leonard hissed.

At that moment, Rebecca walked into the living room and Storm knew she must have heard the commotion; she leaned down to grab Butch who was padding behind her. Storm took that moment to act and he pulled Jules behind him.

"Stay right there, Rebecca," he called out, holding out a hand to stop her as Leonard reached into his robe and pulled out a plastic squeeze bottle of a yellowish liquid. Rebecca stopped in her tracks as Butch began barking like crazy. Jules shrieked as he pointed it at Storm and began dousing him with it. The pungent scent of gasoline filled Storm's senses as his world turned upside down. "Get back, Jules!" he cried out, turning just in time to see her step out of the range of the squirt bottle. He was ever so grateful she was out of the way as Leonard began squirting the liquid over his own bald head. It ran down his face in rivulets as he cackled gleefully. *He's lost his fucking mind.*

No sooner had he thought it, than he saw him throw the bottle aside. They were both dripping in the foul liquid as the man reached back into his robes, pulling out a Zippo lighter, and began shouting.

"You think I have anything to live for after you've destroyed my dream, bitch?" he screamed. His eyes were wide and maniacal and for the first time, Storm felt very real fear creep up his spine.

"This isn't going to solve anything, Leonard," he heard himself saying, shakily. His own words sounded hollow and filled with trepidation. *I'm about to burst into a tower of flame in front of Jules and she will never be able to live with herself.*

"Yes it is. It's going to kill me and hopefully it's going to kill you," Leonard screamed. "If nothing else, it's going to burn that beautiful body and face of yours so that no one will ever want to look at you again!" He held the lighter out in front of his body as his thumb flicked open the metal top with a scraping sound. He shook the lighter in front of his body. "Do you know how badly I wanted you? The superstar!" he spit with hatred. "The bad gay boy who thought he was better than everyone? The skanky bitch who got his rocks off with everyone he ever met? I can't wait to see you burn!" he screamed, shaking the lighter.

"Leonard, don't do this," Storm pleaded, somehow knowing that the man had taken total leave of his senses. "Let's sit down and talk about this like men."

"Don't call me that! I am not Leonard Melkowitz anymore. I am Guru Shamsa, a respected member of society! If it hadn't been for that bastard bodyguard of yours, nosing around in my business, I would still be the man I've made myself out to be… respected, beloved by all… I could have been your man!"

"You wanted me?" Storm asked, shocked to his very bones. He hadn't even known the man was interested in him, hell, he hadn't even known the guru was gay but he was smart enough to know that if he kept the guru talking long enough for Taz and his friend to return, there'd be a chance he could live through this without Jules and Rebecca being scarred for life.

"Yes, I wanted you! Every time I saw you in your yoga shorts, I wanted to tackle you to the mat and take you the way a real man would take you, not like those pretty boys you fuck. I would make you forget any man but me!" he shrieked.

"You never told me you wanted me, Leonard…" Storm realized he made the mistake of using the man's name the second he said it.

"I told you never to call me that!" the pseudo-yogi screamed, shaking the lighter again.

As if in slow motion, Storm watched the man's thumb scrape over the metal wheel. As it sparked, he closed his eyes and sent up a silent prayer, picturing Taz's beautiful face in his mind. *I'll always love you, baby.*

****

"Son of a motherfucking bitch!" Taz shouted as he pulled the Land Rover up to the gate. Leonard

Melkowitz's car was parked right behind Jules's in the driveway. She must have let him in through the gate.

"What is it?" Ranger growled from the passenger seat beside him. "Is he here?"

Taz had filled in his good friend on all the happenings since the last time they'd seen each other at the Emmy Awards and Ranger had been shocked to learn that Taz and Storm had fallen in love with each other.

"That's Leonard Melkowitz's car parked behind Jules's car! That's Storm's friend I told you about. She must have let him in. We didn't even have time to tell her what was going on, dammit! Storm could be dead even now," he said, frantically punching in the gate code and watching the iron gates ever so slowly open.

Not wanting to wait, he jumped from the vehicle, reaching into his jacket, taking hold of his service weapon as he ran toward the house. He heard Ranger right behind him and he was ever so grateful he'd made sure to tell his friend to bring along his gun with an extra clip. They got to the front door to discover it had cracked open from the high winds on the blustery day. Taz had always hated the Santa Ana winds that plagued southern California firefighters every year but today he could have kissed Mother Nature. The open door would give them the element of surprise as they entered the mansion. When he pushed open the door, the strong smell of gasoline hit his nostrils.

God dammit!

Taz took in the sight of Storm doused in gasoline standing in the foyer of the large house and his heart sank as he recognized the guru in yellow robes, standing right in front of him, also doused in the foul liquid. The lighter he held in his hand and his thumb on the wheel gave him the fright of his life. He knew the next seconds would prove to be the most challenging of his life. He couldn't rescue Storm and Leonard at the same time. The room was filled with flammable, noxious fumes meaning he had to get Storm as far away from the fiend as possible if he ignited the lighter or drop him where he stood; he took a chance.

"Leonard!" he screamed at the top of his lungs.

"I got Storm!" Ranger shouted from beside him and as the guru turned to see the commotion at the front door, Taz's friend streaked by him, leaping at Storm and tackling him to the ground where they went sliding on the marble floor out of the puddle of gasoline just as the guru managed to spin the metal wheel on the Zippo. Taz raised his gun but before he could even get off a shot, the yogi was engulfed in flames. The scent of burning flesh and black smoke filled the room and Taz frantically tried to see through it to where Ranger had Storm's body blanketed with his own. Leonard's bloodcurdling screams filled the air while Taz rushed around the ball of flame, his heart in his throat when he reached his lover's side. Ranger was cussing like a sailor as he rolled off Storm and Storm was crying when he spotted Taz.

Taz instantly reached down and grabbed a hold of Storm's shirt, yanking him farther away from the screaming human ball of flames. Ranger scrambled on hands and knees as he followed right behind them, and Taz only stopped dragging Storm when they were twenty-five feet away from the dying man.

The three men fell in a dog pile and turned back to see that what was left of Leonard had crumpled into a ball of black smoke and orange flame in the middle of the foyer where Storm had been standing only seconds before. It was only then that Taz registered Butch's frantic barking and heard Rebecca and Jules screaming. He noted them running toward the three and when they reached them, Jules dropped to her hands and knees beside Storm.

"Storm! Storm!" Jules cried out, reaching for them. She would have pulled Storm's gasoline covered body into a hug if Taz hadn't had such a desperate grip on the man he loved.

"I'm okay, Jules. Taz saved me," Storm squeaked.

As Taz's senses returned, he looked down at the man he loved. Storm had reached out a hand and was squeezing Jules's with a death grip. When his beautiful blue eyes looked up at Taz, the love mirrored in the depths was incomprehensible to him. They stared at each other for a second and Taz leaned down ever so slowly, and took Storm's lips in a desperate kiss.

I love you. I'd die for you. And at that moment, he knew he would.

EPILOGUE

SIX MONTHS LATER
WESTBURG, TEXAS

"And… that's a wrap!" GA Hauser, the producer and director for "Silver Bullets", Storm's movie debut, stood up from the director's chair where she'd been watching the last scene they'd filmed through a huge camera lens. "You did great, Storm," the tiny woman said, walking up to him and Laredo Stevens, the man playing his costar in the role of Tyler Winston. The tall native Texan was dressed as a cop, muscles bulging from his arms though the sexy black uniform he wore. Storm was dressed in tight jeans and a western style shirt to look like his character, Michael Francis, world famous super model.

"You think so, Ms. Hauser?" Storm asked, smiling. He'd come to love the tiny long-haired woman who wore her hair in a bun tucked into a baseball hat. Her director's credentials in a protective plastic covering were pinned to her belt.

"You and Laredo were spectacular. That love scene is going to make you famous, Storm," she said, laughing.

Storm lit up with happiness. The six weeks they'd spent on the set in the blistering hot Texas sun had been worth every minute and with Taz waiting for him on the sidelines, he had never been happier in his life. He glanced over to see his fiancé standing and watching them along with the rest of the crew as they milled around carrying sound equipment and ladders, readying the next and final scene for shooting.

"I'm sure glad you thought so," Storm said, breathing out a long breath in relief. Shooting a movie had proven to be much more work than Storm had ever believed. Twenty hour days, seven days a week, when you counted three hours in the makeup chair, had begun to tax even his young body. All he wanted to do was wrap up the last scene which was scheduled to be filmed the following day, and go home to Malibu where he could rest. Taz had been with him every step of the way and he'd never felt so grateful in his entire life.

"I am telling you, this movie is going to be a hit, Storm. You and Laredo are magnificent together. I can't remember seeing so much chemistry between costars."

Storm grinned. "Well, it really helps when you give such fantastic direction," he said.

The small woman laughed, patting Storm on the shoulder. "You are too kind, Storm... Okay, we're done for the day. I can see a very patient man waiting for you in the wings," she said, cocking her head at Taz who stood some twenty feet away. "See you bright and early."

"Yes, thank you, ma'am," Storm said.

She waved him off and he nodded to Laredo before walking over to Taz. His beautiful lover lifted the tape which roped off the onlookers from the actors on the set and Storm ducked under it. When he straightened, Taz had his arms out and he walked right into them. Only a second passed before his lips were taken in a desperate kiss. *This never fucking gets old.* After two whole minutes in Taz's arms, someone yelled, "Get a room!"

They separated, laughing, and Taz slung his long arm around Storm's neck and began walking them off toward the trailer where they'd been staying in the cramped double bed for the last three weeks. For one person, the bed would have been perfect, but every morning they'd woken up Taz's legs had been hanging out of the bunk. Storm usually ended up laughing his ass off before breakfast.

"Hey, I'm starving. Let's eat before I change," Storm said, nodding toward the mess tent.

"There's plenty of time for sustenance, Storm. I have a surprise that can't wait," Taz said, looking down at him.

Storm looked up as they walked and he could see the look of mischief in his lover's eyes. "What is it? Oh, is it that letter you got this morning?" He was bouncing on the balls of his feet.

"Yeah, come on. I've been waiting for this."

Storm acquiesced and he let Taz unlock the door to their trailer. They stepped inside and Taz walked over to the counter and picked up the envelope as Storm climbed onto the bed, kicking off the cowboy boots while he watched Taz pull out some papers and unfold them. He sat down beside Storm looking like the cat that ate the canary.

"What is it?" Storm asked, taking the papers Taz held out.

"Remember how you told me you wished you knew your birth name so that when we get married in the spring, it would be all legal?" Taz asked.

"Yeah," Storm said, feeling his heart begin to pound. His birth mother had never passed along his real name to The Children's Home Society when she'd given him up for adoption. "You found it?" He started scanning the paperwork which seemed to be his birth certificate until he found the name. When he did, he looked up at Taz who was grinning from ear to ear. "Sebastian Meyers?"

"Yes, Storm, that's you. Sebastian Meyers. What do you think?"

Storm burst out laughing and as Taz's expression screwed into a puzzle, he laughed even harder. "Sebastian?"

"Yeah, what's wrong with that?" Taz asked.

Storm laughed even harder until his sides began to ache. Finally, he gasped, "That means we are Balthazar and Sebastian. We sound like fucking vampires!" Storm collapsed in giggles as Taz finally seemed to get it because he burst into laughter as well.

"Sebastian and Balthazar Grant," he gasped. "Yeah, that's rich!" Taz roared.

They must have laughed for two or three minutes, breaking only for kisses and sexy groping when there was a rap on the door of the trailer.

"Who is it?" Storm called out, irritated by the interruption.

"It's mee, Meester Storm!" Rebecca said through the door.

"Oh my God, that woman has the shittiest timing, Storm," Taz growled. His hand was on Storm's dick, slowly stroking it through his western style jeans. "You had to bring her along, didn't you?"

"Meester Storm! I have a deener for ju!" she yelled through the door.

"What was I supposed to do? She said she has relatives in Texas," Storm smirked.

"Meester Storm! I have a deener for ju! They have a twelve eench hot dog for ju! Just for ju, Meester Storm!"

Storm looked at Taz, no longer able to hold in the laughter as he dissolved in giggles. *The woman is too much!*

She pounded on the door harder. "Meester Storm… they have a twelve eench meat between the buns! Ju like the twelve eench meat between the buns, Meester Storm!"

"Oh for Christ's sake!" Taz screamed and Storm roared with laughter, happier than he'd ever been in his life.

The End

If you are intrigued to learn more about supermodel Michael Francis and his hot cop lawman, Tyler Winston, please check out their story in "Silver Bullets"

If you enjoyed reading about Rome Wilkins and would like to know more about his story with his two beautiful lovers, Pepper Rawlings and Thom Akecheta, please check out their story in "Silver Secrets"

And if you are interested in fine wines from the "Lazy E Vineyards" which will make your clothes fall off, please check out their origins in "A Very Good Year" starring Dmitri Hernandez and Carlo Degli Esposti

ABOUT THE AUTHOR

Patricia Logan resides in Los Angeles, California along with her husband, four children, her grandchild and ever increasing number of cats. When not being stage mom, baking cookies, or scooping kitty litter, she writes steamy, award winning, gay erotic romance and tries to lead her readers on a journey of discovery with more than a little angst.

OTHER BOOKS BY PATRICIA LOGAN

The Armadillo Series
Leather Nights
Undercover Nights
Warrior Nights (MMM Menage)

The Westburg Series
Captive Lover
A Very Good Year
The Cowboy Queen

The Silvers Series
Silver Bullets
Silver Secrets (MMF Ménage)
Silver Ties (BDSM)

The Master's Boys (Serial) (BDSM)
Trick
Jett
Kaden
Grit
Stix
Con
Secrets
The Invitation Only (Serial) (BDSM)
Red
Trask
Heath
Wyatt
Dallas (Dec 2014)
Worth (Jan 2015)

The Assassins Series (BDSM)
Verified Kill
Confirmed Kill
Demonstrated Kill

Civil War Romance (BDSM)
The Slave's Mask
Unmasked

The Bodyguard Series
The Superstar

Stand Alone Novel
Gypsy Knight (Medieval MMF Ménage)

Stand Alone Shorts
Hot Summer Hogs
Over the Road (MMM Menage)
Love Letters
Wounded Warriors

Anthology Submissions
Dinner with Frankie (Vesper's First Date) Part of the
Authors off the Shelf Anthology

In French
L'Amant Captif (Captive Lover)
Une Tres Bonne Annee (A Very Good Year)
La Reine du Cowboy (The Cowboy Queen)

In Spanish
Lazos de plata (Silver Ties)

In Italian
Catene d'argento (Silver Ties)
Trick
Jett
Kaden
Grit
Stix
Con (Dec 2014)
Secrets (Dec 2014)
Chasing Deuce (Dec 2014)

Made in the USA
Las Vegas, NV
05 December 2022

61228169R00168